Blood of Beelzebub

A Novel

James Seymour

Trenton, Georgia

Hardcover ISBN: 978-1-958889-86-2
Ebook ISBN: 979-8-88531-509-8

Published by BookLocker.com, Inc., Trenton, Georgia.

Printed on acid-free paper.

BookLocker.com, Inc.
2023

First Edition

For Alex and Dick

Celtic Druids are most infamously known for burning people in large wicker effigies. But they also strangled, drowned, poisoned, stoned, beheaded, dismembered, and buried them alive. The sacrificial act could vary, with different means of dispatching used for different ceremonial purposes – and sometimes the gods called for a bloodbath. One particularly gruesome Druidic ritual shares certain similarities with the Walton murder. Known as "the threefold death," multiple killing methods (such as strangulation, head injuries, and throat-cutting) would be used in an act of ritual overkill to either appease multiple gods or ensure maximum bloodshed.

Chapter One

Nuneaton
Tuesday Evening
October, 1970

No man or woman alive will deny they are privileged with certain truths, beliefs that justify their actions, even when others may disagree or have abandoned any belief that such truths exist. Such are the exigencies of all beliefs, be they mundane, religious, creative, judicial, or criminal.

I trust you may think me a philosopher or high-minded academic, flaunting my verbiage so enigmatically, but, alas, I claim no such heritage. I am nothing more than an ordinary constable, a simple believer in justice, the sort attached to the more sordid acts of individuals lacking in either moral fortitude or the emotional capacity to regard others as they would wish to be regarded. In other words, a mere copper whose life has been devoted to criminal investigation. And, while my career has not reached the epic proportions of some of my more illustrious colleagues – one of whom you shall come to know quite intimately between the jackets of this literary opus – I expect you may come to appreciate my certainty that the privilege I hold is well-justified. I shall not be discouraged in my pursuance of the truth in this matter, even while more renowned parties have decided they are not up to the task.

Allow me to properly introduce myself: retired Superintendent Alec Spooner, Warwickshire C.I.D. As might be inferred, some individuals – be they intimate or mere acquaintances – fall to the temptation of openly referring to me as "Spooner," "Spoon," or, if they are especially tactless or loathsome, "Spoonful." I generally reply to all three, as I am quite satisfied – even honored – to be considered a public servant, though I tend not to forgive any lengthy references to dinnerware.

Following a mercifully short career as a miner in Staffordshire, I spent more than thirty years conducting mostly murder investigations in and around my beloved Stratford-upon-Avon. Though I retired in 1964, the case related in these pages has never failed to escape my ongoing attention. Its extenuating circumstances illustrate the human need to believe in the unseen; in fact, our willingness to kill in the name of that belief cannot be fully explained by examining the chaos of the criminal mind or religious zealot. It is far more generic.

Was I relocated because I would not give up my determination to find a conclusion to this heinous crime? I never publically accused that in 1959, as I have always considered myself a loyal Englishman who does not disobey his superiors. Apparently, though, my die had been cast.

That year I agreed to leave my duties in Stratford to become Divisional Superintendent in Nuneaton, far removed from the territory I had served nearly all my life. I was, of course, livid, but concurrently civilized.

Today I am no longer associated with the C.I.D. Though my finances require I freelance as a security officer for the National Coal Board, I am free to pursue those truths that certain people – including those who controlled my career –

seem convinced should never see the light. Your proper attention to the following summary of facts, I expect, may enlighten those of you interested in truth.

My acquaintance with Stratford and its environs has understandably endowed me with an appreciation for all things Shakespearean. I cannot ever recall walking Henley Street without wondering how the Bard might have treated the circumstances surrounding this particular crime. Having frequently considered the ramifications of medieval superstitions and witchcraft, Shakespeare rarely failed to illustrate the ways in which the supernatural affected his characters, revealing truths about ourselves that remain as relevant today as they were in the 16th and 17th centuries. While I never attended university, I did become a learned enthusiast of all his plays that put the paranormal under a microscope. Who says a civil servant must merely indulge in *The Mail*, *The Mirror*, or the Teds?

Since the reopening of the Shakespeare Memorial Company Theatre in 1932 – the same year I began working for the Warwickshire C.I.D. – I have been a regular attendee, though on more occasions than one, the work of policing preempted my viewing the company's latest production. And, of course, the war years prevented all of us the pleasure of their company. One of the greatest advantages of retirement – and world peace – is the uncompromised capacity to appreciate the work of England's greatest contributor to the Lively Arts, an indulgence I share with several of the characters in our story.

Perhaps, Mr. Shakespeare's greatest contribution to the world has been his appeal to all levels of social and economic advancement, even to those of us perennially scraping by in our modest communities of South Warwickshire. I shall forever be indebted to his wisdom regarding the fantasies of the masses, information that has helped confirm my suspicions in this and other investigations.

Where to begin? Or, perhaps, more accurately, where to end? Since retiring in 1964 I have made it my responsibility to return each year to Meon Hill and the hedgerows of Lower and Upper Quinton. The murderer still walks these streets, awaiting, perhaps, an older figure like myself in pursuit.

In fact, despite the discouragement of Scotland Yard's "Famous Fabian," I have attempted to prove their literary star was badly mistaken. Having done so, I have made myself quite unpopular in this neighborhood, as I'm reminded every February 14, Valentine's Day, when I make my way back to the site of the murder.

Not for the purposes of seeking passion or companionship. My last encounter with a woman just after Valentine's Day that same year proved I could still find love if I remained open. No, I'm afraid my age and health preclude anything of that sort. I want only to hold responsible the monster who brutally, bloodily, and ritualistically hacked to death an innocent person with a thoroughly decent soul. For this I am annually ridiculed by my "friends" at The Yard, not to mention the various shopkeepers in Quinton and Stratford who would rather I fade away, truth be damned.

Why, you may ask, has this one crime led me to blindly pursue a perpetrator that nearly everyone – almost all the five hundred townspeople queried about their knowledge of the crime – claims to know nothing about. They show no eagerness or willingness to assist any inquiry. This reality alone should raise enough red flags to keep the Metropolitan Police on top of this case in perpetuity. However, even though the case remains technically "unsolved," no one will lift a finger to continue the investigation.

Why has no one, excepting yours truly, found the resolve to dedicate himself to the case's disentangling? I believe I have addressed the first part of this question; its second part requires us to examine some very basic realities about English history, religion, culture, and legal system. Let me even suggest that a reliable, more complete understanding of the very fabric of British society may be at stake.

Consider – and forgive – the freedoms I employ in telling this story. On numerous occasions I shall take you into the private spaces of various parties pertinent to an understanding of these events. You will be allowed the privileges of a silent bystander, as if you'd paid for an orchestra seat for the drama.

How, you might ask, would I have the advantage of knowing the words of our cast? Trust me. As a veteran investigator I have taken great care to consider the contributions of all our actors, to carefully craft their language so that it represents the details of my research, as both an experienced sleuth and longtime Stratford resident assigned to this case from its beginning. Besides, since all other interested parties have chosen to abandon any search for justice, my narrative appears to be the only one available.

The trouble is, dear friends, my future seems to have dwindled. In a matter of days, I shall be entering George Eliot

Hospital in Nuneaton for what I'm told is a rather serious procedure. Hence, the words of this tale are told with a certain urgency from one who clings to the hope that some of you will take heed. And, since this book may never find the commercial success of Mr. Fabian's thread of questionable conclusions in his bestseller *Fabian of the Yard*, should circumstances determine that I have come to the end of my investigation and my life, I trust enough of you will follow my lead by bringing this disturbing affair to its proper conclusion.

Chapter Two

Lower Quinton
Wednesday Morning
June, 1944

The clouds of war had not yet cleared, and memories of the apocryphal fires of Coventry and Birmingham were still fresh in the minds of everyone in Warwickshire. The Yanks had their hands full in the Pacific and Allied troops had just landed in Normandy, so there was hope in Britain that the worst doldrums of war were in the past. The Nazis seemed to be on the run and the sirens of Luftwaffe attacks had not been heard in the Midlands for over two years. Still, many Englishmen and women wondered if the tides of war had truly reversed.

No less fearful than the rest of us and struggling to maintain their meagre livelihood, seventy-four-year-old Charles Walton and his thirty-three-year-old niece Edith were early risers. The blessings of a spring morning that featured glorious buds of magnolia, tulips, and lilies seemed duplicitous, if one considered the tens of thousands of young men facing death across the channel. However, their domestic lives needed to continue. Everyone understood the necessity of standing together against the greatest threat to human decency in anyone's memory. Few were aware of the strains of intolerance lurking in the pastures of their own backyards.

Charles Walton had spent his entire life within the confines of the same few square kilometers, working as a day laborer recognized as extremely talented with animals, especially, as a young man, horses. Many found these gifts extraordinary, even supernatural. He was a gentle man, always in tune with those around him, especially when he was with a horse, a heifer, a dog – of any color – or, as his closest neighbors would attest, frogs.

Niece, Edith, with whom he had lived since the death of his sister in 1927, was equally modest and devoted to her uncle, whose hard-earned three shillings per week provided rent for their small, thatched cottage opposite walls of warm Cotswold stone. For these and other small expenses, Charles depended on ten shillings per week from his pension, a small income as a day laborer hampered by rheumatic joints, and whatever Edith could make when work was available. To make sure she had something during lean times, Charles paid her one pound a week for housekeeping.

"Your tea is on the table, Charles," chirped Edith, emerging from the bedroom at half past six on her way to their primitive gas stove to prepare eggs and crumpets, as she had every morning for as long as both could remember. A full-breasted blonde with a twinkle in her eye, she could not help but remind Charles of her striking resemblance to his sister.

"You're too kind, Edie," he replied, just as he did every morning. He gingerly moved to the table in the tiny kitchen, his joints aching, and sat stone-faced looking towards the fields in which he would be spending the day cutting hedgerows for his neighbor, Alfred Potter, for whom he had recently begun employment. Potter had been managing his father's property, The Firs, for five years, and while no one would have called them friends, Alfred had shown a new interest in Charles, having heard of his special affinity for farm animals, of which Potter had more than a few.

"You should wear your jacket at least till noon, don't you think?"

"Yes, love, capital idea," said Charles, finally showing the glimpse of a smile. As Edie served their meagre breakfast, her small, swarthy uncle – twisted on his left side due to rheumatic illness – opened the window and raised it a few inches, as he often did when weather permitted. Then he began a series of calls, odd sounds somewhere between a cluck and coo.

"Kleeyeeew… kleeyeeew," he gently repeated, and within seconds several wrens appeared on the sill of the window, only inches from their table. He tenderly offered his finger to one of the tiny birds that appeared to be at complete ease with its human friend. He offered his lips to its beak, while massaging its feathered wing with his forefinger.

"This one's the male," he announced. "A better breadwinner than me, I would imagine."

"Now, don't say such things, Uncle. You are my savior and the grandest breadwinner in all of Warwickshire."

Charles chuckled, put the tiny, warm creature back on the sill, and returned to his meal. He always made sure to leave very early during the spring and summer, to take advantage of the cool mornings. Edith, who had been fortunate to find work as a printer's assembler at the Royal Society of Arts, relocated from Stratford to Lower Quinton during the war, always remained at home for another hour after his departure.

"How did you know the wren was a male?"

"Oh, well, he told me, of course, dear," Charles answered casually, before wiping his chin with a napkin and reaching for his jacket.

"You'll be home around four, Charles?"

"As usual, Edie," he mumbled before kissing Edith, grabbing his walking stick to temper the pressure on his spine, unlatching their heavy wooden door, and heading for his neighbor's farm, his exotic scythe in hand.

Edith treasured the next hour in her day above all others. Nearly all the rest of her schedule seemed set in stone. There would be the sometimes tedious and mechanical work of assembling artifacts and exhibits for the Art Society, though she was constantly reminding herself how lucky she was to have found such an interesting job. She hoped once the war was done, she'd be able to continue when they returned to Stratford.

She also appreciated the lunch break when she would generally meet Edgar Goode, her boyfriend of nearly a year, at their small town's café, The Tea Cozy. Once her afternoon's duties were done, she would return home in time to prepare tea for Charles, with, more frequently of late, Edgar, who appeared to have adopted the Walton family. But that one hour after Charles left for work was hers alone.

She often took the time to arrange her picture catalogue, glimpses of a world she barely remembered. Having lost her mum at age three, nearly all her memories were embedded in the few photographs still possessed by Charles, in addition to the newspaper items saved by her mother. Edith also included letters her mum had received shortly after the First War from her cousin in Covington, as well as those she'd written, but never sent, to Edith's father, who lived in nearby Stratford. He had cut off all relations with his daughter even before her mother's death and remained a shadow in Edie's dreams.

She would read and reread these letters to her father, still unable to determine the meaning of his unwillingness to have a relationship with his only daughter, leaving a scar on Edith's character that angered Charles, generally the sort of man who shunned such grudges. On several occasions after turning age fifteen – soon after the death of Charles' wife, Isabel Caroline, his first cousin once removed – Edith queried Charles about her father. He would explain that such a man was unworthy of her love and that those feelings should be redirected.

This one hour of her morning allowed her the privacy she needed to revisit her parents' ghosts, curled up in the bed with her tea. She had to admit that her emotions had recently become less intense since meeting Edgar. Perhaps, she considered, one day this ritual would no longer be necessary.

***

At one o'clock sharp Edith was seated outside The Tea Cozy sipping her chowder, taking full advantage of a sun that was happily drenching the three tables set along the sidewalk. From just down the block, free to take a break from a secure position as clerk at Andrews Insurance, appeared Edgar Goode, installing a full smile on Edith's face. A big man who dwarfed both Edith and Charles' slight frames, he appeared delighted to be in her presence again, though they had only left each other after sharing supper with Charles the previous evening.

"You trying that new tea you thought you'd like?" asked Edgar.

"Yes, it's quite nice after all. I can't think of what led me to put it off so long." She gazed into her partner's deep blue eyes. "What's the book you've got, Eddie?" Eddie and Edie, quite the pair.

"Oh, it's a library copy of *King Lear*, the one I mentioned at dinner. I finally had a chance to pick it up."

"Yes, yes, I remember."

"Rumors abound that the Shakespeare Memorial Company will be presenting it as their first mounting after the war, so I wanted to get a head start." Not that Edgar didn't know the play. He'd been named after the good Gloucester son and had seen it several times since childhood, though both had been school productions. Hence, he was especially excited about seeing what he expected would be the penultimate experience of that classic. Those in the know expected either Gielgud would reprise his 1940 performance at the Old Vic or, perhaps, even Olivier would take a stab at it.

"Olivier is way too young, but the size of his ego should make up for his age," Eddie chortled.

"Will you be looking to get another role when the theatre reopens?" Edie asked.

"Oh, I dunna know… I've only done that twice, just as a supernumerary in *Henry VIII* and *Henry IV Part I*; when they need to fill the taverns, they seem to think I fit right in."

"Oh' Eddie," Edie replied, laughing aloud with pride for her actor boyfriend, "you're such an amazing scholar when it comes to theatre. I'm so awed; I know so awfully little about such things. You've simply charmed me and Charles with all your knowledge."

"Well, we do live in Stratford, or very nearby, so isn't it our duty to know its history?" Like Charles and Edie, Edgar had never been able to afford university. All three, however, shared a fierce curiosity that surpassed many of the more fortunate in the upper class unable to appreciate their station.

"I do wonder, though, if this nasty business on the continent will ever be through and such things as Shakespeare will ever be ours again," said Edgar, who had failed his military physical due to heart palpitations, an ailment that would shorten his life by several decades.

"Oh, surely we're near the end, don't you think?" Edith quietly pleaded.

"Well, I do hope so, my dear. I think I'll just have the chips."

"I do love these lunches, Eddie."

"As do I. You know, Edie, I spent so many years on my own that it's hard to believe I'm sitting across from someone who truly cares."

"I do! I do!"

"Other than my mum – who I never saw – I felt mostly alone. Everybody was always out working and mostly I was there alone, as if I was some kind of orphan. Thanks to you I'm not alone anymore."

"And thanks to the Shakespeare Memorial Company."

"Right, love," replied Eddie, with a big smile across his face, "thanks to them, too."

Following another of their delightful luncheons, each of them retired to their afternoon's duties, with the promise that Edgar would be joining the Waltons for dinner again the following evening. Any longer than a day or two and both Edie and Eddie would be pining away for each other. So, too, would Charles be wondering why the dear man was "staying away."

***

Charles felt a certain vigor that morning as he slashed away at the endless hedgerow surrounding The Firs in Upper Quinton. His spirit had been on the upswing since beginning his work for Potter, a position that would hopefully insure his and Edith's wellbeing until at least the end of the war. Edgar had joined their lives, and Charles was feeling nearly buoyant for the first time since the death of his wife nearly seventeen years earlier. He had always been a bit of a loner, but following his wife's death, Edith noticed a more profound dislocation. Was it possible now that he was actually whistling?

About half an hour before he usually took his lunch break, he noticed a man walking towards him along the side of the road. He had never seen him before. A rare event, for sure, when you've lived all your life in the same, small community. As the man got closer, Charles thought what a pleasure to be imagining such a gathering with someone new, as if the bonds of the town had somehow been shattered.

"Beautiful morning, isn't it?" he addressed the friendly looking man, a few inches taller and wearing some kind of kerchief around his head, definitely a sign of distant customs. The olive-skinned gentleman stopped just a few yards away and stared in his direction, showing no signs of hostility, only slight bewilderment. After more than several moments he waved.

"Buon pomeriggio," the man exclaimed with a broad smile.

"Yes, indeed, sir." Charles was delighted and slightly perplexed, as if he had hopped on an airplane (having never done so) and landed in Rome, thinking the gentleman sounded something like the Pope, whom he'd heard on the wireless during dire moments of the war.

"Well, ok, good day to you, too, I suppose. What am I to do?"

"Ok, basta va bene, cosi!" his new friend said, laughing.

"Ok, ok" Charles repeated. "I guess that's a word everyone knows." With little else to bridge their cultural distance, he took out the sandwich Edie had prepared for him the night before and offered half to his new friend. Just as he did, he heard a voice behind him.

"Move on, you! Just keep walking to where you's going before I call the authorities. Do you'm hear?" At which point Charles became even more puzzled, unable to understand why anyone would so disdain an innocent individual obviously a long way from home. Alfred Potter, disheveled and scowling, was standing directly behind him, a stern face in support of his stinging orders.

"It's quite alright, Mr. Potter, I was just…"

"Listen 'ere, Walton. Let the man be. He don't belong 'ere." The stranger had immediately received the message and was already a long way down the road with no aim to hear more from the farmer. Charles was reluctant to get into any squabble with his boss. It wasn't the first time he'd been a party to Potter's nasty humours, so he returned to his duties.

"I told 'em at the Leet this'd be a problem," snapped Potter. "Never mind, just keep an eye on. There'm more where that one come from about a kilometer down the road. Bloody Nazis, right here in Quinton! They'm worse than useless!" With that, Potter began walking back across the field in the direction of his farmhouse, before stopping and turning around.

"Oh, Walton, you takes a look at that sire later, right? See it you do."

"Yes, sir, just as I said, sir." What a stiff old wart he is, thought Charles, as he watched the younger man disappear. He supposed, since he'd already been interrupted, that he'd eat his sandwich, rather than wait. He wished he still had the company of the foreigner to share his lunch and quietly cursed a world so mired in cruelty and hate.

Chapter Three

Lower Quinton
Thursday Evening
June, 1944

Edith had been so bold as to buy a rather expensive wine for dinner, justified by the notion that they had a guest. This excuse was becoming more difficult to defend with each passing week, since Edgar's presence had become *di rigeur* (you see, even I can sound as though I've been properly educated), but none of them seemed to be bothered by the gesture. Even Charles, who had been a teetotaler all his life, seemed not to mind the new tingle he was experiencing several times a week. Edgar was regaling them with some of his new interest in Shakespeare's references to farm animals, sounding more and more like the English professor he would have liked to become had he been reared by a family with wealth.

"I couldn't help thinking, Charles, about the mention of goats in several of his plays, especially after your telling us about the one you were nursing the other day at The Firs."

"Oh, goodness," Charles chuckled. "I had no idea I's in anyway related to the Bard."

"Well, I'm beginning to understand that there's wee little he doesn't tell us about," replied Edgar. "When Lear is up on the heath…"

"Another old man wondering what's happened to his kingdom," Charles chortled, quite pleased that he could at least indicate he knew Lear's basic story.

"Indeed, convinced he's adopted a 'goatish' disposition," Edgar clarified.

"Oh, I knows how that feels," replied Charles, laughing out loud.

"Charles, you're so funny!" Edie was delighted to see her uncle lighthearted, so unlike the reserved senior she'd been sharing a home with nearly all her life.

"He seems to associate his state of fear – his goatishness, as it were – with the horns of a cuckold."

"A what?" asked Charles.

"That's a man with an adulterous wife," said Edgar.

"Oh, well, gar, I suppose I wouldn't know about such things, am I right, Edie?" he countered, enjoying every moment of his newfound edification.

"So, I decided to find other places where he goes on about horns and goats and such," Edgar continued.

"I knows about'm rams, the sires, they know when they own their kingdoms, they's the ones with the biggest horns."

"Exactly," said Edgar, "until some lecherous knight with bigger horns comes along and – like the devil, says Shakespeare – takes a cudgel to the husband and dis-horns him."

"Yes, I seen'm at each other. The goats, I mean, not the husbands. Quite upsetting, especially if I've made one of'm rams a friend."

"We must get to the next show in Stratford, Charles. Perhaps *Henry IV* when that comes around. Falstaff has lots to say about cuckolds and horns and all that."

"Well, I'd be happy to give a report, Eddie, next time I'm up to the farm. In the meantime, folks, I've got a early rise tomorrow, so I'm gonna let you kids finish up here. Not used to feeling so bubbly, if you knows what I mean."

"That's fine, Charles," Edith assured him with a laugh. "We'll take care of things," after which he retired to the bedroom.

Once they'd cleaned up the few dishes, they sat opposite each other at the window holding hands and finishing the final dregs of wine. "I just love seeing Uncle so cheery, Eddie, and all because of you!"

"Well, I think he's happy about you getting your new job, and his getting the work, too, don't you think?"

"Yes, yes, but Edgar, he's been a different man since you… you've come our way. I'm so happy now." She sat up, reached over the table, and gave Eddie a kiss. They sat for a long while, just gazing at each other, like those who have just discovered love, before it has become *de rigeur*.

"Will you stay? We could have a bite to eat together at the Cozy in the morning before work," Edie suggested.

"Yes, why not. I'd like to." And so, the two of them also retired, after a thoroughly enjoyable evening together, the sort none of them had known prior to that spring, bringing with it new hopes for a fresh tomorrow.

Chapter Four

The Court Leet, Stratford
Monday Afternoon
July, 1944

The Steward of the Manor and several bailiffs had agreed to meet at the courthouse after Alfred Potter insisted crucial matters needed their attention. He had only been a twice-elected bailiff of the Alcester (Warwickshire) Court Leet over the past four years, having become a resident of Quintin shortly before the start of the war. This court had replaced the Stratford Leet famous for its kerfuffle with John Shakespeare, father to the playwright. That legend held that Shakespeare senior, a glover, had left "a hidden muck-heap in a place called Henley Street, against the ordinance of the court," for which he was fined. This court document is one of the few historical clues to his son's early life.

According to the court's by-laws, designated since the 13th c. to "take cognizance of grosser crimes of assault, arson, burglary, larceny, manslaughter, murder, treason, and every felony at common law," any bailiff could convene a meeting. Lately most of the court's attention had been directed towards international turmoil, so few imagined what could be so important that this junior member would bring the group together that afternoon.

About eight of them were assembled around an enormous oak table that was apparently only slightly younger than the

Magna Carta, and while the magistrates were not quite that aged, many of them seemed nearly as heavy and possessing as wide a girth. Given the inconvenience of the hour and its impromptu nature, many disgruntled jowls were in attendance. Steward of the Manor Sir Geoffrey Milner was the first to break the silence.

"What's the nature of these grumbles, Mr. Potter? Several of us is on rather short notice here today with properties waiting our attention."

"Yes, well, Geoffrey, I's had several concerns I need to bring to this distinguished and learned body." One could hear a hushed chorus of groans, responding to Potter's brand of mouth manure, with which these farmers were well acquainted.

"Best to get right to it, Alfred," one of his closer confidants on the council offered.

"Awright, Thomas. I would like to first bring up the matter I introduced at our last meeting, som'it I spoke to you'm about a couple of times, but's gettin' worse w' time. These criminals they got camped down'm road is no longer tolerable and needs remedy. It ain't safe to walk me property no more. They's threaten' the wife, nearly attacked one'm workers just this week! I had to run him off before he did harm to me or me animals. Me and m'neighbors can't wait till we's get assaulted and I've warned'm as I's gonna shoot'm if I sees'm again."

"When we addressed this before," Geoffrey interjected, "we decided the prisoner camp was justified as our contribution to the war effort. Has anyone else changed their minds about that?" There was no one to step up.

"Well, that'm all very well, but I've got m'safety – and me neighbors' safety – to be thinkin' bout, but you's tell'n me I ain't got no way to protect m'self, 'm that it? These Italian Nazis are comin' and goin' on as if they's free men!"

"I think it was determined that given the security forces available they had to be free to get lunch during their work in the fields and that if there was any shenanigans, that prisoner would be put in confinement. I've not heard about any problems with said prisoners, have you Mr. Potter?" said the Steward.

"Yeah, well I's tellin' ya that don't make me safe and if'n I sees one of'm again, I's gonna bleedin' shoot afore I asks their name. Understand?"

"Well, I trust, Potter, that you'll give such actions careful thought before you put us all 'ere in the middle of a difficult international incident," Milner continued. "Remember, while we continue in the Alcester Leet to hold considerable influence on judicial matters in our jurisdiction, it's not what it used to be, and our actions are generally outflanked by the Crown. Now, as to other matters?"

"I's not ready to put this to rest!" Potter objected.

"You are now, Sir," Milner said with considerable authority. "If you're not ready to move on, then I'm ready to adjourn this meeting."

"How are your crops, huh? I's talked to sum of ya about what's happenin' in your fields. Ain't normal, is it?" Alfred insisted, vigorously shaking his head, and looking to his friend Thomas Burns for some agreement.

"What's this about?" Milner asked, looking to all the members for some kind of answer. He did note from several of them a general agreement with Potter that something was amiss. Thomas again voiced his support for Potter.

"It's true, Geoffrey, that some of us in Lower Quinton, especially those of us adjacent to The Firs, have noticed an unusual amount of dead trees in our orchards, and wheat and soybeans just don't seem right."

"It's been a rough year all around for crops," one of the other bailiffs offered.

"Looks here," Potter enjoined, "I ain't seen it like this since I come to Firs."

"All of three years ago," offered a snickering Constable Winters, not one of Potter's closest associates.

"Six years! And you say that, Winters, but you just wait. Bloody blight might be headed your direction afore the summer's done and don't come cryin' t'me."

"Have you got any theories, Mr. Potter? asked Milner. Potter remained uncharacteristically quiet, as if the generally impulsive farmer was actually giving some consideration to his response.

"There's something of the devil afoot, if yous ask me," he finally said, a claim which only a few of the bailiffs seemed to dismiss. "It could be somethin' put together by these Nazis…"

"Mr. Potter, I asked that we leave that matter alone," added Milner.

"But that ain't my biggest theory. I think we may have some visitors from the dark side, someone – or many – who see this as a good time to draw on the powers of witchcraft we understand so well in these parts," Potter exclaimed.

Everyone in the room was speechless. After several long moments of reflection, the Steward of the Manor concluded the gathering with these remarks:

"Bailiff Potter has introduced a serious claim today and one we have heard before during the history of this distinguished body. We are all familiar with prior incidents in which the powers of evil have created great harm for the citizens of Warwickshire and we must always be diligent in looking for ways to protect ourselves from these darker forces. I think we cannot overlook these dangers, and even in these desperate times when we face such treacherous forces of the devil in Europe, we must remain diligent in searching for any evil here at home. I am, therefore, asking Mr. Potter to organize his suspicions, provide some evidence, and present them to us at another meeting within a fortnight. If that is all for now, I hereby adjourn this formal meeting of the Alcester Court Leet."

Potter and Thomas lingered outside the courthouse, watching as others dispersed into the streets. A lingering cloud cover darkened the late afternoon.

"I meant to ask you," said Thomas, "how's your neighbor Walton working out? How's he helping out with the animals?"

"Well, I'm not ready to dismiss him yet."

"What do you mean? I thought he was doing magic with your heifer and the ram?"

"Yes, yes, you call it magic, and I wonder. That sire did get cured, but I ain't convinced it be him," countered Potter.

"We've all seen what he can do, Alfred."

"I wonder what else he can do," Potter answered.

"He can talk to them, as if he speaks their language. I've not ever seen…"

"I've seen him! Comin' in and out of that house at all hours with others. And living alone with that woman…"

"That's his niece," said Thomas.

"Yeah, that's what I mean. The three of them down there stayin' together, 'm and his talkin' birds. We'll see. I've got my eyes out."

Thomas was quite surprised by Potter's negative attitude towards Charles' work, as he had been one of the first of the neighbors to recommend his hiring. Though Charles was no socialite and somewhat shy, he'd been residing in the same cottage for as long as anyone could remember and was well-liked and respected by everyone in Quinton. He could not fathom why suddenly Alfred was bothered by the man simply because he was raising his niece.

"Y'aint seen'm smiling away lately down in the field?" Potter asked.

"I have noticed he seems 'specially cheerful of late. I always thought it was due to Edie's new boyfriend, a good man, so as I hear, so maybe he's countin' the days till he can get her married off, as she ain't no spring flower."

"More likes a fading, prickly cactus, if yous ask me. And I's seen the man comin' out their door in the mornin', I did. Wid only one bed in the'm house, as far as I can tell," added Potter cryptically.

Thomas was beginning to tire of Potter's paranoia and decided to find an excuse for moving on. "I've got an errand 'ere in town, Alfred, so you'd best get on home without me."

"Alright, alright, but I be looking for yous soon to help put things right for'm Leet. You'll do it, I expect" insisted Potter.

"Just give me a call," Thomas assured him as he moved down the main street, leaving Potter alone amidst the wavering crowd, as if he saw himself a pillar of decency standing against a stream of depravity.

Chapter Five

Lower Quinton
Thursday Evening
October, 1944

"It's usually 'bout this hour just afore twilight when the fields come alive," Charles instructed Eddie, as they settled in to one of his favorite spots, underneath a copse of silver birch not far from the hedgerows surrounding The Firs. The two of them were sitting by a stream where Charles seemed intent on showing his new friend, who had come to feel more like a family member, the ease with which he is able to call together a regular herd of frogs.

"The time of the eve is the chief element 'ere, when they'm congregate to make sure all the yougins 'ere not far removed. Let me see if they won't come round to meet you, Eddie." The older man began humming, creating a unique sound manufactured from the depths of his throat and thorax, making the vicinity of his neck and mouth noticeably vibrate.

"Edie's talked about your friendliness with all living things, Charles, and I'm so excited you've agreed to bring me here." The elder man, during these moments in which all else seemed transcended by the doors to our distant cousins of the animal kingdom, seemed happier than ever introducing one of his magical realms to a new believer.

"I've not shared this place with anyone but you, Edgar, not even Edie. I knows how most folks 'ere think I'm some kind of witch."

"I'd love it if you were, Charles! How magical."

The frogs were not as promptly responsive to Charles' calls as were the wrens, but then this sound, being so much lower than the bird calls, did not reach as wide a territory. Charles had to crawl along the stream with his head only inches from the surface of the water to spread his sound. Edgar noted after several minutes the frogs' eyes just below the water, as if they were congregating outside a meeting hall. To his wonderment it took very little time for at least twenty to thirty of them to feel comfortable enough to skuttle up the rocky sides of the stream and gather round Charles' elbows, as he was now lying on his stomach, still humming.

"Do you feed 'em now?" Eddie asked softly.

"Not always 'bout food. These creatures, unlike the birds, appreciate company. They like joining a group of others, as we do as humans, you could say, couldn't you?"

"Indeed, you need only ask the audience at Stratford," confirmed Edgar with a broad smile. "No long speeches or recitin' in verse, I assume?"

"Guess I'm not the one could do that, me boy. Yous could give it a try." Eddie gave another chortle, at which point the two of them settled into a long period of frog-staring. It turned into an experience Edgar never forgot, something like meditation, moments during which he and the wider world were one, communicating – at Charles' direction – at a spiritual level, seeing into each other's souls. Why shouldn't they – him and the tiny amphibians – understand each other?

"What's that?" Edgar hesitated, listening intently. "Did ya hear?" Charles was unmoved, as if nothing else existed beyond his small gathering of live creatures bound to one another, lost together on another planet. Eddie couldn't help feeling they were being observed and raised himself to walk up a nearby ridge to view the golden field beyond Meon Hill. In the distance he saw, running towards the farm, a distant figure he assumed had just been spying on them. Afterwards, he rejoined the congregation, gingerly positioning himself again next to Charles on the ground. Several frogs noted his return with a look in his direction. He also regretted the probability of not finding any reference to frogs in Shakespeare, but he wasn't going to hesitate to get to the library to look for one.

On their way back to Charles' cottage their conversation turned to matters that proved their friendship, compared to a few months earlier, had deepened and become increasingly intimate. Having garnered enough courage to speak openly with Charles, Eddie felt a deep need to reveal a new emotional attachment.

"You've come to mean so much to me, as if I've found the family I never had," he said to Charles. The older man stopped after a few moments of silence and looked up into Eddie's eyes. It had been many years since Charles had felt so off-guard, nearly naked and unmasked. His relationship with Edie was natural, though equally intense, a marriage of minds and mutual needs. His feelings for Eddie were startling, awakening a desire he never realized he possessed. Could it be that using his abilities to converse with the animal world had revealed to him an essential lacking in intimacy with another man? His only male friend was Harry Beasley, a neighbor his age he'd known nearly his entire life whom he visited sporadically. Eddie was there in front of him, nearly daily, and Charles felt completely safe sharing a world in which he heard voices and never felt alone. Without realizing it, he took Eddie's sizeable arm and squeezed, then reached for his hand and gently held it. No words, it seemed to both of them, were necessary to communicate the very deep emotions they shared exclusively.

Chapter Six

Lower Quinton
Monday Evening
November, 1944

Thomas drove up the hill towards the farmhouse at The Firs, unnerved about the kind of devotion Potter might be expecting from him. He had been a tenant farmer as a child until he was an adult able to purchase his own cottage with a small field, but he was still beholden to Potter, both senior and junior, subject to the wrath of quirky overseers. While he may have reached the social level of a cottage owner, he was still regarded by the village – and Potter himself – as a tenant, dependent on the manager for work.

As he entered the mudroom, a passageway to the kitchen reserved for the farm help, he nearly ran over Judith, Potter's wife, who was on her knees cleaning something.

"How be it, Judith?" he exclaimed before moving into the kitchen itself. She just skittered away, a tiny mouse evading a hungry cat. In all of the maybe dozen times he'd been in Judith's presence he couldn't remember her saying more than a few unintelligible words, so this encounter seemed unremarkable. He was afraid to mention her to Alfred, who'd never said anything about her, except to acknowledge the diminutive woman's existence. A single man himself, Thomas had few references for what should or should not be a proper marriage or a loving wife.

"In here!" exclaimed Potter from his business office just down the hallway from the kitchen. "Sit."

Having been in Alfred's office several times previously, he was struck by its uncharacteristically unkempt condition. He knew Alfred to be a meticulous manager, adamantly dedicated to knowing every detail of his over five hundred acres of rich orchards and farmland, as well as the health of his estimable herd of Herford cows and egg-bearing hens. He noted Potter's large oak desk covered in maps, accounting sheets, and indecipherable notes written in untranslatable scratch.

"You've noticed'm fields of mine, 'aven't yous? A disgrace. And yours, too, 'm right?"

Thomas hesitated, remembering Alfred's hyperbolic pleas at the last Leet, equating the harvest and field conditions to the drought of 1893, as if every speck of moisture and nitrogen had been leached from the soil down to the roots. He had noticed, as had the other farmers nearby, that the harvest was one of the poorest in the past few decades, but agreed with most of them that the war had curtailed the delivery from the continent of much needed agricultural additives. And there simply wasn't the manpower to properly maintain many crops. Like most suffering Brits praying for an end to endless death and destruction, he accepted that the price to be paid by all citizens of the Kingdom was small compared to that of the husbands, brothers, and fathers who gave their lives.

"A've noticed it's not been what we expected since the war," Thomas remarked.

"Not the war and you's know it!" barked Potter. "I've been tending these fields in Warwickshire all m'life and 'ave never seen it like this is 'ere. We's need to make the Leet aware of the darkness 'round us, it's ar duty. Cause it's also 'bout my heifers, the sickness in them's eyes, and it's not like they's usual sick.

"A've not seen anythin' with my stock."

"You've not the trainin' t'see what 'm talkin' 'bout, so you'll keep that remark to youself, understand?" Thomas said nothing, knowing any resistance was futile.

"And I knows 'bout them's that makes it 'appen, understand?" Alfred drew Thomas to a table on which he spread a map of the land directly north of Meon Hill. "This 'ere's the camp of them Nazis."

"I thought they was Italians." Thomas offered timidly.

"You never 'erd of Benito Mussolini!" shouted Alfred. "Look 'ere. See this path? They's always comin' through the farm to go t'town to get they's lunch and see movies. And nobody stops'em. I knows what they's do. They'm poison us!"

"Course I'd not like 'em."

"You heard what I says 'bout 'em, right? And you saw 'em when they'm came after Judith and Walton, din ya?" Thomas nodded slowly, wondering how much he'd actually have to say or if he'd just be able to nod his head when he spoke before the Leet.

"And you knows what they'm bring with 'em, don ya? The darkness. Sure as I'm standin' 'ere, you knows how the devil lives in these fields," Potter insisted.

"I do."

"An' you knows what cleanses those fields, don ya." No answer was necessary.

"Come'n soon, you'n Judith 'n me will finally be testifyin' at the Leet about the curse that's come upon Meon Hill, won't ye. I need to knows you be there. There's a long history of evil that lurks in this corner of the Empire, lest all of yous forget, which ain't 'appenin longs as I'm runnin' this farm, you got that Burns?"

"I 'spect you'll be 'avin' Walton there, as well?" asked Thomas. Potter hesitated, as if he wasn't sure if he was going to answer.

"We'll not be callin' him as he'll 'ave work to finish." Thomas thought this strange, if Potter wanted to prove his theory, but he sought a brief meeting and simply waited for any last instructions. "Besides, I's not be needin' the words of Walton." Reaching for a letter from underneath the pile of maps, Potter continued to weave the narrative suggested by his recent discovery.

"E'en before I went through these 'ere maps where dees prisoners of war runs around free, poisonin' our own rich fields, I gets a letter from one Richard Clarke whose own father was eyewitness to the murder of the old woman, Ann Tennant."

"Oh, yes, 'Bloody Nancy,' everyone knows the story of that witch they killed back in what…"

"1875 in Long Compton, right by where them prisoners are."

"That were a famous murder I's heard a million times over a pint at the King George," Thomas noted excitedly.

"It were more like a liberation, I says, and it was Richard Clarke's old man who saw wid 'is own eyes the cleansing of that soil, but maybe they missed other hags, I's think. Cause Richard Clarke tells us more. The god-fearing son tells me 'bout Granny Faulkner who could transform herself into different kinds of animals, can ye believe! He writes 'there are enough witches in Long Compton to draw a wagon of hay up Long Compton Hill' and 'the influence of witches comes and goes like the full moon.' There's somethin' they won't ignore at the Leet, ah can tell ye."

"It's frightenin'," Thomas agreed with a slight shutter.

Before Potter could continue, they heard a knock on the door followed by the calls of Judith from beyond.

"Alfred! Alfred!

Potter swiftly exited the office, shutting the door behind him. For the first time Thomas found himself alone in Potter's sanctified inner realm. He wished he could carefully examine every detail found in the papers around him, there being many things he wondered about the workings of the farm. But he feared Alfred's re-entry, so he had no choice but to sit and listen intently to the sounds coming from the hall and kitchen beyond. All he heard was whimpering, to which Alfred seemed to be admonishing, then all was quiet.

Thomas wished he could be anywhere else, tending his small herd or spreading mulch in his home garden, because he knew this was the beginning of a new chapter in an old story that had defined his village for centuries. Weren't there enough evil forces at work in the world that year without stirring up this history? Thomas Burns knew the answer. He also knew he was helpless to stop them.

Chapter Seven

The Garrick Inn, Stratford
Saturday Evening
Late November, 1944

"You looks lovely this evenin', Edie," declared Charles with an enormous grin, due partially to his consumption of two pints of Guinness, more than he'd had in one sitting since his '20s. He couldn't have been happier were it his own birthday, not Eddie's, who had insisted the three of them have dinner somewhere other than in their kitchen, so Edie wouldn't feel responsible for washing up. Besides, he wants the opportunity to pay for their meals, as this is the first birthday on which he feels like a whole human being looking forward to a future with a new family of his own and an end to a war they all fear could destroy their lives. And soon, he imagines his beloved Shakespeare Memorial Company will be returning, giving him back the life he loves on the fringes of fantasy and literature.

"I've not been here in so long," said Edie, "not since our second date, right Eddie?" He nods his head, remembering how nervous he'd been when he first brought Edie to the oldest tavern in Stratford, named for England's greatest 18th c. actor-producer, having come there on many occasions with the casts of his SMC shows, savoring his second life as a professional actor, not insurance salesman.

"I think I's spent the best nights of my life here," Eddie added. "I used to pass the early evenings with Falstaff on stage drinking water under lights and the late evenings with Falstaff in this room drinking real ale."

"You're so lucky, Eddie. I can't wait till you can come back after shows again."

"With you, next time, love."

Charles seems to have escaped a fog of weariness and fear for himself and his beloved niece. Now, surrounded by friends and neighbors whose spirits are loosened by alcohol and conviviality, a new personality begins to emerge. Where previously one would expect him to listen intently with a perpetual frown, he was that night generously offering stories of his history, perspectives on his shuttered life that fascinated Edie, who knew him best, but had never imagined his freedoms as a young man.

"This pheasant is grand, Eddie, but you won't be tellin'm if I order another Guinness, just to help get the bird, bless it's heart, down to the belly?" Charles asked, to the hoots of both Edie and Eddie. Neither of them had ever witnessed this newly liberated day-laborer, who seemed to have shed years, revealing a man who would have been as comfortable as Eddie in the company of a laughing and bragging Falstaff.

"Have you been 'ere before, Uncle?" asked Edie.

"'Course I'ave! Is the Pope Italian? There's many things I'ave not told ye, love. Remember, I dinna marry 'til I's in my forties, so there's few places like this ah dunna know in these'm parts."

"I'll bet your uncle was quite the ladies' man, were you not, Charles?" Eddie asked, trying as hard as Edie to temper his horselaughs.

"Well, I's not quite that, but I knows a few unattached ladies, yes, a course." It was hard to tell if his ruddy face was from the sun, the ale, or embarrassment.

"Oh, tell us, Charles, don't be shy," coaxed Edie, as they all settled into their main dishes. Her uncle, so used to staring at the same four walls, seemed as moved to reveal his early years as he was in eating a really good meal.

"Long before I settled down wid Isabel, who I'd never dare bring 'ere, her not bein' the sort who'm comfortable in this kinda crowd, I had reasons to forget things, if ye knows what I's mean. I'd come 'ere ee'n in my teens, when I'd hoped to find a lass…"

"I love him, don't you Eddie? Who uses that word anymore?" Edie shared with Eddie between bites of meat pie.

"I suppose ye think I'm out of 'em dark ages, don't ye, love?"

"Don't mind her, Charles, just feel free to tell us all," countered Eddie.

"Well, there was one occasion…"

"Yes, tell us," Edie cajoled.

"Perhaps more than one, if I's bein' truly honest. Now mind ye, I were barely old enough to hold the Guinness down, but ee'n then I seemed able to reach others – not just four-leggeds – but folks, as well, without words. I's had, 'specially at that age, what some folks later called "the evil eye," do ye know?

"What did I tell ya," said Eddie, "your Uncle Charles knew how to charm 'the lassies,' am I right?" They were both relishing every detail of his admissions.

"There were one, and maybe the reason I kept comin' each night, whose eye I'd caught early on. Ann Smith, 'er name, as luvly as the night I first give her 'the evil eye,' older 'n me, course, with sweet auburn hair 'n lips as red as the blood of a heifer."

"I can see her now, Uncle!"

"I dinna have to say a word. She all but knew exactly what I's thinkin' and me her, like if there'm electric wires a tween us, carryin' our thoughts to and fro. It give me shivers now to think of't. E'en others sittin' by us seem to know and stared."

"Did you see each other outside, away from the Inn?" asked Eddie. Charles hesitated, almost as though he didn't remember.

"Funny… I's almost no memory of that, as if'n it were all a dream, but yes, I's suppose we must have had, as what we was feelin' were so strong as to take over me whole mind, it did. It were always dark though, a bright light only shinin' on her. We talked, for sure, yet I's felt we did not need it, as bein' our minds knew all e'en without the words." Charles seemed lost in his own reverie.

"Close your ears, Edie, but did ye… well, did ye touch each other, if you don't mind me askin'?"

"Oh, yes…" Charles responded, as if the touch were happening at that moment, "but it were not what you may be thinkin'. I's held her hand fer hours and once, just once, did 'er lips meet mine. It were my first real kiss an' the sweetest this mouth did ever taste." He had found a place of peace that neither of them dared break into, until Edie could no longer endure it.

"What happened, Uncle?"

"It were as strange as the day is long, 'specially if yous think about me bein' married t'Isabel. I'd felt so long as if we had shared a world before we's were born, like'n if she were a soul sister in a previous life, so I's asked 'bout her family. Turns out, she told me, she were the namesake of her great-grandmother, Ann Smith, whose maiden name was Ann Tennant, would ye believe?"

"Who's that," asked Edie.

"Oh, bejesus!" Eddie burst out.

"I's never told ye, that bein' the story of a connection I's afraid would scare ye, love. Ann Smith, her great-grandma, was married to Thomas Walton, who were my great-grandfather, which a course made us cousins a some kind."

Edie looked at both men, bewildered by her uncle's concern and by Eddie's outburst. "But why was that so surprising, Charles? Weren't you and Isabel some kind of cousins, as well? It's a small town and I know several friends whose parents were distant cousins."

"That weren't my concern, love."

"Do you not recognize the name, Edie? She was the woman who… well, you tell it, Charles."

"As I'd heard the tale, and I heared it many times in places like this, it were in September of 1875 that Ann Tennant at aged eighty walked out for a loaf of bread and came upon a herd of farm workers headin' home from the harvest, includin' one crazy, drunken idiot James Heywood, who attacked Tennant – Smith, me great-grand – killin' her with a pitchfork and then himself gettin' hung after bein' declared insane.

"Why, Uncle?"

"She were a witch, they says."

"She became known as Crazy Nancy, though I'm sure I've no idea why," added Eddie.

"That's awful," said Edie.

"Indeed," followed Eddie.

There followed a silence that left Edie and Eddie completely downhearted, as they'd wanted so badly to cheer the old man, who finally emerged to complete his tale of first love.

"Afterwards, as it were, Ann – my Ann – never felt the same, makin' excuses, and I never saw her likes at the Inn again."

Edgar sensed the man was on the verge of a revelation. After all, Charles had never felt so able to share his secret past and Eddie had become a confidant, a witness to his speaking with all creatures of the animal kingdom.

"So after meetin' Ann, and losin' Ann, I commence to havin' these dreams 'n visions." Almost immediately an even deeper cloud engulfed the small, aging man, revealing a dread that made it difficult for him to continue.

"What is it, uncle? Is it your pheasant?"

Charles took a huge gulp of his Guinness and made an effort to suppress the fears that seemed to have returned sixty years later. "I'd found if I come 'ere and sat with others who dinna know me, I could get by in the world, alone as I was. But then I'd have to walk home, a long ways at night in darkness and mist, and it were then that the images come. I'd finally reach the bottom of Meon Hill and I'd see it. I'd see him."

"Who, Uncle, who did you see?"

"It were a dog, a huge, black dog who'd be standing 'bout half ways up the hill staring at me, waiting, every night, in the same place."

"But why, Charles, if you saw the dog every night, did ye keep coming here late at night if you feared the dog?" asked Eddie.

"It become like a cycle. The more I seen the dog, who never threatened me, the more I needed to come 'ere 'n drink, so I'd forget the dog, who was always there." He grew silent.

"What did you do?" asked Edie.

"It were the last night I saw the dog, a cold, cold night, as I recalls. Maybe it were the drinks that night, and the cold, but next to the dog I saw clearly, I swear as clear as that night were, next to the hound, a headless woman. I stared at'em both for the longest time… I'd never seen… till I turned and they'm gone." Neither Edie or Eddie dared question the truth of his vision.

"Don't let your bird get cold, Uncle," Edie quietly reminded him.

"That wasn't the end, was it, Charles?" Eddie cautioned.

"The next mornin' I wake late, it bein' Saturday after me be'n out late and no one payin' mind. I's come to the table t'find me mum alone and she tells me… your sister's died, Charles. Just like that. And all I can thinks about were the big dog. And the woman... with no head."

Bits and pieces of the pheasant remained on Charles' plate, but he lacked the will to finish it.

"So, Ann, your great-grand-mama, and my great-great, I suppose, is the same that's part of the tales they're always talking about in Warwickshire?" asked Edie, now unable to touch her own half-finished pie. Charles simply nodded and reached for another large gulp of ale.

"We live in such a lively, imaginative corner of the country, my dears," Eddie jumped in, "full of the inspired workings of great minds. It's a wonder we're all not consumed by fears of the devil. Macbeth imagined Banquo's ghost and eight kings, the result of demons, inciting him to sin and crime. 'Sleep no more! Macbeth does murder sleep!' The devil and his angels create illusions, which lead to his betrayal and destruction. These demons, they live here in Warwickshire, don't you think, Charles?"

"I's no scholar like you, Edgar, but these visions… I'm sure I's not the first to see 'em."

"These ghosts are sometimes demons that lure men to death; they come in horrible forms and unsettle reason when the victim is close to unseen destruction. Like you, maybe, Charles. Shakespeare understood this."

"I'm beginin' t'think I should know much more about your Bard, Edgar."

"And I remember, as I've been readin' it again of recent, Edgar in *King Lear* saw Beelzebub, what they sometimes called the devil, with eyes like two full moons and a thousand noses, with horns waving like the sea. So, it's not so odd as one might think, right Charles?" Eddie added. "Some think today we don't believe in God as willingly as the Elizabethans believed in the devil."

"I 'spose I should be more regular in gettin' to the chapel, but I's havin' me problems supposing either God or Satan," Charles replied.

"Satan comes in many forms. Just ask Macbeth, though I should not be sayin' that name so close to the theatre as we are," said Eddie. "But havin' now said the name, he reminds us of the phantoms that ride the wind and mingle with the mist, just as did your dog and headless woman. You're not alone."

"I's suppose that'm some kind of comfort," said Charles, feeling slightly better after hearing Eddie's acquaintance with literature's apparitions.

"And his descriptions of the devil I learned after our last talk about Shakespeare's references to animals," Eddie added, reaching into his pocket for a note he'd written himself. "Edgar's fiends in *Lear* included 'hog in sloth, fox in stealth, wolf in greediness, dog in madness, lion in prey.' You see, Charles, 'dog in madness.' Surely these visions were brought on by your unhappiness about losing Ann."

"But these animals who tell me their secrets, their fears, they'm no fiends, I swear!" exclaimed Charles.

"Fiends in the minds of those that may be mistaken for devils themselves, Shakespeare may teach us," said Eddie.

Fortunately for the revelers celebrating Eddie's birthday, they were able to recover from Charles' upsetting revelations to enjoy their pudding desserts topped off with brandy. But their return that night to Lower Quinton in Eddie's car, not by foot, featured as they passed, a new look at Meon Hill, which would forever appear forbidding in the minds of all three.

Chapter Eight

Lower Quinton
Wednesday Afternoon
Early December, 1944

Though it was not yet winter by the calendar, the winds had picked up and the temperature dropped, making Charles' hedgerow chores more challenging. Once the morning sun had vanished, he would now head for the barn to check on the herd, clean their stalls, and feed the strays. But before he could get away that afternoon, just after his luncheon sandwich, he noticed someone looking at him from across the road just beyond the stone fence, half protecting himself from view behind an oak tree. His pulse quickened, as he noticed what he thought to be the outline of the stranger he'd met earlier that autumn who'd been so hastily chased away by Potter.

He wanted the opportunity to tell the Italian that he did not feel the same as his boss, but first checked to be sure Potter was not watching nearby.

"Hello, friend," he shouted, as he moved to the middle of the road, hoping the man would oblige and meet him halfway. "Ciao, ciao," Charles called out. He'd asked Eddie for some basic Italian, in case such a meeting occurred again, as he'd hoped it would. "Buon pomeriggio!"

The prisoner, this time more confident and wearing no scarf around his head, slowly emerged from behind the tree to stand just feet from Charles. Again, they both seemed baffled by the encounter and remained cautious about their next moves.

Then the oddest thing occurred. Deep in their gaze during which each seemed to lose himself in the other's stare, the two began conversing in a language all their own. Charles, without speaking, seemed to have found a way to make himself understood, just as the stranger's thoughts became decipherable to him. Had they found the same wavelength that allowed Charles to understand his animal friends?

- *I am Roberto*, said the Italian prisoner, without as much as a quiver from his gentle mouth. Their conversation continued, as if each thought was being shared regardless of which man was speaking.

- *Charles. I am Charles.*

- *I see you here each morning. You are working so hard. A man your age must be careful. A good man like you must be spared, as we live in a world where so many are not good men.*

- *I am grateful, Roberto, for your kind thoughts. I have sensed your presence during my work and have desired these words with you since first seeing you on the road. You are not a free man, are you?*

- *No man is free these days where I come from. They can put me in chains here in your country or they can give me freedom to walk your roads, but either way we are not free men. I am no freer if they send me home.*

- *I know so little about your ways or the reasons my people and yours turn to killing each other. I have spent my life cutting and digging, touching animals, learning their ways, seeing to their meals, raising the crops they eat, so that we all may eat, survive until the next season, when it all repeats itself, as it always has.*

- It is the same in my country. Until our leaders achieve complete power and their hunger turns on themselves, we are left to follow these fools. What are we to do but watch them destroy everything around us?

- I listen to the sounds of the animals, to their codes of respect for other living things. Yes, they kill, but their killing is for survival, so that they may feed their offspring and endure the dangers of the natural world. These men kill for the sake of self-aggrandizement, to mimic the powers of our maker.

- You are wise as well, old friend. There is, in both your world and mine, a fever that has spread and poisoned the minds of men who are so distanced from the labor of righteous souls they now intend to destroy all the world in the name of progress.

- And who will inherit the charred earth we shall leave behind? The smallest of creatures speak to me in the night of their need to gather and feed, to protect and defend their families as they have done for millions of years, long before humans existed. Are not the forces that subjugate these minions – our creator's minions – are they not the very personification of evil?

Charles felt more fulfilled than ever before, as if he were a learned philosopher communicating with a clarity that had always eluded him. Finally, he had found an individual who understands him and can share with him the ideas betrayed by the old and uneducated armor of flesh he must wear in this life. Whatever should occur now during the short time left him, he has succeeded in creating a bond with this man that has vindicated the silence he carries with him.

As might be expected, this moment of transcendence is short-lived. Charles suddenly believes he is being watched and with the deepest regret signals to Roberto that he should walk away quickly. He is left no opportunity to touch the man, to make any material link, the kind he has sought his entire life. He feels an emptiness engulf his being.

He waits along the empty road expecting Potter to descend, then berate him again for befriending the Italian. He never appears, though Charles is sure the man was nearby watching. Had he become such a threatening force that Charles fears him even when he is nowhere nearby? If so, then he has let his boss win, let him poison his world, at a time when so much was seeming to change for the good. Charles became determined not to let this happen, imagining ways Potter might pay for his sins without knowing the source of his troubles.

Chapter Nine

Stratford, Court Leet
Friday Afternoon
Mid-December, 1944

"So much for a fortnight. Will anyone, I's ask, tell me why we've waited five months for dis body to meet again? No. And these men'm taken wid demselves," Alfred grumbled, sitting upright on the bench outside the great hall where a coterie of Leet bailiffs were conferring. Thomas had gotten through the entire process of Potter's complaints to the Leet by remaining as silent as he could, appearing to support his overseer, while not alienating himself from others in the body he valued as friends. With everyone other than Potter fully taken by the holiday spirit, he hoped anxiously that the entire controversy would be settled that day, so that the new year could mean he would no longer be required to uphold Potter's obsessions and their winter chores could continue without interruption.

"They listened, but did they hear? Not a one, if me eyes don't deceive me. They'm not wanting to hear what they know, that the earth is still soaked with the devil's blood – in their own fields – and they be no spring crops without we cleanse the soil. What else they'm want to know?"

Thomas pretended to be listening, thinking of little but the strangers coming and going around them, all, he was convinced, believing the man to his right was mad. He was sure they were keeping their distance, completing their civic duties in the grand hallway constructed with slabs of near-ancient marble under excessively high ceilings and windows way above them allowing for a minimum of natural light. He longed to be back on the festive streets, mixing with the holiday crowds, finally able to purchase the few gifts required for his several nephews and niece.

"These bailiffs'm near blind to the truth staring them in they's eyes," Potter continued, "they think themselves weak, as if they'd been neutered like me diseased bulls." Thomas couldn't help but smile at this analogy, thinking how many of the bailiffs, in fact, resembled old, lame cows.

With no warning that the Leet had come to the end of its conference, what had been in medieval times the work of a jury, the Low Bailiff of the court burst out of the door opposite their bench and signaled for the two of them to join the communion. Finally, thought Thomas, this wrought period of indecision would be settled and Potter, either verified or negated, would accept the decision of the Steward of the Manor.

Alfred and Thomas entered the hall, noting that many more bailiffs were in attendance than during the initial meeting, momentarily convincing Potter that his argument had sparked the concerns of all the farmers in his district, and they had come to support his outrage that the devil's forces were again loosed upon the land. They found the two seats in the first row set aside for them.

Steward of the Manor Milner addressed the two of them directly as the members of the Leet looked on without expression.

"While all the members of this court owe a debt to the scrutiny of Bailiff Potter, who has vigorously sought to protect us from the possible intervention of age-old forces of evil, after scrupulous debate and careful consideration of his presentation, such suspicions have been deemed to be hyperbole. While the harvested crops of Quinton have not been as satisfactory as in years past, a majority of the Leet believes the causes have more to do with cycles of nature than with any demonic authority. While few of us can deny the possible sway of the devil when it comes to personal temptations, we agree that the proper venues for the expulsion of such powers are still our houses of worship, which are best equipped to stand firm in the defense of virtue. In these times of great consternation, when half of the continent remains hostage to the ills of National Socialism, we believe all our energies must be devoted to the expulsion of this palpable evil, and not misdirected by concerns beyond our control. This meeting of the Alcester Court Leet is, therefore, adjourned."

Alfred sat motionless, his blood pressure rising, determined not to betray his outrage at the incompetence of this outdated and incoherent so-called body of justice. He knew he had no chance of defying the Leet's final verdict. None of his cohorts would ever recognize the existential dangers threatening their livelihood and Potter feared he would forevermore be shunned as a throwback to medieval practice. Should the true nature of justice be determined, he knew it would never happen here amongst a stilted, self-interested cluster of dead souls blind to the devices of a local demon hellbent on indecency and the destruction of a quintessential British village's way of life.

Charles and Edith's Home

Chapter Ten

Lower Quinton
Monday Morning
Christmas Day, 1944

As the morning light drifted through the small window of their kitchen, one would have noticed a bright green cloth atop their small breakfast table adorned with sprays of Norfolk Island Pine delicately arranged around a pot of Christmas Cactus with red and white blossoms. To its left, hiding the other rather smallish window in the living area, stood a tall Balsam Fir adorned with strings of cranberries and popcorn, even some mistletoe balls artistically spaced. Prior holiday decorations in the Walton household would have dimmed in comparison to this year's. Never had their tree been so large, the quantity of decorations so plentiful, or the number of gifts under the tree so numerous.

Dickens' dark views of "Christmas Past" would have been farthest from the minds of both Charles and Edie in 1944. As if he were Father Christmas himself, Eddie's presence made this year's cheer more glorious than ever before, even by the more modest standards of a wartime Christmas. In fact, the sheer audacity of the room's adornments nearly sent Charles into spasms of guilt, after so many Christmases on which he and Edith had scrimped. As neither of them was a devout churchgoer, they respectfully minimized their celebration. Their last Christmas had included little more than an extra glass of rum toddy and an evening visit to Charles' atheist friend and neighbor Harry Beasley, never known in the village as either a banner of virtue or the life of any party. In hopes of cheering Charles' lonely friend, Edie had invited him to this year's Christmas dinner, for which Eddie had spent the previous day preparing.

"You'm spoiling us, dear boy," Charles, seated in his one upholstered chair, said to Eddie as he opened a large bottle of champaign he'd brought with him the day before. "It bein' shortly past noon and me not attendin' chapel."

"Harry will applaud you, Uncle," Edie replied with a chuckle.

"Well, sometimes, when I do gets to chapel, I feels like certain folks are takin' attendance and notin' hows I'm most often absent."

"The Lord is forgiving, Charles," added Eddie, as he stood in the kitchen area rubbing his two small ducks with garlic, adding to the delicious mix of holiday aromas pervading the household.

"Not to mention me current obsession wid all things bubbly," said Charles, unable to obscure his guilty joy anticipating more than one glass of Eddie's festive spirits.

"Merry Christmas, Charles!" offered Edie, as she walked up behind Eddie at the oven to embrace him from behind. "How delightful to finally have Father Christmas within our midst."

And so, the day began, an uncharacteristically joyful occasion for three individuals heretofore immune to any glimpse of happiness, but now, buoyed by the belief that their futures, enabled by the good fortune of having found one another, will be brighter than any of them could have imagined. The war was surely on the verge of coming to its end, they were all gainfully employed, and, though each of them had accepted a life mostly devoid of deep friendship or love, they had discovered love and acceptance were attainable after all.

For several hours, until their guest was scheduled to arrive, the three of them sat around the tree sipping their toddies, attending to preparations for the holiday meal, and listening to Eddie's current thoughts regarding Shakespeare's near- silence about Christmas, or, in fact, anything about being a Christian. For four hundred years scholars and "Bardologists" had been trying to decide exactly what were Shakespeare's religious sentiments.

"But you say there was no Christmas?" asked an outraged Edie.

"Well, no, not the way we think of it today, no," Eddie replied.

"But I thought…"

"Well, of course, they celebrated the birth of Christ, for a full twelve days, in fact, but it would not have looked or felt the way it does today. Easter was their main holiday."

"Seems they was more liked to death than to birth."

"That's actually true, Charles. We mustn't forget how much death there was in them days. Children dyin' at birth, the plague, it was more a part of life than it is today, 'cept of course recently." The Angel of Silence descended upon the room.

Eddie was careful not to lead his new family down a rabbit hole of regret and misanthropy. He was as enthusiastic about

Christmas as the next person. "But there was certainly no reason to think Shakespeare didn't love mirth and celebrations of love! He practically invented them."

"It is about joy, and don't we all need joy at this time of the year, especially in years like this?" exclaimed Edie.

"Of course, love. The reason he avoided Christmas was because their celebrations were all parts of grand, spectacular events for the queen, which he hated. Not that he didn't love the queen, at least as far as her payroll was concerned. It was the spectacle he disliked. The Bard was more interested in character, civic rather than religious spirit. But I expect the way their Christmas was portrayed as an orgy of theatrical indulgence, with numerous sprites and countless courtiers served up in a pageant for a queen Mr. Shakespeare did not necessarily accept as a direct line to the Holy Father or the Lord himself…"

"I love it when Eddie talks about Shakespeare, don't you, Uncle?"

"I'm not sure I's always know the gist of his matter, but I sure do like the sound of his sayin' it."

"Well, you know me of late. Always prepared to offer some of my latest new finds of Mr. Shakespeare." Reaching for his notes, Eddie continued. "He only mentions Christmas three times. In *Taming of the Shrew* he refers to a 'Christmas gambold or tumbling trick.' Doesn't sound like he was a big fan of the queen's version of the Christmas story."

"Tell me if I'm wrong, Eddie," said Edie, "but if I remember right from school, didn't *Midsummer Night's Dream* have lots of fairies and what you call 'sprites' in it?

"Oh, yes, certainly, but there he was interested in marriage, not Christmas."

"There bein' more interest in marriage than in religious celebration by Mr. Shakespeare is the ways you see it?" asked Charles.

"Well, from what we know not likely a huge admirer of marriage either."

"What did he believe in then?" Edie asked bluntly.

"It's truly hard to know, love, about much of anything he personally believed. Which is why so many keep reading, thinking they can find out."

Always the practical one, Edie declared, "Why not just come out and say it?"

"Life's not like that. No one – certainly not God, if there is one – ever tells us the truth, so why should Shakespeare? At least that's the way I see it."

"I's gotta agree with Eddie on that one," said Charles.

"He does give another hint, though," reading from his notes. "In *Love's Labour's Lost* he writes, 'At Christmas I no more desire a rose, Than wish a snow in May's new-fangled mirth.' That would suggest he has a rather serious notion of what Christmas should be."

"Guess we'll never know, right Eddie?" asked Edie.

"Fact is, we know a lot more of what he thinks about devils and murder." At which point the Angel of Silence again settles in the room.

As if it were his Christmas duty to defy that angel, Harry Beasley knocked on their door. To everyone's surprise, standing at the entrance stood two gentlemen: Harry, and beside him a total stranger to Eddie and Edie. Charles, due to his rheumatism, was seated facing in the other direction, unaware of the other guest's presence.

"Good day, Edie. I'll refrain from all the amenities of the day to say I'm grateful for your generous invitation," said Harry, who seemed to have forgotten he was not alone.

"Harry, Harry, we're so glad you decided to accept!" Edie replied. At which point the four of them – all but Charles – stood looking at each other confounded by the presence of the odd-man-out, unintroduced and smiling broadly in their direction.

Eddie finally rejoined, "Who's your friend, Harry?"

"Say what?" exclaimed their neighbor. "Don't get up, Charles, I knows how hard it is to get out of that chair."

"How are you, sir, and welcome. Merry Christmas," said Eddie, graciously acknowledging the stranger dressed in a fine suit and carrying a wrapped gift.

Nodding enthusiastically, the gentleman replied, "Buon natale!"

Charles heard that voice and struggled to get up to greet his friend. "Bless the day, I can't but believe it. Roberto! I never thought to lay eyes upon you ever again."

The Italian pressed on with his smile and nodding head, sure only that he'd been recognized and that it was Christmas. All else was a mystery, his English having barely improved since the beginning of his stay at the prison camp.

"Harry, ye old coot, you never told me you'm knows me friend Roberto."

"I don't know him! Never laid eyes on him till just this afternoon, you old crazy man. On me way here, there he was, standing at the corner he was."

Determined he couldn't explain to any of his group that he and Roberto could communicate without words, as Edie and Harry would think him certifiably insane, Charles continued his queries to Harry. "Well, how, if neither of yous can understand a word of the other, did you know where he was going?"

"He was just standin' there, chantin' your name. 'Charles? Charles?' Well, I assumed you knew him, and I guess I was right, weren't I, as usual, I might add."

For the rest of the day Charles was in seventh heaven, surrounded as he was by his new nuclear family, his oldest friend, and his newest friend, to whom he remained nearly attached during the remainder of their festivities. Though the existing crowd never allowed them to reconnect via their private wavelength and Harry, having found an audience after months of solitude, dominated the discussions, Charles and Roberto remained as content as peas in a pod. Had Roberto – most likely a devout Italian Catholic – understood the language, he might not have smiled so broadly through the day.

By late afternoon, following their forays into duck, fresh squash, and Christmas pudding, along with several bottles of Eddie's fine champaign, they found themselves sprawled on the floor beside the tree. All the gifts – a new pen for Eddie, a bright red apron for Edie, and for Charles, a warm sweater for the upcoming winter mornings working on the farm, reflected their modest means after years of war. Charles, wanting to make sure the Italian felt fully comfortable with all these foreigners, was overly gracious in his acceptance of Roberto's gift, a pair of suspenders in the colors of the Italian flag, probably purchased in one of Stratford's tourist gift shops.

Harry, always the contrarian, became fascinated with Eddie's return to the topic of Shakespeare's lack of interest in Christmas.

"You say he was an expert on devils and demons, do ye?" asked Harry.

"Exactly," answered Eddie.

"What do ye think he'd say about the witches in our midst today?" asked Harry again. "Do you think they disappear at Christmas?" Eddie chuckled and looked to Edie, confirming their expectations that Harry was always a risk for expressing outrageous views, especially during religious holidays.

"Now Harry, don't go spreadin' your crazy notions," Charles interjected.

"Not my crazy notions, the notions of those who still believe in Shakespeare's witches as appeared in some of his plays."

"Yes, especially in *Macbeth*," Eddie concurred. "But this don't mean the playwright believed in them, just that he knew others believed in them."

"Yes, alright, I knows where yous goin'. And what did he believe that others believed, and do yous believe it today?" Harry insisted.

"Alright," Eddie murmured, remembering what Charles had said to him about others thinking he was a witch. He was afraid Charles might think he was pointing a finger at him, the farthest thing from his mind. He also remembered Charles complaining about Harry's growing allegiance to Bolshevism, that he'd favored the new Russian regime since the First War, and that once you got him started, it was never easy taming the tiger, or in this case, the Russian Bear.

"If you takes a look at Christmas today," Harry continued, "it's as if you'd thought Christmas was about anti-consumerism, but then realized it was actually all about consumerism. Good Christians drowning in all the things that Capitalism tells them they need."

"Good Lord," moaned Charles, "here he goes again." Edie was laughing hysterically, fully under the influence and charmed by the perennial bout between the two old friends.

"It's true! It's both an antidote to industrialization..."

"The man can barely read!"

"And a misdirection from industrialization," Harry continued.

"Now what's that supposed to mean?" asked Charles.

"It takes the objects of mass industrial production and wraps them up in colored paper."

"Good lord, he's sayin' this cause nobodys got the poor man a present. Look under the tree, Edie, I thought there'm somethin' there for him."

Edie wasn't quite sure whether Charles was serious but looked around under the tree anyway.

"Christmas takes the sacred and makes it material," said Harry.

"And there," Eddie interrupted, "enters the devil."

"Yes, you could say that. Christmas sublimates the injustices of capitalism. And who does that better than…

"Here it comes," warned Charles.

"I've put it into a song."

"God help us!" Charles hooted.

"*Where do we find the gifts from our Lord? In Santa's Claws.*"

This bit of wordplay sent Edie into further convulsions of laughter, revealing to Eddie a sense of humor that confirmed his adoration for the woman. They fell into each other's arms on the floor, savoring the further verses Harry sang decidedly off-key.

"*Where do we find the promise of more? In Santa's Claws.*"

"Enough!" cried Charles.

"*What takes the sacred and makes it profane? Santa's Claws.*"

There was a twinkle in Harry's eyes. Years of consuming recent Russian history was finally making him the life of the party. "It's the truth and we's all know it. Santa gives us gifts in return for our souls."

"Which truly makes him a first-class fiend, wouldn't you say," Eddie suggested to anyone who'd listen. "I can't believe I'm agreeing with Harry."

"That's right," agreed Harry. "He wants our obedience and goodness. He wants our "self."

"And traditionally – like Santa – the devil was always the most fun character in medieval plays, the most colorful character, just like Santa," Eddie added.

"All one's gotta do is listen – and it's impossible not to hear these days, if you turn on the wireless – just listen to that Mr. Crosby and his *White Christmas*."

"They do plays that one an awful lot, I'll give you that," Charles reluctantly agreed.

"If you's really listen, what do ye hear? All that nostalgic yearning, the snow, the tree, the sleigh bells, and togetherness…"

"But I love all that, I really do!" cried Edie.

"Of course, you do, love," Eddie assured her.

"But Harry says he's the devil!"

"Not Bing Crosby, love. Santa Claus."

"Christmas takes us into this kind of dream state, capitalism's dream of itself, with all its hopes and terrors, all of it out of reach, just not quite there."

Roberto grinned through it all, as if their celebratory words were right out of the liturgy.

"And I do begins to see your connections to the traditional picture of the Anglican devil, Eddie. Charles has told me about your studies of the Bard and his love of witches." It was here that Eddie hoped to steer the conversation towards something other than witchcraft, old or new, afraid once again of a subject he believed to be sensitive for Charles.

"Charles, tell us more about how you came to know Roberto."

"But you know, Eddie, you've struck a bit of gold here," said Harry. "I'd never imagined Santa in quite that light. Think about it. Wasn't he, just like witches, a person who made a pact with the devil to disguise consumerism in exchange for supernatural powers?"

"That's a bit of a stretch, isn't it?" Eddie objected.

"And Santa had all those animals around him, all his reindeer," Harry said. "Elizabethans believed witches had pets – a toad or a bird – to be their demon advisor." Eddie looked closely for any response or change of expression from Charles. Could all this be going over his head due to his state of inebriation?

"People often accused witches of being old and poor…" Harry continued.

"And of being a woman. Santa was neither poor nor a woman," objected Eddie.

"And witches were so convenient, am I right, Eddie? If your cow was sick or your beans wasn't growin', all you had to do was point at a witch."

"That's right," Eddie agreed.

"And it were legal to kill witches, too, according to the Witchcraft Act of 1563. I can't believe I remembers that date."

"One year before Shakespeare was born," added Eddie.

"They considered it a cleansing," replied Harry, "as if the blood of a witch could purify your fields and make the crops grow again." Once again, as if the topic had been thoroughly explored, the Angel of Silence descended for the third and last time, and again Eddie saved the day.

"I don't think I'll ever hear Santa's bells in quite the same way," he exclaimed to everyone's rather nervous laughter, even that of Roberto, who seemingly gathered the gist of their last conversation.

Once the evening's darkness became apparent through the windows and Harry's stories of the glorious success of the Russian army in Stalingrad the year before had been exhausted, there seemed little else to hold the group together. Harry agreed to make sure Roberto safely found his way back to camp and Charles, having again consumed significantly more alcohol in one sitting than he had as a young man, excused himself for a "wee nap." Soon enough, their cozy celebration having ended, Edie and Eddie found themselves alone under the tree. Both exuded the sense that all was right with the world.

"An all-around success, wouldn't you say, love?" asked Eddie.

"I would say, yes. And I loved Roberto, though I don't feel like I got to know him very well."

"My guess is we'll see more of him, don't you think?" Eddie wrapped his arms around Edie, warming her neck with his breath and cherishing the quiet of their Christmas night. "One thing, though, hasn't happened that I thought would happen."

"What's that?"

"I haven't asked you to marry me yet. Will ya?"

Edie didn't seem surprised or even overly excited. The moment was simply too sublime to spoil with excess emotion. She responded as if it was already written in stone, merely the next line in their preordained dialogue. "Yes, Eddie, I will." Inside, she was screaming with joy.

Chapter Eleven

Lower Quinton
Wednesday, February 14
Valentine's Day, 1945

Edie couldn't recall a more optimistic time in a very long while, since well before the beginning of the war in the late '30s, during which everyone understood war was inevitable. The buzz around the Royal Society was that their work would soon be reflecting a resurgence of arts-related committees that had been on hiatus, including The Arts Council of Great Britain, which included funding for the Shakespeare Memorial Theatre. She couldn't help but beam with happiness thinking of her soon-to-be husband shining on the stage with, who knows, maybe even Lawrence Olivier! Eddie didn't need lines to impress Edie.

The day seemed to zip by. She'd gotten Charles off to work in the morning, dressed in his new sweater carrying a large slice of fruitcake for lunch, still delicious despite being a Christmas leftover. Her usual lunch with Eddie had been cancelled, since it was their plan to celebrate Valentine's Day at a restaurant in town, the identity to be Eddie's surprise. The euphoria set off by Eddie's proposal was still very much alive for both Edie and her uncle, to the extent that Edie no longer huddled with her pictures in the morning and Charles was talking about getting a dog, an indulgence he hadn't appreciated since his marriage.

So, when five o'clock rolled around it was almost as if she'd never gone to work, her mind overtaken by thoughts of a new life in which a husband would be waiting at home for her after work and once a week he'd whisk her off to test the menu of a new Stratford restaurant. A short distance from the relocated work site, she would often take her time walking home, meandering to appreciate the beauty of her neighborhood. This late afternoon, though, looked as if it was turning into a cold, misty evening, so she wasted no time reaching the warmth of her kitchen.

"Charles?" Edie called out after dropping her purse on the kitchen table, a bit surprised her uncle wasn't sitting by the window after returning from feeding duties at The Firs. It was often an optimal time to attract his birds. She was also frazzled as she had less than hour before Eddie would be picking her up. She needed to shower.

"Charles, are you in the shower?" she called again as she stepped into the bedroom, but there was no one there or in the WC. Nothing in the room reflected any change since morning. No one had been on either of the beds. Perhaps he'd gone out with Harry or been delayed at The Firs, she thought, but this would be highly unusual for someone who's life seemed set to a timer, its rituals attuned nearly to the minute, providing comfort and continuity for the older man.

Edie began to panic, though she resisted. She knew she had to worry less about her uncle, especially if she was going to be living with Eddie. They hadn't decided yet on any change in living arrangements, if there was to be any. So, she took several deep breaths and followed the most logical steps to find him.

First, she needed to contact Eddie by phone without causing further alarm.

"Eddie? Hello, love. Yes, I'm fine. No, no, I was just slightly concerned because I can't find Charles. Yes, well, but you know him. Yes, alright. I'll wait. Perhaps I'll just quickly check to see if Harry knows anything. Yes, alright, we'll wait right here. Yes, love."

She was gauging the level of concern she'd heard in Eddie's voice, as she was dependent on him to temper the level of her own distress. Charles had become everything to Edie, her mother, father, roommate, confessor, advisor, even lover, in a platonic, familial way. The thought of life without him frightened her to the core, even considering her upcoming marriage.

Intent on moving forward despite the knot at the pit of her stomach, Edie walked the short distance to their neighbor and knocked on Harry's door. Part of her hoped no one would be home or that she'd discover the two of them sharing a pint inside, though she honestly regarded each scenario as highly unlikely.

"Who be it?" asked Harry after her first knock.

"Edie. It's Edie."

"Enter." His first remarks reflected an observation that would have occurred to any witness of Edie's demeanor. "Good lord, woman, have you seen a ghost?"

"Have you seen Charles?"

"No, he's not been here. Probably up to the farm, don't ye think?

"He's never been late like this in all the time he's worked there." She sat in the empty chair opposite Harry, not because she'd relaxed at all, but fearing she was about to collapse. "I'm so frightened."

"Now, listen, Edie, I'm sure there's some reasonable…"

"No, Harry! I know my uncle. Something terrible's happened and I… I don't know what to do!"

As an unmarried man of advanced age, he had scant experience with any woman, much less one who was near hysterical. "Edie, now calm yourself, if ye can, I really think he must be somewhere safe and be home soon."

Edie was in no mind to be appeased. She leapt from the chair and ran outside to look for Eddie, who happened to be pulling up just as she appeared in front of their home. Harry followed her out the door as she ran towards Eddie, distraught.

He enveloped her in his long arms. "Edie, Edie, try to calm yourself. Let's take this step by step. Harry, can you get in the car with Edie? We're going up to The Firs where I'm sure we'll find him or, if not, we'll find there's a good explanation, don't you think, love? Edie said nothing, obeying Eddie's direction, but remaining convinced no one really understood her fears.

Moments later Eddie's old Chevy Coupe was pulling up to Alfred Potter's farmhouse, dark and forbidding in the foggy mist. One feint light shone through the kitchen window. They waited at the front door after forcefully knocking until Alfred appeared.

"Yes?"

"We're looking for Charles," Eddie said. Alfred was silent. "Charles Walton."

"Not seen him. Not here." They stared at each other. No one seemed willing to go further. Until Edie could no longer bear it.

"My uncle never came home," said Edie, nearly breathless, "and I know he usually comes here to feed the steer, when he's finished down by the road, but he's not come home, and I don't know what I'm going to do, what I'm going to do if..."

"Have you seen him? We really need to know if you've seen him," Eddie asked, while trying to calm Edie, who was on the verge of losing all control, which seemed to alarm even Potter.

"I sees him earlier, cutting, or at least I assumed it'm him. He was in the distance, a long ways off, but I'm sure it'm him." While Potter was not one to exude empathy for anyone, his wife included, he seemed sincerely concerned and suggested they take several of his torches from his mud room and drive down to the spot near the hedgerows where he had seen him earlier in the day. While the three of them returned to Eddie's Chevy, Alfred took a moment to put on his jacket before getting into his truck to lead them to the edge of his farmland where Charles had been cutting.

There was very little to see in the darkness, especially with the heavy mist hanging overall. Alfred moved slowly along the slender road, his arm through the driver's window with torch in hand. Eddie's car followed close behind. He hadn't gone long at that pace when he pulled to the side, stepped out, and walked slowly towards the other car. His expression revealed he'd seen something. Eddie stepped out of the car.

"You. What's your name?" Potter said, frowning at Eddie.

"Eddie. I'm a family friend."

"A word." He gestured for him to walk towards him, so they could speak privately. "Yous oughta know, I thinks what you're about to see, well, it could be the worse thing you'll ever see, maybe, I don't knows yet, but… if what I sees off to the right, on the other side, is what I think it could be, yous oughta tell your sister – or who is it, the niece?" Eddie nodded his head and swallowed. "Tell 'er… well, hell, I don't know what yous can tell her. Just you come wid me. Alone. Hear?"

Eddie turned, knowing he had to make Edie understand she needed to hold back to let him see what Potter had seen, and then come back for her. It seemed to him a near-impossible assignment.

"No, Eddie! I want to see!"

"I know, love, and you will! But please, let's not get on Potter's bad side, he's an erasable old crow, and we can't know what trouble he'll bring." Edie's tense fingers dug into Eddie's jacket, the tears streaming and lips parsed.

"Go, please. I need to know!"

A mere fifteen meters up the road, just to the side, a long, wooden rod shot up from the earth. Alongside it, a walking stick. At the base of the fiendish-looking slash hook he found what appeared at first sight a bundle of dark clothing, but when observed more closely revealed the sharp teeth of the fork hook severing the neck of a wasted corpse that could only be Charles Walton, so close to the spot from where he'd seen the huge dog and headless woman so many years before.

Eddie could only look at the body for a brief moment before being overcome by grief and he knew – his fiancée in dire need of his strength – he could not allow the moment to overwhelm him. He stood a long time at Charles' side, without looking directly at him. Now was not the time.

Then he turned and walked towards Edie. Almost as if he and Edie had found Charles' direct line to communicate without words, she understood. By the look in Eddie's eyes, Edie knew Charles was dead before he was able to say a word. She fell to her knees and crumbled to the ground, as if she could sink into it and meet her uncle somewhere beneath.

Chapter Twelve

Upper Quinton
Wednesday, Late Evening
Valentine's Day, 1945

In as small an area as Warwickshire one might assume someone with my career longevity and experience as head of C.I.D. would be acquainted with nearly everyone in Quinton. Truth be told, most of the homicidal crimes to which I was assigned occurred in Stratford-upon-Avon proper, given its large population and international prominence as a major cultural center. Quinton, on the other hand, was comparatively remote with its own rural codes, allegiances, and superstitions. So, when I received the call at about 9 pm on Wednesday night to go immediately to Upper Quinton, I was surprised and certainly had no knowledge of the victim or his family.

By the time I arrived about an hour later the victim's niece, having been allowed a brief viewing of the crime scene, had been taken home, sedated, and put to bed by her fiancé and their neighbor Harry Beasley. Alfred Potter remained the sole watchman over the crime scene, and fortunately he had the sense to leave all the particulars mostly untouched. At least, that is what he told me. Next at the scene was PC Michael James Lomasney with several of his local underlings, neither of whom had ever witnessed such a bizarre and bloody mass of human waste. They hovered away from the body, witnessing, perhaps, their first corpse. Lomasney also stood off to the side taking notes. This may have been his first homicide, as well.

The trouncing or slash hook was deeply embedded through the center of Walton's throat, above which one could read the look of shock and utter terror, eyes wide open. His shirt had been torn open to reveal what appeared to be a cross scratched into his chest. His belt and fly had been opened, pulled down to show his upper groin. The area surrounding the body was soaked with blood seeping into the ground, almost as if the upper body had been placed at an optimum angle for the blood to drain. The nature of the crime suggested some sort of ritualist intent, though at that early stage in the investigation, I was unfamiliar with any rituals that could have inspired such bloodthirsty violence.

Standing to the side stood Alfred Potter, who seemed transfixed by the gruesome remains, unafraid to look at what was left of Walton, as if each detail deserved considerable contemplation. Neither of us said anything for the longest time.

"You found the body?" I asked.

"Yes. He worked for me."

"I'm Superintendent Alec Spooner, Warwickshire C.I.D."

"Yeah, I know whose you are."

"You do look familiar."

"Court Leet. I'm a bailiff," Potter replied.

"Of course. What time was it?"

"Say what?"

"Time you found him?"

"About 7 pm, I'd say."

"Hmm. And when was the last time you'd seen him alive?" I asked.

"Saw him around noon, or maybe it was a bit later."

"You spoke to him?"

"No, no. I's drivin' up to the farm in my truck, and I sees him in the distance." I decided at that point to leave further questioning for the formal investigation which would follow directly.

My next concern was making sure James Webster of the West Midlands Forensic Lab was contacted. At this juncture Detective Inspector Tombs, who had arrived at about the same time as Lomasney, also took a statement from Potter, who seemed increasingly bothered by the cold temperature. His statement to Tombs was mostly a recounting of his history managing the farm and a confirmation that Hillground, the field on which Charles had been working for the past few months, was the last hedgerow that required cutting.

Webster arrived about 11:30 pm, by which time Lomasney's constables were more than ready to transfer the body to town, which they did once forensics had finished their work. It was clear to me after consultation with Webster and Lomasney about the more inexplicable details of the case that this homicide presented challenges none of us had encountered over the course of any of our careers.

***

Following a night with practically no sleep, I found myself standing on the same few square meters I'd been standing on the night before, now sacrosanct due to the unthinkable actions of what had to be a madman. Fortunately, the weather had cleared to the degree that it was no longer a chore being open to the elements. I was early enough to precede any of the other authorities assigned to the case, so I was able to concentrate on the circumstances I knew so far without being harried by pointless questions. Having reviewed the situation with Webster the night before, I concluded that this case was going to demand the kind of resources unavailable to the Warwickshire C.I.D.

My next move was not taken without some trepidation. As was the case with most of the general public, I was familiar with the career of our country's most famous law enforcer, Detective Superintendent Robert Fabian of Scotland Yard. Why, then, would I question the value of employing the skills of such a successful investigator? Call it hubris, I suppose, or occupational envy. With his great success he'd inherited a certain cache of privilege. Bragging rights, you might say. I am neither too humble nor self-effacing to admit I would love to have reached some of the same heights he experienced. I would be lying if I failed to mention that on the several occasions I'd met the gentleman I felt a certain animosity regarding his rather haughty demeanor and the steadfast certainty of his various theories. That said, I was not so foolish as to believe I had the same investigative abilities as Scotland Yard. This case deserved every resource at our fingertips.

When I learned during my first phone call that morning after the murder that Fabian and his assistant Sergeant Albert Webb already knew about the crime and would be arriving in Warwickshire by train later that day, I could feel the old pangs of resentment rise to the surface. I was wise enough, however, to put them aside and move to the second chore of the day: visit the bookstore.

I had to follow my basic instincts, which led me north to Birmingham, where Chaucer Head Bookshop had been founded in 1830. This iconic spot had become an invaluable resource to me long before the war and would continue to lure me after it moved to Stratford in 1960.

While I was fully aware of the possible resistance to my suspicions about the town's history with the supernatural, I knew instantly I had found gold. I was directed by the bookshop's owner, Lionel Bodware, to a publication from 1929, *Folklore, Old Customs, and Superstitions in Shakespeareland* by J. Harvey Bloom, a local vicar. How I wished I could have interviewed the author, but Lionel informed me that he had died the previous year. Perhaps, I thought, one of the mediums I suspected would be attracted to this case, would be able to put me in touch.

As one might expect from a religious man who spent his life in and around the Bard's playground, Bloom proved to be an eccentric with the skills of a seasoned scholar. I spent the next few hours happily concealed from the rest of the world in a small Birmingham café drinking up the vicar's knowledge of Warwickshire's supernatural past, including his claim that in 1875 "a weak-minded young man killed a woman named Ann Turner with a hayfork because he believed she had bewitched him." I was not yet aware of this incident's direct connection to our victim, but was, of course, brought to its attention because of the murder weapon and the claim of witchcraft.

Later in the book, however, could be found even more astonishing evidence – if one remained open to these kinds of spiritual speculations – of Walton's dark inheritance. There between the covers of Bloom's estimable scholarship were written the words that would haunt me for the rest of my life. He told the story of how a plowboy in 1885 had confronted a large black dog on successive nights returning home. On the last night the dog was accompanied by a headless woman. Now, even I, a rational protector of civic values and balanced justice, had heard numerous claims of black dogs on Meon Hill, but here, as clear as day, was written the name "Charles Walton," the same name given to our victim, whose age perfectly matched the date in Bloom's book.

Revelations did not end here. Bodware had provided me two other books. The first, simply titled *Warwickshire*, published in 1906, I found particularly relevant. In it the author Clive Holland explains the defense of Turner's murderer, John Hayward, later convicted and hung. Hayward claimed he was acting on behalf of the community, as Turner the witch had "bewitched the cattle and land of local farmers." Hayward also admitted to "pinning her to the ground with a hayfork before slashing her throat with a bill hook in the form of a cross," and that these actions referred to as "sticking" reflected ancient Anglo-Saxon rituals intended to prevent the witch from rising from its grave and to cleanse their land.

The second volume titled *Phantom Dogs* brought to life a tiny speck of Warwickshire heretofore unknown to me. Was it possible to ignore such clearly analogous legends? How was I to manage these suspicions that the murder of Walton had a precedent steeped in concerns that dark, evil forces were alive in their community and that actions to end that evil were not just forgivable, but necessary?

The Rollright Stones (The King's Men)

Chapter Thirteen

Phantom Dogs

The brooding mounds of earth known as Meon Hill mark the remnants of early Roman encampments, a place where it is said even the birds won't sing. Arawn, Lord of the Underworld, lies prone at the highest point of the most southern mound. A smile of satanic satisfaction defines his face, as if he were a billboard announcing the kind of pleasure few of us will ever experience. His right-hand wraps around the neck of his chief dog, the finest canine specimen in the land, while the left-hand massages his genitals covered in wolfskin. He rules at the entrance to the Gateway of Hell.

"AArrgh," he barks, as the lead dog in his glorious pack of black beauties. He is about to begin the prowl, his nocturnal hunt to gather the souls of the departed. No mortal is safe from the designs of this slippery, fiendish, and hungry demigod, all that remains alive on the Neolithic and Bronze Age burial mounds, who requires a nightly meal of wayward men or women brave enough to resist his enticing arms and throbbing member.

Arawn locates his prey, a whisp of a woman whose ivory face and heaving bosoms lure him in her direction. She holds in her hands an amethyst stone set in silver. He lifts his lean legs and with his lead dog in tow approaches the young vixen, trying with all her might to show her strength and self-control, but failing from the start to ward off the sort of creature she has always wanted to take her, in just the way her parents warned her would happen.

Words are pointless; the ritual they are about to perform has long been written in the story of the young girl, and language would only muddle the intent of either of them. His lithe arms reach out to grasp the back of her head and pull her forward, forcing her to her knees where she drops her amethyst and slips her hands beneath the wolfskin. He gazes into her pale eyes, his smile unchanged, as if it was etched in stone. She handles him, as if his length of protruding flesh was the love wand for which all her previous life had prepared her. Every stroke represents her greatest effort to please the god, to feed his fire, and bring him down upon her.

He mounts the virgin, tearing apart her slender gown, and enters her, his hands supporting her buttocks and cupping her fleshy dunes. She screams with every thrust, embracing long moments of unspeakable pleasure until his center erupts in a river of semen. He drops her to the ground, delighted by another evening's conquest. She lies in the dust, amazed that the guilt she has been told will follow such a deed never shows itself. How is it possible, she wonders, that she feels freer now than ever before, ready for any consequence, knowing, perhaps, that she has reached the culmination of all that has come before?

He hesitates for only a moment, understanding that any empathy will hinder his ultimate mission: to bring the living into his fold, to liberate this pathetic figure of desire by introducing her to the netherworld and thereby declare himself the ultimate power. He reaches into his boot to bring forth his silver dagger, and with a swift and beautiful motion, he severs her head from her body, watching it roll down the side of Meon Hill. As if on cue, the hounds show their obedience by following the head to the bottom of the hill, circling it, and raucously barking their delight.

Such was the tale that fed the imagination of the 8th c. Viking King who led a hunting party marking the Celtic celebration of fertility on Meon Hill centuries after Arawn had last been seen. Only his dogs remain present to remind all who encounter them that the rule of Arawn must still be respected.

Their revels that night marked a harbinger of death for those who might resist the Devil's thirst for domination and his fury instigated by their nearby construction of Evesham Abby. Meon Hill has become his earthly residence, a launching point for his forays into the night where he wishes to rid the land of newly established Christians.

Unable to lure this new congregation through his gates to the underworld, Beelzebub kicked a massive boulder down the hill to destroy the abbey. However, alerted to the plot, the believers gather to pray, hoping to divert the boulder's path. The boulder misses the abbey and comes to rest on Cleeve Hill, near Cheltenham, where villagers through the ages have carved it into a giant stone cross to ward off further attacks.

Only a few miles from Meon Hill can be found the ancient megalith site known as The Rollright Stones, divided into three sections: The King's Men (a circle of seventy-seven large stones built for ceremonial purposes), The King's Stone (a single monolith that stands to the north of The King's Men), and The Whispering Knights (five upright stones that lay inwards towards each other as if they were whispering behind the king's back). But before these locations were literally set in stone, the Celtic King and his army met their demise.

The old king on his even older stag was riding through the night in pursuit of the fleeing inhabitants of the Cotswolds, intent on conquering all of England. He reaches a ridge near Long Compton, and he spies a local witch, Mother Shipton, the Sovereign, a goddess protector of the land, so angry that she transforms the invading army into stones and herself into an old tree that guards over the army for eternity. On certain nights at the stroke of midnight this curse is briefly lifted to allow members of the king's army to come to life. Some of the soldiers drink at a nearby spring, while others join the faeries from underground caves to dance in ecstasy around the King's Stone, a phallic emblem of fertility.

Lured by the supernatural power of the King's Stone, women unable to conceive come to the phallus and, by rubbing their bare breasts against the stone, are able to give birth nine months later.

Forever present are the dogs. Meon Hill and the nearby Rollright Stones have come to serve as the center of all rituals in which local witch covens gather, overseen by their horde of black dogs. In the 17th c. a witch accused of murder "by the means of black magic" was also accused of joining the festivities at the King's Stone and summarily hung.

While the evidence of hooded figures surrounding a fire and the discovery of the remains of dead animals abound, the dogs – black harbingers of death and misfortune – remain the most feared.

Chapter Fourteen

Lower Quinton
Thursday, Late Afternoon
February 15, 1945

Eddie sat at their small kitchen table where Charles would usually be found at that hour, his elbows supporting a heavy head, exhausted after twenty-four hours of feeling the world had turned upside down. Edie had not yet emerged from the bedroom and Eddie wisely decided not to wake her, but rather let the medication run its course. The fact that Charles was gone and never to return had not yet fully registered.

He couldn't help thinking that at about this time on a near-spring-like day his future father-in-law would enter after depositing his strange trouncing hook just outside the front door. While Eddie had rarely been there to greet him, his imagination provided a clear scenario that included Charles feeding his birds, or, perhaps, waiting to walk his new dog. He quickly banished these thoughts, though, because they made him too sad.

Eddie couldn't imagine how such a sordid crime could occur in his quiet and culturally rich corner of Warwickshire. And no matter how he struggled to make sense of it, he continually returned to the stories Charles had told that night in the tavern: his dark journeys full of ale, walking home along the hedgerows and waiting to see the black dog, then finally beholding the headless woman. Were he to believe Charles' heartfelt tales he would be admitting to a world open to supernatural influence, unearthly creatures more suited to Hades than to Stratford-upon-Avon. He would be accepting the notion that Shakespeare's witches were not fictional characters, but the product of rational observation. It would not be the world he thought he was inhabiting.

On the other hand, if it could be proven that Charles was murdered for earthbound reasons – as wretched as they may be – by an individual who is very much a product of the material world, he would be able to return to his belief in reason, justice, and the power of love. Should no such resolve be found, he and Edie would be forced to accept the dark forces and Charles' place in a universe measured by its enslavery to evil.

With no option but to wait until the investigation was in full swing, Eddie recognized his most important duty was to help bring Edie back from the depths she would surely be inhabiting for the foreseeable future. As he began to consider ways in which such a redemption might be possible, he heard a knock at the door. There I was, standing before him, on my way back to Stratford from Birmingham.

"Please, come in, Inspector."

"Thank you. Sorry to bother you so soon, but I was driving in your direction and had a few questions."

"I'm afraid Edie hasn't recovered from last night yet."

"I expect it will be a very long time before any of us recover from last 'night, though hardest, I'm sure, for your fiancé, am I correct?" I asked.

"Yes, we're to be married this spring."

Eddie directed me to the kitchen table. "Charles would often sit here at this hour and feed his birds," Eddie reflected.

"He liked his birds, did he?"

"Oh, yes, he had a special way with all animals, as I'm sure you'll hear people say."

"I need to ask a few simple questions before we begin the formal investigation. Is there anyone you can think of who would have wanted to harm Mr. Walton?"

Eddie hesitated, knowing full well the tensions that existed between Charles and his quarrelsome boss, but he'd never considered them reasons for murder. Was he prepared to open this can of worms when he had no real evidence of ill will between the two of them?

"Charles very much kept to himself. And I've only known him this last year, but I understood him to be loved by everyone in town, even if some found him slightly eccentric."

"When you say eccentric?" I queried.

"Well, the birds, as I said, and Edie told me that as a younger man, before his marriage, he would work with horses, you know, speak to them, sort of, but I never saw that. Some folks, down at the King George, for instance, suggested he had near magical powers of healing with all kinds of farm animals, so sometimes he would get calls about that, I believe."

"But you never saw that happen?"

"No, sir, just what I heard," answered Eddie. He thought to mention his observing the frogs, but for some reason withheld that information. "Edie would know much more about that, but I don't think she's ready to be questioned yet. In fact, I'm going to seriously object if…"

"No worries about that. I'll be giving her more time to recuperate," I assured him.

"Charles was such a good, kind soul. I can't imagine anyone wishing him harm."

"I understand, but I need to know even the slightest suspicion you might have had about anybody else's feelings toward him. Did he owe anyone money, was there anyone in his past who might have been holding a grudge, had he ever had romantic problems? Things such as that."

Eddie couldn't help but smile at the thought of Charles being romantically involved, after hearing the stories of his marriage to a very modest, staunchly conservative woman who had died seventeen years before. "No, no, he led a very isolated existence. That's why he was so looking forward to the end of the war and perhaps coming to see the shows at the theatre. I sometimes appear with the Shakespeare Memorial Company, and he was excited about seeing that."

"Oh, my, my, I'm quite impressed," I gushed.

"No, well, it's not really much, I pretty much just stand around."

"Well, still. I assume he and his niece had a good relationship, correct?"

"Yes, yes, she loved him dearly, depended on him for so many things. They were like father and daughter, I'd say."

"What about her real father? Dead?"

"No, apparently not. She rarely spoke of him, but I understood he is very much alive and living in Stratford, even if she never sees him. Can't say why, really." I noted this detail in my pad, wondering how and why a father could abandon a daughter. Or was it, perhaps, just a loose, meaningless circumstance?

"What about his boss, this Potter fellow? There wasn't any bad blood between them, was there? Wages owed or anything like that?"

Again, Eddie hesitated, knowing I'd follow any hint of a lead if he offered one. "Not to my knowledge. Not to say they were best friends or anything. Potter's not always the most likeable sort, if you know what I mean."

"I gathered some of that, yes," I admitted.

"He did seem to keep his eye on him, I noticed." Eddie was careful to choose just the right words. "He seemed to me to be somewhat suspicious of something, though that could have been in my own head, you know."

"Can you be a bit more specific?"

"Well, like I said, many thought Charles had certain powers over animals, but others thought it was mostly odd, you know. Potter seemed to take it a bit more seriously. But then, he takes most things more seriously, lacking as he does much of a sense of humor, it seems."

"Yes, well, if we arrested every Englishman without a proper sense of humor, I suppose the jails would be full." I chuckled, glad to be with someone who obviously possessed a fine sense of humor. "Well, thank you, Eddie. May I call you Eddie?"

"Yes, please do, Inspector."

"Please, call me Alec." Which, by the way, he could never quite do.

My next chore before I would finally be able to get a good night's rest included an initial meeting with our two sterling members of Scotland Yard. I was anxious to know what they'd been up to during their first day in Warwickshire. I was also curious to know how well we'd be able to work together on a case that I expected was as mystifying to them as it was to me.

Chapter Fifteen

White Swan Hotel, Stratford
Thursday, Early Evening
February 15, 1945

As I expected, Inspector Fabian and his partner Sergeant Webb had plans to turn their Stratford jaunt into a first-class experience by making their home base the White Swan Hotel, the town's oldest and most exclusive lodgings. Who could blame them? Certainly not me. I often enjoyed meals and drinks there, though I'd only spent one night in one of its beds. So, I was looking forward to meeting them there for dinner to discuss our first actions in the case.

The pub's amalgamation of stucco, brick, and dark cedar beams made one feel he might be in a much earlier century, it's tables small and generally set before roaring fireplaces. After spending much of the day on the road, a good meal and some stimulating conversation were exactly what I needed, even if it was to be a working dinner.

"Over here, Spooner!" I saw Fabian motioning from the farthest corner and moved towards the table, surprised that he'd recognized me. "Have a seat."

"I'm glad you made it safely," I said sincerely.

"Good to see you again," added Webb, with whom I was more familiar.

"Likewise."

"So, it seems as though we've got one we can tell our grandchildren about," Fabian said, with a supercilious smile, as though he'd found a challenge worthy of a feature in his memoirs, still a decade away from publication.

"If the press doesn't beat you to the punch," warned Webb. "Have you seen any reporters in town yet, Alec?"

"My god," I said, "The crime occurred last night!"

"And by the end of the weekend everyone in the kingdom will know the name Charles Walton. You wait," Fabian concluded.

I hadn't given a thought to the kind of interest this case might engender in the press, always looking to lead its readers down some dark, amoral alley. "I suppose it might be just what people are looking for after years of reading nothing but statistics of the dead on the continent," I calculated.

"Yes, human interest," said Fabian.

"Or supernatural interest, rather."

"What do you mean?" Webb interjected. "Granted it's early to say much of anything definitive, but it seems to me the work of some maniac, a loose monster of some sort. Who else would go to go the lengths of this murderer?"

"Why don't you go ahead and order, Inspector. We've already done so," Fabian added. "I suppose I'd have to agree. It's not as if the suspect is hiding his intentions, but who could be driven to such extremes? Everything points to a madman, and we've come across those before."

I took my first sip of some very fine burgundy they'd ordered and tried to map out the ways I would broach the many superstitions that would surely color our investigation. "I've already done some research, but I'm frankly somewhat reluctant to share it quite yet."

"Yes, I wondered if you were quite in your right mind when you called to tell me you'd be spending the first day in a bookstore. Hope you found the perfect mystery to spend your late evenings with," Fabian noted dryly to his partner.

"I hope, gentlemen, you are able to appreciate this rather unique corner of the empire," I ventured.

"I do love my 16th c. literature, if that's what you mean," said Fabian, "though I'm afraid my knowledge of the Bard doesn't go much beyond my private schooling."

"Unfortunately, we haven't seen too much of WS since the start of the Blitzkrieg, but the culture to which I refer actually predates the Bard by quite a few centuries."

"I have to admit to being intrigued, Spooner. I trust you'll be sharing these nuggets of knowledge sooner than later."

"I'll leave you three volumes I found in Birmingham today. I've marked several pages in each that I promise will get your attention, but might, perhaps, demand an imagination beyond what one usually finds in London."

"I look forward to stretching some of those atrophied cerebral muscles, Inspector," Fabian surly responded.

"It may demand instead a more inquisitive heart than a questioning mind," I cautioned.

"Now, there's dangerous territory, Superintendent. In the meantime," Fabian said, looking to Webb, "let's talk about some of the things we know, not the ones on which we can only speculate."

At which point the Sergeant took out his notebook, just as the waitress arrived with two very thick and very rare steaks for my two colleagues. "I'll have the ribs, Miss," I told her, before giving Webb my full attention.

"Following our very brief visit to the incident room after we arrived this morning, we gathered from viewing the body that death was the result of traumatic wounds to the neck and upper torso. It appeared from the look of the victim's face that death was near-instantaneous," Webb read from his notes.

"I understand that Alfred Potter, the victim's employer, was the first to discover the body, is that correct?" asked Fabian.

"Yes," I replied, "his niece and her fiancé, Edgar Goode, went to his home because they were worried he hadn't returned from work. Potter drove them to the spot where he believed he'd been working and that's where they found the body."

"And they left the body untouched, so when you arrived it hadn't been disturbed, correct?" Fabian asked.

"Yes, that's what Potter told me, though I haven't confirmed this with the niece, who was obviously too distraught to be questioned that evening."

"Of course, we'll want to speak to her as soon as possible," Fabian added.

"Well, we may have to wait a few days on that one. According to Eddie she's in no condition at the moment," I answered.

"Yes, well, we'll see. We can start with the fiancé, I suppose. Go on, Sergeant."

"The victim appeared to be in his early '70s…"

"74, I believe," I said.

"We should have the forensics report within twenty-four hours, I expect, not that it's going to tell us much. It's not as if we suspect poisoning," Fabian jested.

"Inspector Fabian and I will be conferring with the central office tomorrow," Webb confirmed.

"I'm going to be asking for some help from our geographical unit, try to get a look at the lay of the land around the murder site," Fabian followed up.

"We weren't joking, Spooner, when we expressed our concern for the press. There's already been a lot of speculation from reporters, given the graphic nature of this murder, so we've got to be prepared for the public and political curiosity regarding this case," Webb continued.

"In other words," said the chief, "we'll be using every tool at our disposal to find this fiend in an expedited manner, so there's no chance of a panic, which could do irreparable harm to the financial health of the region, just as we hope to be returning to some kind of normal. We want this monster, and we want him yesterday."

"I think there's very little doubt," Webb interjected, "but that the killer is a psychopath who lives here in the area and can be found in a relatively short time. I'm confident."

Fabian's considerable fame as a successful sleuth who nearly always "gets his man" reflects an intellect, a natural instinct, that generally eschews confidence to embrace curiosity, instead. No one ever expected a popular memoir with a list of cases in which the killer is successfully found to be penned by Sergeant Webb. If Fabian was as confident as his partner, he certainly never expressed it. For this, I admired the Superintendent, despite his sometimes slightly arrogant presentation.

"Nevertheless,Webb and I will be setting ourselves up in the room just down the hall from your office, Spooner, and we'll be there until we identify our killer."

While I can't say I looked forward to the weeks, maybe months, ahead of me, sharing my workspace, I could not deny a sense of unbridled excitement at the prospect of success in this case. A good deal of that enthusiasm was, however, related to my own curiosity about its more paranormal circumstances, the timeless notion that our human beliefs - and actions - have consequences.

Chapter Sixteen

Upper Quinton
Saturday, Early Afternoon
February 17, 1945

By Saturday afternoon, three days after the murder, the investigation felt as if it had been ongoing for months. Fabian's first measures, far surpassing anything my powers would have been able to put in motion, included calling in aircraft from the nearby RAF Leamington Spa, so that detailed pictures might be taken of the entire area. I'm not quite sure why I was requested to be on the ground to observe these flyovers, other than he wanted to impress me with his abilities to activate our armed forces with one phone call. I had to admit to finding his thoroughness quite remarkable. No wonder, I thought, one's ego tends to grow when he becomes associated with Sherlock Holmes' old office.

While nothing particularly useful was discovered as a result of these photographs, it did come to our attention how close the Italian prison camp was to the crime scene, leading to several avenues of the investigation. It was important, though, that the three of us observe the crime scene together, so each of us could be sure we were referring to the same space and evidence.

After we all stood over the spot where we could still see blood seeping into the ground, even from the air, Fabian walked up a nearby ledge and stood looking across the field beyond the hedgerow that led to Potter's farmhouse. As opposed to Webb, who was always jotting notes in his tiny notebook, Fabian never took notes and almost never conferred with anyone about his current state of mind. After what seemed a very long time, I walked over to stand by his side.

"Beautiful scenery, is it not?"

"Indeed, the very heart of the Crown," he replied.

"I wonder, if I weren't born in this corner of the world, if I wouldn't..."

"You don't suppose the tales you pointed out in those books you gave me the other night aren't precisely what we should rationally consider quackery, do you?"

Fabian's sudden turn towards abrupt truth-telling struck me as uncharacteristic, but then I hadn't gotten to know the inspector very well yet. If his intent was to dismiss these theories out of hand after less than twenty-four hours, I had overestimated his intellect.

"I find it extremely difficult to forget some of the striking details that seem to share times and places in Walton's life," I said to the inspector.

"Yes, well, I like a good story when I hear one, too, Spooner." I had yet to hear him call me Alec, but then I couldn't remember if I'd ever asked him to. "I'm as aware, as are you, of the healthy imaginations of most everyone who's lived their lives in the shadow of our most admired literary giants of Warwickshire. I am also a skeptic when it comes to an over-abundance of praise for either the higher or lower being. As any capable investigator, my first allegiance must be to the power of science and its ability to lead us to the perpetrator, don't you think?"

I was again pleasantly surprised by the man's eloquence, as well as his ability to remind me of our first responsibility to follow every lead in this world before we go looking for leads in another world.

"I expect you're right, sir," I answered, without sounding, I hoped, like some milquetoast supplicant. I still believed our journey was not going to allow us to ignore the signs and signals discovered in the metaphysical journals I'd found.

"I have to admit I can't help agreeing with Webb – not always my inclination, by the way – but I think the identity of our killer will be found if we simply sweep this town with questions, that ultimately not everyone will be willing to withhold information about someone capable of such grisly actions. I might be a natural skeptic, but I do believe in the general goodness of men – and women – when it comes to simple decency."

"Yes, I think you're right again." God, listen to me, I thought, sounding like one of those women who followed Fabian around on his book tours to get his signature in their copy of his literary barnstormer *Fabian of the Yard*.

"In which case, let me suggest that Webb and I begin interviewing a very long list of possible witnesses or interested parties. I'd like to get back to London by Christmas."

"Christmas?!" I asked with alarm.

"Just joking, Spooner. I expect we'll be home for Easter. In the meantime…"

"In the meantime," I interrupted, not wanting to give him the idea I was waiting for instructions, "I'm going to have a long tete-a-tete with Mr. Potter. I have every belief he's going to be a difficult nut to crack." I was quite sure I detected a hint of indignation at my unwillingness to let him make the initial assignments, but I was determined to maintain a balance of power in this endeavor, even if it meant alienating myself from those calling the shots from The Yard. I already understood that this case would prove one of – if not *the* – most perplexing of my career and I was not about to accede all control to my London guests.

"Yes, well, why don't you do that. We'll get around to him eventually, no doubt. Can't hurt to warm him up and then compare our notes, don't you think?" Fabian concluded, as he walked back to his waiting car, never expecting an answer to his final question, thereby missing my wry smile at his departure.

Chapter Seventeen

Upper Quinton
Early Sunday Morning
February 18, 1945

Potter and Thomas Burns were huddled behind a shrub beyond the copse of trees that surrounded the stream running along the southern border of his property. Burns was there to witness the assault, so he could report to the Leet.

"Hold the gun by its shank, you'm fool, be dumb enough to shoot off yous balls," Potter demanded, as they neared the spot that gave the best view of the rise just above the copse. They were both armed with 12-guage shotguns and dressed in camouflage outfits with hats, leftovers from the Great War. It was dark, but not so much that one couldn't define the horizon line.

"What's this about?" inquired Burns sleepily.

"Never you mind. You just keep yous eyes open and ready to shoot when I says, you got that?"

Potter came to the spot he'd chosen earlier and dropped to the ground, pulling Thomas down with him, convinced no one, including the herd of amphibians he was expecting, would see them so closely molded to the cold ground. He pulled out his binoculars – also relics of his fighting days in France and Germany – looking for any movement. His heart was racing. The rage he remembered from Verdun had returned, though this time the fear was replaced by righteousness.

Slowly, as the deep night slowly turned light, he began to see them. Their eyes glowed, as big as tea saucers, moving in military lines, hundreds of them marching slowly up the rise. They seemed as large as dogs, big dogs, their skin a shimmering green.

"God in heaven, do ya see'm, Thomas?"

"I do, I do!"

"From the guts of the watery beast below, set upon us, an army to kill our crops."

"They're frogs, sir."

"Not just frogs, Burns!" Potter barked at his bemused companion. " Them's the devil's militia. Some of them looks as big as horses!"

"What are we to do?"

"Stay low and mark them, remember them so's your report makes the others take notice. Stay low and when they's get close we both shoot and kill more than one at time. Got it?"

"Yes, sir."

As the morning light began to wash over the hill, Potter could see endless lines of these demons, seeming to smile like huge enigmas marching slowly towards them.

"And listen, can ya hear it?"

With the light came the sound of a hundred groans. Or were they growling? He'd never heard a sound like it, as if it were the hum of a chorus from hell. He felt more alive than he had in years, indeed, since facing down the Hun twenty-five years earlier. This was his day of glory. He would kill one of these grotesque creatures, skin him, and show the cowardly bailiffs that the real evil lived in their own backyards, not on the fields of Europe.

But where was Walton? After motioning for Burns to stay to the ground, Potter stood, as bravely as he thought himself all those years ago. How he longed to load his buckshot into the wily witch who'd overtaken his farm, turning even his meekest four-leggeds against him with his secret words and hidden signs. And there, just as he'd wished it, stood the arthritic old man, though today he was tall and robust as a giant oak tree and his eyes as large as those of his amphibious army. He carried no walking stick, but in his arms, held high and aimed in Potter's direction, the deadly hayfork.

"You'll not be leaving this field alive, you fiend!" screamed Potter, before he raised his gun, aimed directly at Walton, and fired! The crack of the gun was no ordinary sound. Rather, a roar ran throughout the entire farm, awakening all the animals, even his sleeping wife next to him, as he jolted upright in his bed shaken, feeling as if he were at the center of an earthquake.

***

Seven hours later, at my behest, Potter walked slowly to his front door to quell my knocking. He was still dazed by his nightmare, his first since those years just after the Great War. He found it impossible to rid himself of its sounds.

"Thank you, Mr. Potter, for meeting me so soon after the murder," I told him, noting that it seemed as though he'd not slept in several nights.

"Yes, well, gotta start somewheres, I suppose."

I was amazed that he seemed so amenable to my questioning, thinking, even then, that he was the most likely suspect, though I had to admit he seemed quite incapable of such a heinous crime. A slight man in his '50s whose physique resembled that of the victim, he drew us into his sitting room, offering me the most comfortable armchair opposite a slight, wooden straight-back he chose for himself.

"I'll begin with the most obvious question. Do you know anyone who might have wanted to harm Mr. Walton?"

"I didn't trust him," said Potter.

We both fell silent. I was bewildered. Was he pointing a finger in his own direction? Was this some kind of confession and our work now complete?

"I'm not sure I understand," I replied.

"What's to understand? I never liked the man. Since the day he arrived at my farm after bein' recommended by other farmers. I'd asked him to tend to one of me sows, which he did, I guess. But I still didn't like him."

"So, you slaughtered him?"

For the first and only time I can remember, a huge smile commandeered his face, followed by a deep chuckle. "Wouldn't that make your job an easy one, Inspector? No. 'Suppose I wished I had, though."

"Why should I believe you didn't, if you're the only one who seems to have a motive?"

"Cause he wasn't worth the trouble he'd make for me if I did kill'm."

"But you'd have no trouble killing a man, would you?"

"I've killed men, if that's what ye mean. Many men, perhaps, in case you've forgotten those of us who fought in '16," he said, looking straight into my eyes.

"I was just a bit too young for that one," I told him, unable to hide a deep-seeded guilt that had remained heretofore unrecognized. "You seemed to know just where to go when the niece came to get you. You knew he was there, didn't you? And you knew he was dead."

"I told you, I seen him there earlier, so I knew where we'd find'm."

"You knew where you'd find him cause you knew he was dead, and you know who killed him," I stated bluntly.

"I guess I've done all your work, then. Case closed," he replied, seeming calmer than he had since I arrived. "Ceptin' you got no evidence, has you? Nothin' that ties me to any crime, am I right? Nothin' I'm hidin' either, right? I don't know nothin' and I'll just state that to anyone who wants to listen. I'm not your killer, Inspector."

My problem was that I believed him.

"What was it about him that made you dislike him so much?" I asked.

"Not a fair question."

"Fair? Why not fair?"

"What do we know about such things?"

"What things do you mean?"

"What happens when a man enters the room and yous know such a man is poison. Nothin' he said or what anyone's said about him, just a feeling as true as yous ever had, that no one is safe because this man walks among us. Yous never felt like that with someone you didn't know?"

I hesitated because I wanted to tell him that he'd described my exact feelings upon meeting him, but I thought I'd best hold that card close. It seemed more reasonable to let him go deeper.

"Yes," I replied, "I suppose I have felt that way. But society is held together because one can't simply act based on a hunch or abstract feeling, otherwise we'd have chaos."

"At's right, Inspector, and why we have people such as you to what… keep the peace?"

"How am I doing?"

"I can see you'm an honorable man who'll listen to reason and then see such an act as we've witnessed only verifies my sense of this dead man."

"You didn't owe this man money, did you?"

"I didn't owe this man nothin'. A job, a payment, an apology, nothin'," Potter affirmed without blinking. "But I can tell ya who did kill the man."

I wasn't quite sure I'd heard him correctly. "Excuse me, you said what?"

"I said I knew who was the killer."

"Why have you not said something earlier?"

"Do yous want to know or not?"

"Yes, of course, I'd love to hear your speculations."

"Speculations... It's one of them Italian Nazis at that camp just down the road from my field. I seen him many times, botherin' Walton, threatenin' my wife, sneaky little bastard. He's the one you're lookin' for."

"Have you got any proof, Mr. Potter? And why didn't you say anything to me right after the murder?" I asked.

"What more proof do yous need? He was there with the man many times and he was a Nazi! Walton brought it on himself, makin' friends with a foreigner like that."

"You mean he had it coming to him, is that what you're saying?"

"I never said that." He seemed to have come to the end of his accusations, most of which only confirmed my general impression of the man as a snake.

“Well, again, thank you for the time. I’m sure this won’t be the last time we’ll need to talk.”

“My door is always open, Inspector.” And it was through that door that I departed, for the time being, anyway.

Chapter Eighteen

Lower Quinton
Monday Morning
February 19, 1945

Edgar sat in Charles' old, upholstered chair in the living area, solemnly resigned to the string of questions he knew would follow. He had objected to bringing Edie to our office so soon after the murder, thinking the questions would be easier to swallow if they occurred in her own space. Hence, Webb, Fabian and I agreed to coming there.

Fabian had buried his indignation, believing an office interview would give him advantage. He needed to know everything. Settled into the niche by the window where Charles ate his meals, he stared at Webb with his notebook in the straight chair, and I moved around freely, unable to settle in one place. Edie tried to relax in the chair opposite Fabian, who'd been drilling her with questions for over an hour.

"I wish I could be more help," said Edie.

"You're being very helpful, Miss Walton," Fabian insisted. "Do you remember hearing anything about someone needing anything from Charles?"

"No, no. He was a giver, Charles was, as I've said. He was kind and loved making new friends."

"Of course, he was," Eddie chimed in. "You remember him at the pub that night, Edie? People smiling and loving him as they always have."

"But surely over the years, there must have been some suspicions about his way with animals. What about the people who thought he was odd, even psychotic maybe?"

"What do you mean, psychotic?" asked Eddie with an edge.

"He saw things that weren't there," Fabian answered.

"Yes, well, don't we all.

"Very well." Fabian took a long breath and moved down his list of questions. "Is there anything you'd like to do with his personal items? I understand you've not viewed the body or those things we've kept. Surely, you'd like to keep some of them."

"There was one thing. Have you seen his watch? It was a cheap watch, but he loved it so. I'd like to have that."

"Webb, have we got a watch in the mix there?"

"I don't think there was any watch," Webb replied.

Then, impulsively, he decided this watch was his ticket to the suspect. "Then we'll find this watch. And if we find this watch, we'll find some prints. Correct, Webb?"

Webb agreed. "You wait, Miss Walton. We'll find that watch for you."

"So, we shall," concluded Fabian, equally pleased they'd completed their first formal interview and ready to take the investigation to the rest of Quinton.

I remained behind after agreeing to visit several merchants, as well as members of the Court Leet, whom I'd told Fabian were Potter's fellow bailiffs. First and foremost, though, I could not escape believing that Potter's state of mind was central to the conclusion of this affair.

Once Fabian left, I took Charles's seat by the window, hoping Edie would remain in place long enough for me to explore a few remaining threads.

"You've had a long life here with Charles, haven't you?" I asked.

"I have, Inspector. Thank you for recognizing that and realizing how difficult it is for me to accept this."

"How well did you know your uncle? Did he speak often about his life before marriage or the death of your mother?"

Edie looked at Eddie, who, apparently, harbored some of the same suspicions; he seemed just as anxious to dig a little deeper into Charles' impressions of Ann Turner's murder and his understanding of Charles' encountering the black dog and headless woman. But then something snapped.

"I don't know! Why is everyone asking all these questions?" Edie asked frantically.

"I'm sorry, love," said Eddie. "I know how upset you are."

"No, it seems you don't, Eddie!" Edie was determined to make herself understood this time and slammed the door after going into her bedroom.

"I'm sorry, Inspector, I expected this might be the opportune moment to better know Charles, whom I believed had come to an understanding of his special powers."

"So, you believed he had these powers?" I asked.

"Oh, yes, absolutely. No question."

"Was he a witch, then?"

"How can I know this? We are not in the 17th c., Inspector.

"Do we have no witches in the 20th c.?"

"I may be the wrong person to ask. I know I have walked with them in the flesh on Shakespeare's stage."

"So, you would recognize that such forces exist in our time, much as they did in 17th c.?"

"I have little doubt Shakespeare was observing human behavior that was as relevant to his times as it is to ours, if that's what you're asking."

"I'm not sure what I'm asking, frankly," I said, hoping to get beyond the allusions to Shakespeare's characters. "Perhaps, I'm asking where you think might be the best place to start our investigation. I'm not as sure as Fabian that once we find his watch, we'll find his murderer. You've been around these parts all your life. Where would you begin?"

"Well, if you're looking for someone who knew Charles the longest, I'd talk to Harry Beasley," Eddie said. "The friend who was with us when we found Charles. They've known each other since they were both in their '20s, maybe longer."

"Yes, of course. Maybe he's the one to confirm a few suspicions I have."

"Suspicions are exactly what Harry Beasley is about," Eddie confirmed.

"Splendid. Then that's my next stop. I'd love to speak more with Edie, too, but only when she feels more comfortable. You'll let me know when you think that might be possible?"

"I will try, Inspector."

Chapter Nineteen

Lower Quinton
Monday Afternoon
February 19, 1945

"Paradox. I think it's me favorite word."

I'd been in his miniature garden for what felt like half the afternoon, long enough to sense the onset of evening, it's red ball fading into the western horizon. I'd only intended to stay an hour after he graciously accepted my offer to come right over from Edie's, but I was greatly enjoying nearly every moment of what seemed a cross between a comic's cabaret act and a history lesson.

"How do we survive, the Bolsheviks asked themselves, starving as they'm were in the midst of a war, the second part of which sits with us like a prolonged bowel movement," said Harry, his hands full of dirt as he finished planting another row of strawberries.

"I shall forevermore never again think of this war as anything other than a bowel movement," I replied.

"This were a young communist state on the verge of a great experiment, determined, according to their illustrious leaders, to create huge state farms to feed their newly liberated millions. Yet, were it not for the tidy, small-scale farms they kept hidden in the family lots in their back yards, they never would have survived those first famished years. Them's the paradoxical realities, Inspector. A little dose of the independent farmer helped these humanists create the greatest socialist state to succeed on the international stage."

Harry was like a little kid in a sandbox, one he seemingly preferred keeping to himself, having lived alone his entire life. I'd asked about his childhood and became so entertained that I'd failed to reach my third question related to the Walton murder, wanting nothing more than to hear the rest of his personal tale.

"Harry, you're a naughty boy. I came here on business, and you've given me nothing but a lot of pleasure in its place," I scolded.

"That's because you'm stayed for the second act; you didn't cut out after detecting me "dangerous political leanings," said Harry with a smirk.

"Do you think people regarded Charles the same way? Were people afraid of him because he seemed different?"

"Only because he preferred spending so much time with me, I 'spect. They couldn't tolerate such a looney and disagreeable chap who lives alone, shuns both marriage and church, and can frequently be found on the corner preaching revolution. That's what most of 'em were thinkin', I 'spect."

I was now getting slightly irritated, as I imagined part of Harry's diagnosis reflected a large dose of "solipsism" (You see, I told you I was self-educated).

"But Harry, this doesn't always go back to you. Lots of folks knew Charles and apparently many loved him. But wasn't he also a threat to certain people?"

"Well, he was a smart, open-hearted individual who loved a few people, but loved animals more. Such a good soul would have made many people uncomfortable. Another lager, Inspector?"

"But why, Harry? Why would such presumed goodness make other people uneasy, or, even, vengeful? That's the question I have."

Harry seemed to unwind a bit, sat with his back against the garden bench, and gave my question some serious thought.

"Charles always listened. To the earth, to the thoughts of others around him, to the language of the unseen. To the murmuring of all animal creatures, who found themselves unable to escape his natural lure. He understood he was a part of them, not so much a part of any human family, because… well, look what humans have done in his lifetime. He lived through two wars! I think he heard the animals of the earth screaming in denial of the destruction mankind has wrought. He would say this to me. I believed in the possibility that man could create a truly moral and fair socialist state. Charles would never give that much credit to human beings. People sensed that, I think."

"When did you first meet Charles?"

"That be a funny story, seeing as we both grew up so close. We was both linin' up for to join the military in '16. There was I, as eager as anyone to lend his body and soul to the destruction of the Hun. And there were Charles, conscripted as he was, thinkin' of nothing but ways to 'scape the draft. One would've thought we'd be in opposite positions and there be the irony, the paradox. We became life-long friends. I swore I'd never laid me eyes on Charles before that, and he didn't know me, 'cept we grew up doors away."

"How could that have been?"

"I guess we were both wearing our own kind of blinders. Neither of us believed anyone else existed who could understand us. But we understood each other when we finally met. And here's another irony of that meeting. The British Army seemed ready to do anything they could to get Charles and anything they could to keep me out. Seems they appreciated neither me politics nor me inclination for making fun of their superiors."

"But Charles… he didn't serve in the war, I thought?" I asked.

"He did not. Appears they discovered his true age, 44, at the time, and lost interest. Or they may have heard some of the chit-chat about him, even then in '16."

"By chit-chat you mean…?"

"Charles told me about his encounter at the pub, the woman he'd met and then discovered was a distant cousin. I 'spect this is when the voices began.

"After discovering his sister's death, you mean?" I asked.

"Yes."

"But, Harry, why would this incident mark him for so long? He'd just lost his sister. Why would there not be anything but sympathy for him?

"Look. I consider myself an expert on man's abilities to create a socialist utopia. I have no understanding or interest in these hopeless dreamers who read in books of witchcraft they believe is undeniable, irrefutable truths sanctioned by their ancestors. These people are mad!"

"Didn't Charles believe these claims?"

"Charles was not a madman! He saw these visions and yes, in that one case I believe a premonition of the girl's death occurred, nothing more, nothing less. People have been seeing black dogs and foggy visions on these grassy hills for hundreds of years."

"What is it about this vision that marked him as a witch? Why a witch?"

"When people gather in churches they conjure ghosts, old stories of good people sacrificed for the betterment of the community. Babies in a manger, etc. When people gather in pubs they conjure ghosts of another kind, those that live beneath the stones on places such as Meon Hill who, in this case, have chosen Charles because they can speak to him. Why Charles? Because he's listening! Simple as that. Because such witches can be done away with, if you gets me drift. It gives these people powers they cannot find in a church, which, of course, had given up hanging witches."

"But if Charles can hear these voices, are not these voices real? If you believe Charles to be honest."

"Real to Charles, yes, no doubt. He could hear these and other voices. Real to the church and its dependent loonies, yes, why not?"

"Who do you think killed Charles, Harry?"

Harry became exceedingly quiet and began digging rows again for something else he was putting in the ground. He seemed happiest with his hands in the earth, clearing a way for new things to sprout. Like many in Quinton, though, whose voices we'd yet to hear, Harry was silent. Perhaps, he was listening to the same voices as Charles.

“Is there nothing you can offer?” I sensed I may be pushing him too hard.

“You disappoint me, Inspector,” Harry growled in my direction, holding a trowel in his left hand, standing over me and nearly threatening me with his personal philosophy. “Why must everything have a reasonable explanation? Or a logical conclusion? Of course, if we are to have an organized society, we must try to find those who choose to break our laws. But what about the other laws? The natural laws? Are you all so naïve as to believe you can march into Warwickshire and solve the crimes against natural laws you know nothing about? This is an unorganized territory Mr. Spoon and …”

“That’s Spooner, Harry,” I interjected, to little avail.

“Yours is a ship of European explorers pulled into a harbor where you know none of the natives and if you’re not careful you’ll have a full Indian war on your hands. It will be a war you have little chance of winning and you will leave many people wounded or dead. You should be careful to see that you are not one of the casualties.”

Neither of us said much following Harry’s tirade. I had thought him to be the greatest of outsiders hiding out in his own home. However, it seems he was more the gatekeeper, keeping his village safe from interlopers like Scotland Yard. Funny thing. I respected him even more, thinking he was probably right about most of what he said. But his objections were certainly not going to curtail my interest. Indeed, his ambiguous responses piqued my interest, insuring me that I was on the right track, like it or not. And I can say without question – especially as it related to our Fabulous Fabian – I felt I was the person to solve this case.

Chapter Twenty

Warwickshire Police HQ, Stratford
Tuesday Morning
February 20, 1945

Fabian's interviews, having revealed little or nothing in the way of leads, were now to be followed by more of the tools available only to Scotland Yard. In order to discover the whereabouts of Charles' watch, the Superintendent ordered an army of metal detectors to cover a vast area around the crime scene. Fortunately, Fabian did not request my presence for this exercise, but it was one of the several latest measures on a list for discussion at our weekly case meeting. Our leader sat at a large table casually reviewing several maps and notes, enjoying his pipe and sipping tea. Webb sat opposite, obediently waiting to fill his notebook, when I walked into the room.

"Inspector Spooner, welcome," said Fabian. "I trust you spent the evening enjoying your latest crime novel."

"I wish I had the talents to create a few of those myself. It would give me a good place to put a plethora of facts and figures to good use," I countered.

"I have always felt the same. Perhaps, one day we shall both make our mark as leaders in this genre. In the meantime, I'm afraid we'll have to satisfy ourselves as mere chess pieces in a game with no winners."

"An excellent metaphor, Robert," Webb remarked.

“Thank you, Albert,” said Fabian. “Moving forward… in the matter of our victim’s watch, Albert has informed me that we are in possession of what appears to be the cheap, metal fob once attached to Walton’s time piece. We’re checking it for prints, but believe our item is too small, so we have continued into our third day of metal detection in and around the crime scene. Though it appears we might not find our watch, this search and the numerous pictures we received from our flyovers, has brought to my attention how close Walton was to the prisoner of war camp down the road. Spooner, when you spoke to Potter, you say he made accusations about an Italian Nazi from that camp?”

"Yes, as I stated to you after my interview, he seemed certain that this one Italian Nazi was the killer. Of course, he had no evidence and appeared to simply be vetting his hatred."

“Yes, well, the Sergeant and I have an update on that matter. It appears we’ve gotten some calls suggesting a few of these prisoners had been harassing the Potters.

“Calls? Calls from who?” I asked.

“Strange as it may seem, calls from Mrs. Potter.”

“I didn’t even know there was a Mrs. Potter,” I announced. “She never made an appearance during my visit.”

“I took the call,” said Webb. “She was nearly incoherent, going on about how they’d threatened to hurt her after coming onto their property.”

“Which means it’s time Albert and I plan to visit our only suspect.”

“It seems certain that Potter was responsible for that call,” said Webb.

"Has he now become "our only suspect?" I asked.

"I haven't told you, but I think we're closer to wrapping this up than I could have imagined only days ago. Mr. Webster from the forensic lab has informed me that Potter's fingerprints are all over the murder weapon. And he told you he'd never touched anything while waiting for you to arrive at the scene, is that correct?"

"Yes, that's what he told me," I said.

Fabian believed this was a case he could bring to a natural conclusion in a timely fashion. I was astonished how he continued to see himself as invincible.

"Item One: Potter's prints. Item Two: the Italian's prints. And Item Three: the Court Leet. You are aware, Inspector, of Potter's association with the Alcester Court Leet?" asked Fabian.

Perhaps he was doing his homework, I thought. "Yes, I am, as I'd mentioned previously. I'd seen him several times prior to the murder with some of his fellow bailiffs around the courthouse."

"I have to say I'm amused," said Fabian with a smirk. I assumed that Stratford had moved forward and left their Court Leet in the 18th c. where it belongs. Having spent my entire life in London, I've forgotten how far we've come since our lands were overseen by Lords and our citizens were at the mercy of the King's inner courts."

"I think you'll find," I told him, "our Court Leet is regarded as more of a museum than a court of justice. It seems no one wants the duty of informing them they are as obsolete as their wigs and robes. Most here would say they are simply out of fashion, harmless, as long as their judgments and declarations don't get in the way of the law."

"How quaint," answered Fabian. "Another matter to address when we finally revisit this Potter gentleman. You see, Alec, we've followed up on Potter's claims of the dangers of being so close to the prison camp, suggesting someone from that group posed a threat. In order to verify these claims Sergeant Webb and I had a visit to that camp which, by the way, was filled with as many Germans, Ukrainians, and Slavs as Italians. I had my doubts from the beginning, as most seemed to be rather descent human beings. We did, however, come across one individual who happened to be Italian. He admitted to knowing Walton, so we questioned him further, and when we asked to see his clothing, we discovered one of his shirts was covered in blood."

"So, it seems our Mr. Potter may have found our suspect after all," Webb added gleefully.

"Yes, I admit to feeling as though we might have finally found our killer. He appeared to be the only human being along that road on any given afternoon, so we've taken a sample of his blood to compare it to Walton's. The authorities are going to keep their eye on our fellow until we get the results, as there's no way we can hold him for having blood on his shirt. So, we shall see, shan't we."

"That's tremendous news, Robert!" (I actually heard myself calling him Robert).

"Yes, we may actually be getting home by Easter, correct Sergeant?"

"Music to the ears, Chief."

"Item Three involves speaking with someone who knows more about the Court Leet meetings, correct?" I asked.

"Yes. I'd like you to take on that one, Mr. Spooner, as you're familiar with this town and its inhabitants. They'll be more inclined to share truths with you than they will with me." It seemed he had finally reached a conclusion to which we could both agree.

"Alright," I concurred. "I think I know just the person to begin with. He serves as their Steward of the Manor and would probably have the most informed perspective of their last few meetings."

"Excellent," added Fabian. "Then, depending on any nuggets of truth we take away from our visit with Mr. Potter, Webb and I will begin to interview every resident in their community, minus, of course, those you've already visited."

I wondered if it was not yet time to suggest we add to our questions certain suggestions of the town's knowledge of the Ann Turner murder or Walton's visions of the black dog ten years later. Had Fabian simply dismissed the contents of Bloom's *Folklore, Old Customs and Superstitions in Shakespeareland* or was he saving that angle for a last-ditch effort when all other avenues for prosecution had been exhausted? I was not ready, as was Fabian, to wait and I looked forward to keeping that narrative close by when I was conducting my interviews. I imagined if I brought up the subject again in his presence, Fabian would dismiss me even faster than he dismissed the Court Leet. Perhaps, he was right and I, too, was a throwback to medieval times, ready to listen

– as was Charles – to the first suggestion of a paranormal intervention.

Chapter Twenty-One

Lower Quinton
Wednesday Afternoon
February 21, 1945

On their way to Potter's farm, Fabian was sharing with Webb the odd nature of Potter's response to his phone call asking for a meeting. Apparently, the farmer was overly anxious for their meeting to occur, as if he had information that was essential to the case. Was this anxiety related to his wife's phone calls? What could be so astonishing about any knowledge he had, considering he'd been at the center of the investigation since right after the crime? The nature of his behavior further hardened Fabian's belief that they were close to finding the killer. While he'd not yet even met Potter, he seemed to have a strong opinion of the man's culpability. Potter was walking out the kitchen door headed for the barn when their car pulled up.

"Mr. Potter, I'm Detective Superintendent Fabian, Scotland Yard," he said, cutting him off in the drive. "This is my associate, Sergeant Webb."

"Yes, I'd heard you was up from London," said Potter in his curt manner. "Heard it from a reporter whose been snoopin' around. You's mind if we stay out here? The wife is trying to get a nap."

"Yes, about that, I may need to have a word with your wife. That might be possible, do you think?"

In what Fabian and Webb found to be an astonishingly rude gesture, Potter failed to acknowledge the Chief Inspector's question. Was the man deaf or just ignoring a simple request for the purpose of hiding important information? The three of them walked towards the barn and settled at a gate leading into a fenced paddock beside the barn.

"How long had Mr. Walton been your employee and what led you to hire him in the first place?" Fabian asked sternly.

"He'd been working for me for about ten months. I hired him because some of me herd become ill, and someone suggested Walton would be useful as a laborer and someone who could heal animals." Fabian waited, thinking Potter had more to say. He didn't.

"And were you pleased with his help?" Fabian asked.

"He were a hard worker. I'd seed him cutting hedgerows at all hours of the day. And yeah, he seemed to've settled some of the sick ones, even a sow. But, likes I told your partner, I dinna like the man."

Fabian was a detective, so, just as I did, he knew exactly where to go next. "You didn't like the man, so you killed him. Correct?"

"That would be convenient, wouldn't it, Inspector? But I'm not your man," Potter countered. "If I were, why would I be confessin' I didn't like him?"

"I trust you've got an alibi, Mr. Potter, as your comment means we'll have to consider you a suspect," Fabian rejoined.

"Several alibis won't be a problem."

Fabian could feel himself shifting into a new gear, sensing that he'd found a real force to be dealt with, not some weakling he could easily collar.

"Mr. Potter, I need you to tell me exactly what happened when you arrived on the scene with Ms. Walton, Mr. Beasley, and Mr. Goode. Please take your time."

"Like I's told Inspector Spooner, I'd seen Walton working along the hedgerow earlier in the afternoon, so's when they comes to the house looking for him, I naturally takes 'em there. It were gettin' dark, so I grabbed a couple of me torches and they followed in their car. We drove kind a slow first, but it weren't long till I sees the body on the other side of the road. I stopped and asked to speak to Goode, and I said he needed to come wid me. It were kind a shocking, a course, so when she fell to the ground and then had to see the body herself, I told him to take her home. Then I spoke to the other man…"

"Mr. Beasley, you mean?"

"Yeah, that's right, then he called the inspector and others."

"Alright, so what happened then?"

"Well, after the three of 'em drove the lady home, or wherever, I stayed with the corpse, looked at it really close, you know, to see for any clues, but it were dark. I tried a couple of times to remove the fork from the ground. I mean, it were upsettin' to see it sticking through the man's throat like that, but it wouldn't budge, not an inch."

"You're saying you held the fork in your hands and tried to remove it?"

"That's what I just said, ain't it?" answered Potter, whose revelation truly complicated any case against Potter, so he chose to defer to Potter's supposedly new information.

"You had something you wanted to convey to me, Mr. Potter? Or so it seemed when we spoke by phone."

"I couldn't help but thinkin' hows in the past several months I been bothered by them Nazis down the road,"

"Yes, we've heard from you about your Nazis," Fabian replied.

"Them Italian prisoners everyone likes so much. I thinks one of 'em might just be the man yours lookin' for. I found him two to three times, at least, harassin' Walton at the very spot we's found him dead."

"By "harassin' you mean?"

"Well, beggin' after him, ya know, tryin' to get his lunch and… cursin' him and such."

"Why didn't you mention this right after the murder?" asked Fabian, trying to control his anger.

"Just slipped me mind, Inspector."

"The same way your mind slipped over those fingerprints, Mr. Potter?" the inspector asked under his breath.

"What's that?"

"Never mind," he simmered.

Fabian wanted to smash the insolent cockroach, but, as he'd had to do on numerous prior occasions with other cockroaches, he catalogued the urge and moved forward.

"You understand, I hope, how that action confuses the investigation."

"I'm a farmer, Inspector, not a detective. How would I know this?" snapped Potter.

"That's not what you told Inspector Spooner. You told him you'd never touched anything before he arrived."

"He's hearing what he wants to hear. I never said that."

"You're telling me," said Fabian, "you never said anything to him about touching the evidence while you were alone with the corpse?"

"Yeah, that's right."

Potter's denial left Fabian frustrated and furious, understanding that the prints found on the murder weapon were demonstratable, provable evidence in a case with little or no workable leads. In contrast, the suspicion that prints on a lost watch could be even more incriminating evidence but might also lead the investigation down endless alleys, leaving them further behind than when they arrived in Warwickshire. Here, only feet away, stood a person Fabian was convinced knew much more than he was revealing. Or, perhaps, he was the actual murderer. He was determined to use any pressure he could to uncover the evil he believed was physically within his grasp. After he'd taken a breath to control his urge to throttle the farmer, he took his next steps.

"You've been a member of the Court Leet for a while, is that right?" he asked Potter.

"Yeah. Since I's been lookin' after The Firs, once me father stepped aside."

"If I were to speak to someone about the Leet, who would you recommend?"

Fabian immediately sensed Potter's unease, giving him the notion that he'd found a crack in the farmer's resolve. Was there some clue in his reluctance to tell the inspector whom he should speak with? His silence seemed to suggest he may have opened a vein, though Fabian couldn't imagine how the crime could be in any way connected to the Leet's recent meetings.

"Perhaps someone might be able give me an idea of what you've all been debating lately," Fabian suggested.

"Nothing of importance. Just some complaints about the effects of the war on crops. I wouldn't waste your time." Potter's recommendation further indicated to Fabian that this Court Leet avenue was worth pursuing. Besides, he wasn't getting anywhere following up on the murder weapon's fingerprints.

Just as the inspector was about to give up trying to find the person from the Leet to speak with, Potter blurted out his name.

"Thomas Burns. Talk to him." Fabian looked at the man for the longest time, analyzing him, trying to determine just by his physical properties if the man was capable of telling the truth.

"Very well, Mr. Potter."

"Ahem." Fabian had forgotten his trusty No. 2 was standing just to his right, furiously taking notes. "Mrs. Potter?" Webb reminded Fabian in hushed tones.

"Yes, Mr. Potter, I'm going to need to speak with…"

"The wife is asleep, as I's stated. She never leaves the kitchen."

"That may be the case, but I'm afraid I will still need a few words with her…" Fabian said hastily.

"Listen here," interrupted Potter, his nerves beginning to shatter in visible pieces," I'm not about to..."

"Sometime in the future. You'll be hearing from us." There followed several uncomfortable moments as the two men faced off, as if they were heavyweights before a championship fight.

"Nazis, Inspector," Potter hissed, before the two men turned away towards their car.

Fabian had wanted to close his remarks by addressing them to "you cheeky bastard," but decided it would be best to retain some kind of professional – but by no means, respectful – distance. They hadn't left with what they were looking for, but, at least, they may have implanted a fear in their suspect, a warning that they knew what he was up to.

Chapter Twenty-Two

White Swan Hotel
Wednesday Evening
February 21, 1945

Clair Dunham had heard that Fabian was staying at the White Swan, so he was able to convince his editor that he should be as near to the inspector as possible, allowing him to be on top of any scoop. He'd always wanted to stay there during previous visits to see the Shakespeare Memorial Company but hadn't been able to afford it. Now *The Mirror* would be picking up the bill.

On the evening of Fabian's first visit to Potter's farm he found himself in the hotel bar, hoping to get a glimpse of Scotland Yard's envoy. It was the young reporter's first major assignment, and he was determined to make a splash when the mystery of this crime was revealed. Perhaps, his research might even help bring the killer to justice, he imagined after several gin and tonics. Other sheets had reported the bloody crime, but a week later none of them had committed to a long-term expose tying the murder to the town's long history of supernatural skullduggery. Like his editor, Clair understood the story had the markings of a first-class series that would sell heaps of papers throughout the Commonwealth, putting a major feather in the newsman's cap.

For a Wednesday night dinner hour, the crowd was rather subdued. Several businessmen commandeered a few tables, and a roaring fire drew stragglers in from the nearby lobby. Clair was weary from his trip up from town and anxious about all the locations he had to cover the following day. At the same time, the sojourn felt oddly like a vacation, a week to enjoy the cultural jaunts available to all visitors of Stratford. Or would have, had the war ended.

Only a few other men, mostly older and more monied, stood nearby awaiting the barkeep's attention, when Clair noticed a woman squeezed into the opposite corner. She looked to be in her early thirties, dark hair, dressed in a black… what was it? A rather plain, very short cotton dress. Attractive. Still, plain. He began noticing her because it looked as if she was noticing him. How long had it been, he thought?

Just as he was about to get the nerve to move to her side of the bar, Fabian and Webb walk in from the lobby and … could he be so lucky? They settle at the bar directly to his left.

"I imagine tonight you'll be ordering a double, Robert," quipped Webb, as they stood facing the potpourri of poisons facing them in front of a mirror.

"For starters, at the least," Fabian answered. "I'd love to get that worm in a corner and beat the truth out of him."

Clair knew the inspectors' identities, having encountered them several times at various press conferences in London, so he began plotting the best course for him to get any case updates. He wasn't sure if they'd recognize him, and it might be easier if they didn't know he was press. His first step would be simply to listen.

"Do you suppose we ought to let Potter simmer in place for a while and move on to some of our other interviews?" suggested Webb.

"My thinking as well, Albert. Give him some time to suspect we know more than we do."

Clair was familiar enough with the case to know that Potter was one of the only suspects. He'd even made a phone call to the farmer before leaving London, so he decided not to make acquaintances with the inspectors quite yet. Rather, he would gather some information from Potter himself and remain undercover for a while. Besides, he hadn't yet fully investigated the woman in black, whose interest in him intensified after the entrance of Fabian and Webb. He reminded himself that inhibition in a reporter was a career-killer, so he cupped his drink and deserted Scotland Yard for the mystery woman in the corner.

"Excuse me, but I don't suppose you'd allow me to ...?"

"What? Buy me dinner?" Clair's face broke out into a broad smile. He already liked this woman tremendously, thinking that such abruptness was reserved for Americans, not plain, unassuming English women who lived in the hinterland. Nor had he expected his social life might be shifting into more fertile territory.

"I'd hoped for a drink at the very least," he said, finding her even more alluring a foot away than from across the room. He reached out his hand and she took it. "Clair Dunham," he announced.

"It *was* then," she said.

"It was? I'm afraid I don't..."

"A foregone conclusion conveyed to me during my last session."

"You are a creature of mystery."

"It's merely vocational vocabulary. You'll understand. I'm Sam. Sam Zawalich. A woman with a man's name speaking to a man with a woman's name. A sign. A signal," the woman of mystery proclaimed.

"I'm beginning to feel sure our meeting here is not wholly coincidental."

"You catch on quickly, Mr. Clair."

"You were looking at me. As though you knew who I was."

"Guilty as charged. I knew I was looking for someone, a gentleman from out-of-town, someone with particular interest in our visiting lawmen. So, when I saw you take an interest in Scotland Yard to your left, I had the sense I was on the right track. Now that I'm told your name – received the sign – I'm convinced I've found who I'm looking for."

"Now, one moment. How did you know about my interest in Inspector Fabian? Are you a mind reader?"

"That's an easy one. Body language. Am I a mind reader? Yes, I suppose. One of the tricks of my trade," said Sam, with an easy smile.

"You're a spiritual medium, aren't you?"

"Again, guilty as charged, Mr. Dunham. Now, about that dinner."

In fact, Clair wasn't surprised. He'd assumed that a gaggle of psychic practitioners would show interest in this case. Given the history of parapsychological phenomena in this corner of the empire, he would have been astounded had the investigation gone unnoticed by this community. He'd never imagined that interest would be represented by such a disarming individual, who happened also to be hungry. And wasn't he fortunate that dinner's chit would be covered by his employer. After a few more drinks they settled into one of the corner tables by a fireplace. Fabian and Webb were having an evening's meal at their usual table across the room.

"You knew who they were. Scotland Yard," said Clair.

"I'm not a novice. Neither am I immune to the mythic doings of their greatest sleuth. I'm quite certain, like you, he has no idea of my identity, if that's your concern," answered Samantha, though she preferred being called Sam.

"You must also be an expert on local lore," Clair suggested.

"Born and bred Warwickshire. One might even conclude my location was the impetus for my work."

"Did you know Walton? I understand there's a lot of gossip about his abilities to talk to animals. Could that be one of your hidden talents, as well?

"One of my talents that I certainly don't keep hidden. In fact, many a cat or dog owner has asked me to be a conduit to either their lost or deceased loved one." Clair could not escape a rather broad smile at the idea of her ability to translate the thoughts of a purring kitten. "I did know Walton, in fact. And I found him to be the real thing."

"The real thing?"

"A caring, very open and committed, individual whose conductivity – sensitivity to unheard voices and ghostly urges – I found to be authentic, nearly electric. I truly believe Charles was able to channel human and animal spirits, and I intended to learn from him, as one would study under any spiritual leader."

Clair remained still, quite unable to register this new information or his good fortune to find a very special view into the subject of his piece. He was speechless.

"I suppose, even before dinner's first course, that you find me a terrible fake," she concluded.

"Not in the least. I have the utmost respect for psychic practitioners, be they connected to the human or animal world, dead or alive, for that matter. You must be excited, as it seems such talents – like those of Charles Walton – are at the very heart of this case."

"Yes, exactly. At some point, sooner or later, the relevant parties are going to recognize the importance of our powers in discovering who committed this monstrous crime."

Clair remained dazzled by this small woman who claimed such astonishing powers. And, for as many personal as professional reasons, he wanted to know more about her. As they lingered over their salad and main courses (Sam had remained a vegetarian since the age of seventeen, when she discovered her "unusual abilities"), the medium provided her backstory.

Raised by her spinster aunt after losing both her parents to the Spanish Flu in 1918, she intended to go to medical school, but couldn't abide the myopic view most scientists adopted when it came to the spiritual destinies of their patients. Instead, she took a lengthy trip to Ireland where she immersed herself in the study of Celtic Christianity, "more spiritual, friendlier to women, more connected with nature, and more comfortable dealing with Celtic polytheism than the Roman Catholics." Sam found this Celtic practice naturally led to the discourse of the parapsychic community, even if the British Psychological Society found most claims of paranormal mediumship were fraudulent. Apparently enough British citizens disagreed, and Sam Zawalich found her faculties not only brought her financial security, but popular legitimacy, as well.

By the end of the meal neither Sam or Clair was thinking much about Walton's murder or its subsequent inquiry. Once it came time to choose, late in the evening, whether they would have after-dinner coffees, both opted in, believing their conversation was a long way from concluding. Before they'd considered the wisdom of mixing business with parapsychic pleasure, the covers on Clair's bed upstairs were pulled down and the shades on the window shut tight.

Chapter Twenty-Three

Lower Quinton
Friday Afternoon
February 23, 1945

Eddie was still treading gently around Edie's home, not quite sure how much she had evolved from a grieving niece to a budding bride. No funeral service or burial had been scheduled. She had not yet been able to accept the finality of the murder and was simply not ready to say goodbye. Her mother died after a long illness and the young girl was able to prepare for an after-life. No such agenda for a future existed in this case. Charles was simply there one day and gone the next, as if he was still walking his neighborhood and attending the hedgerows as a ghostly shadow.

Still unable to undertake even the smallest daily chores around the house – cooking, cleaning, or responding to Eddie's verbal attempts at normality – Edie had taken several weeks off from work and Eddie, in order to oversee her mental stability, was working part-time. Both knew that such arrangements would need to be short-lived, or they would lose their jobs, so each day revealed a greater urgency. By noon Edie had still not emerged from the bedroom, having returned to lengthy periods on her bed perusing her mother's letters and photos. Denied her company for breakfast, Eddie sat alone at the table drinking his fifth coffee, drained of hope that life would ever return to anything like the jubilation he'd been feeling two weeks before. Was there no remedy for her desolate state of mind?

Meanwhile, just down the block, parked in front of Harry Beasley's home, sat Clair and Sam, behind the wheel of her new sedan. She'd not wanted anyone at the Walton home to know they were nearby, as they'd not yet determined exactly how they were going to approach Charles' niece.

"I don't think I need to say it again, but she won't talk to me. I've tried to reach her by phone, but the man…"

"Her fiancé," Sam corrected him.

"The man hangs up when I mention anything about the case."

"Of course, he does. Wouldn't you?"

"And it did no good to try to reach her at work, because…"

"They told you she'd been out since the murder."

"Good lord, how much did I drink last night? I must have told you everything. I can't remember."

"Clair, you told me many things, yes, but I knew lots without your telling me."

"Right, right, special skills. How could I forget?"

"Listen. I've thought a lot about this," Sam said.

"Yes, all those hours between 9 pm last night and 11 am this morning."

"More than enough time for me to know that ours is not just a marriage of convenience…"

"So, I'm a fiancé, too!"

"Shush now. Ours is also a marriage of necessity. Edith will probably not remember me very well, but enough so that I can get us in the door."

"That's why you bought the flowers this morning?"

"Exactly. From here you simply need to leave it to me. She's the only one close enough to Charles to help us reach him. But we must work with alacrity and stealth. The longer we wait, the less likely we'll be able to make contact."

"You astonish me," said Clair in awe.

"This means for the time being you're going to have to proceed incognito."

"I suppose I can do that. No one knows who I am except...'

"Except me," insisted Sam. "And let's keep it that way. Just follow my lead, all right?"

Sam drove her car thirty meters to the entrance of Edie's home. A few moments later she was employing the knocker at the front door. Eddie was intrigued but determined as ever to protect Edie from anyone who might upset her. Reluctant to respond, but curious, he opened the door, leaving it ajar just enough to see Clair and Sam, her arms holding a bright bouquet of red roses.

"Yes?" announced Eddie sternly.

"Mr. Goode? What a pleasure to finally meet you. Charles spoke of you so often and with such fondness," Sam said with a warm smile, making sure the flowers were practically in Eddie's face.

"I'm sorry, but…"

"Oh, I'm the one who's sorry. Foolish me, to burst in like this. What am I thinking?" They both took a moment to consider that question.

"You were a friend of Charles?" asked Eddie.

"Yes, yes, I'm so sorry, for you and Edith." Another long silence.

"I see…" Eddie didn't know what to say or do. "You're…?"

Sam broke out in nervous laughter before handing the flowers to Eddie. "Forgive me again. I'm Samantha. Sam Zawalich. I've known Charles a long time and was completely devastated when I heard the news."

"I don't remember Charles ever mentioning you."

"Oh, well, I knew him since I was a child and hadn't seen him so much these past few years. I thought so very much of him."

"Yes, he was very special… to me," answered Eddie, who began to lose his composure after being flooded by recent memories.

"Oh, dear man. He was so right about you. Such a caring individual."

Determined not to fall apart in front of two strangers, he pulled himself together enough to address her directly again, referring to Clair standing behind her.

"And your friend?"

"Oh, yes, this is my associate, Clair Dunham. Clair was also extremely fond of Charles."

"Yes, awfully," inserted Clair, right on cue.

"Yes, well, I'm afraid Edie is… unable to take guests."

"Oh, I can imagine, the poor dear, please don't bother her. But why not let me put these flowers in something." Sam edged her right foot beyond the door jam.

"I suppose… for a moment, yes, please come in," offered Eddie half-heartedly. "I'm not sure what we have for flowers."

Sam surreptitiously commandeered the kitchen area, reaching up into the cabinets for some kind of vase, sensing which objects Charles may have used recently and holding them in her hands to receive any vibrations that might give her a clearer sense of his life there. Clair and Eddie were left staring at each other, at a loss for words.

"I'm sorry, we don't generally have flowers and I can't think of where she might have something."

"I'm sure we'll find something," said Sam, hoping she could get to as many objects as possible before she actually found a vase.

"So, you knew Charles as well, Mr.….?

"Clair. Oh, yes, he and I were… friends, yes. My condolences to you."

Down beneath the sink Sam finally found a glass container that would do the trick, though she was sure it wasn't meant to hold flowers.

"Ah, here we are. Let me just get these babies cut down a bit. I don't suppose you have a pair of gardener's shears?"

"No, I'm sorry, let me see." Eddie went through the kitchen drawers and came up with some scissors, then settled his large frame into the chair by the window, resigned that he'd never rid himself of his new guests.

"Oh, don't they look beautiful! I do hope they cheer Edie's heart a bit," said Sam as she settled into the chair opposite Eddie. Without a seat, Clair leaned against the door beside Sam, hoping he would look as if he belonged there.

Closing her eyes, Sam took Eddie's hands in hers, surprising him. Especially when it seemed she was experiencing something more important than merely the touch of another hand.

"I think you've let us in because we've been called."

"Called?"

"We're here for a reason, Eddie. Because Edie needs us."

"Well, she is despondent, so very despondent. I've tried everything to get her to recognize her future is bright, that Charles would want us to accept his death and move on with our wedding. But she won't hear anything and simply locks herself away, the way she used to before we met."

"I can help," declared Sam. "I know what Charles would say and, perhaps, I could get him to say it."

"Say what? How could you do that? He's dead."

"Edgar, do you know anything about Charles' special abilities?"

Eddie found himself at a further loss for words. He remembered making promises to Charles not to reveal their meeting by the stream or his coterie of frogs. How often he had tried to direct conversations away from concerns about the power of witches and the assumptions of others that Charles' history of clairvoyance meant for sure that he himself was a witch. But now Charles was gone, never to return. How much did those suspicions matter now?

"I knew some things about it, yes, but…"

"Edgar," Sam gently coaxed, "I believed in Charles, in his goodness and the powers he possessed to communicate with all creatures, human and otherwise, alive or dead. I believe I can help you and Edith find Charles again, speak with him, begin to understand how and why he was taken from us."

Then, remembering his fear that others would take advantage of Charles' knowledge of the unseen and then accuse him of witchcraft, he began to see his visitors as interlopers intent on blaming Edie for her uncle's powers. He couldn't let that happen. He didn't know these two people who had barged into their kitchen making promises to bring back the dead. Nearly upsetting the small table, Eddie stood and, raising his voice, motioned for them to leave.

"I'm sorry, Ms….? I think you ought to go. You're simply going to upset Edie more. She's not well and I don't think what you say will help, so please leave before…"

At that moment Edie emerged from the bedroom, alerted by Eddie's booming theatrical voice.

"Eddie, what's the matter? Who are your friends?" she asked sheepishly, recovering from her nap.

Sam jumped on the moment, rising from the table and moving towards Edie, her arms open, ready to embrace.

"Oh, Edith, I've thought of nothing except you since we lost Charles," she said with tears in her eyes. Edie had no idea who the woman was.

"I'm sorry, I don't believe we've met," Edie replied simply.

"Edith, I'm terribly sorry, it has been some years. I used to help Charles with some of his gardening duties before he worked at The Firs. We both loved animals and often talked about raising a horse together. He loved horses so."

Edie vaguely remembered a young woman Charles had mentioned was interested in horses, but as much as she tried, she couldn't recall meeting her.

"Yes," Edie replied. "Horses were his first love. And dogs, of course."

"I remember," said Sam, "how he talked about his dog who had passed on many years before, and how he was determined to get another."

"Oh, my, yes. I often encouraged him to get another one, but he never did. He talked about it a lot after learning that Eddie and I were getting married. I suppose he imagined he'd be alone then and need the companionship."

"I'm so sorry for everything, Edith. What a catastrophe!" Sam then took Edie's hands, the way she'd taken Eddie's, and stood for the longest time searching Edie's eyes.

Still concerned that Edie's recovery would be impossible should she get a whiff of the woman's scandalous promise to bring back her uncle, Eddie made one last effort to see them gone.

"They were just on their way out, Edie, and we don't want to keep them." He took Sam's arm and with his large frame that gave him authority tried to escort them both from the room.

But Sam would not be overruled. "Edith, I can find you Charles. You can speak with him again," she said abruptly, bringing to Edie an instant joy, relaxing her tired facial muscles so that suddenly the dark shroud she'd been wearing since his death fell away. Eddie couldn't bring himself to disappoint his wife-to-be again, afraid that no other avenue to her salvation existed outside this woman's mad plan.

"Eddie, do you hear? Could it be possible? Charles did have those kinds of powers. Why couldn't we speak with him? He's here, around us, for sure. We've still not put him in the ground, and he could speak to so many of his other creatures. Why then couldn't we speak to him, too?"

Eddie had no response. He walked slowly back to the table and sat, unable to remember why he had any objections at the start. Perhaps, he thought, it would be possible to reach Charles, remembering the way the frogs had certainly heard him that afternoon by the stream.

"Edie, listen to me. I understood the way Charles communicated with the beyond, because I have those powers, too."

"It's true, Ms. Walton, she does, and she…" interrupted Clair.

Determined that Clair's input would only confuse matters, Sam plowed ahead. "Edie, if you let me, I can bring you to him." She longingly searched Edie's face for an answer and only became diverted once she realized Edie was ready to make the journey.

Chapter Twenty-Four

Warwickshire Police HQ, Stratford
Monday Morning
February 26, 1945

The prior weekend had been the first since the murder that I'd found some time to relax or any diversion from the many exigencies involved in a very complex – and potentially career-changing – case. Of course, as soon as I'd found the time to take a breather, I remembered all the other office work and newly accumulated matters on my desk that remained untouched since Fabian and Webb had arrived from London. It was these concerns that brought me into the office that next morning.

Upon entering the station early that Monday, as I had for many years, expecting a few officers sharing a coffee and a fag in the public waiting area, I was surprised to see a lengthy line of people, mostly middle-aged couples, citizens of Upper and Lower Quintin. Because my previous work had been performed predominantly within the confines of Stratford-upon-Avon, most of them appeared to be strangers, though a few I recognized from The King George or other watering holes around town. My question to everyone as I moved beyond the line and into my office, past the temporary Scotland Yard HQ, was why such a line was forming before 9 am? I got the answer from Gertie, one of our secretaries, in a thick North Country dialect.

"He's gone and ordered half 'a Quintin to 'peer front and center on a Monday morning."

"Inspector Fabian, you mean?"

"Yes, your Mr. Conan Doyle, there. I 'ope he's not planin' to be runnin' for any town offices in the near future. Them's folks out there ready for blood."

"Oh, dear." I couldn't help but smile imagining a mob dicing Fabian into multiple pieces, serving him up to the masses, and Gertie having to clean the mess. "You'd best keep an eye on them, Gertie, make sure they don't get too restless or unhappy."

"Not me job, boss," Gertie demurred with a smile.

"I'm sure you can command the troops, Gertie."

"Yes, Inspector."

I gave her a smile and moved down the hall where the Chief was sitting in his usual spot at the end of a large table. His pipe was billowing smoke.

"Ah, Superintendent Spoon…., "

"Er," I said under my breath.

"Spooner, yes," Fabian intoned through clouds of tobacco. "I'm glad you're here."

"Yes, well, Monday morning," I answered.

"So it is, so it is." Once we were joined by Webb and a few other officers, the Chief Inspector shared his goals for the remainder of the day. "We're going to take this first bunch of residences before noon, try to keep each interview to a minimum fifteen minutes."

"So, they've been scheduled then?" I asked, somewhat alarmed that we had already filled the waiting room and a line was snaking outside the front door.

"Well, yes, of course, what do you mean, Mr. Spooner?" asked Fabian.

"Each of the... what, 'respondents' have been given a time, correct?"

"Yes, I expect, scheduling is scheduling. Mr. Webb, can you explain?" Fabian deferred to his second in command.

"Well, Chief, I gave distinct instructions to several of the very cooperative staff in Superintendent Spooner's office to have the first group of houses, Quintin citizens, here on Monday morning. I thought my instructions to be clear and it seemed as though they all understood... perfectly well."

I realized that because of miscommunication practically half the inhabitants of Lower Quintin were expected to be in these offices before noon. Somehow it was forgotten that these citizens were not used to being called to the police station to stand for hours before being interviewed for fifteen minutes. In fact, revolutions had begun for less.

"I wondered, Chief," I asked.

"Robert."

"Robert, yes, I wondered if we might have a word in my office?"

I needed to remind myself that I was addressing a superior officer, though I found it hard not to blame the Chief for such a calamity.

"I'm concerned, sir. You see the folks here are not used to these procedures."

"What procedures?"

"Well, generally, in the past, if we had a series of interrogative sessions with, what, people of interest? Well, we generally went to their homes or offices and didn't expect them to devote quite so much time to us, if you know what I mean?"

Clearly embarrassed, but not quite willing to admit any blame in the matter, Fabian wiggled his way out, maintaining his stature… and status.

"Well, I'm sure I don't know how such a thing happened, but I don't believe it will make such a large impression on them. I'm sure they realize the importance of this case and will be more than happy to participate in this quest for justice," intoned the Fabulous Fabian. "And I know you've heard me say many times the importance of having these suspects…"

"Not suspects, Robert," I dared.

"No, not strictly, but to have these potential witnesses on our own territory gives us a greater advantage of getting the truth. These are things I know, Mr. Spooner."

"Yes, sir, of course, I know this, as well.

"I am the Chief Inspector."

"You are, sir, and thankfully working on this case. Amen."

I gave up any hope of trying to amend what had long been in the planning and was glad that I had scheduled a meeting with the Steward of the Manor for 11 am. This would allow me to escape much of the mayhem this mishap had caused. Apparently in London, residents have nothing better to do than spend their morning in a line with their neighbors, nowhere to sit, unaware of how their information could make any difference to any case. It was my distinct impression that

Fabian regarded such rough, uneducated farmers as little more than tools to be played with, pawns in his chess game. And the earful I got while leaving the office for my meeting convinced me our fabulous leader was about to learn a bit about country ways.

"Superintendent!" cried Ted Benson, whom I knew from the pub. "What's this? I can't leave my shop, Mr. Spooner!"

"I know, I'm sorry, Ted. I wish I could be of help, but I've got to run," I sheepishly called out after colliding with him by the inner door.

"Officer Spooner, what are you going to do?" begged Eleanor Bigsby who worked in the clerk's office. "I can't miss my job! Can you help me get in early or sumfin?"

"I wish I could, I'm so sorry," I said, trying to move through the crowd to the sidewalk.

And then just as I was about to reach the outer door I was stopped by Harry Beasley, who looked as though he might be ready for a good fight.

"Where is this Mr. Fabian, Mr. Spooner?"

"Mr. Beasley."

"I'm organizing," said Harry. "This 'ere has the makings of an uprising."

I couldn't help but enjoy the prospect of a proletarian rebellion as I moved out the doors and into one of my safe police vehicles, glad to be free of the uproar.

Chapter Twenty-Five

Lower Quintin
Monday Morning
February 26, 1945

Happy to be conducting our investigation according to protocol in place for many years in Warwickshire, not as I imagined Scotland Yard was regularly doing under the Detective Superintendent in London, I pulled into the long drive belonging to Geoffrey Milner, owner of Quintin's largest dairy farm. It was a magnificent property, uncharacteristically prosperous and huge compared to most of the smaller family-run farms in the area. As far as the eyes could see were grazing herds of Holsteins and Jerseys, the pride of the Milner family for over five generations. No wonder Geoffrey was Steward of the Manor of the Court Leet and had been for as long as most could remember.

While I'd known of Milner and even met the gentleman some years back, he was for all purposes a stranger to me. I had not imagined such a stately mansion in what was by comparison a rather modest pocket of Warwickshire. Certainly, no castle in a land known for castles, the structure was made of stone and had been built in the 18th c. I imagined, if one paid close attention to the details, a great deal of care had been given to all twenty-four rooms, the sort that guarantees any guest will be left in awe – even slightly out of breath – after being given the tour.

My response was no exception and I fully appreciated that my tour had been led by the master of the house, a stately and properly rotund gentleman in his late fifties who by my estimate had never spent a minute of life in doubt of his supreme authority in the world. He wore such certainty well, but I couldn't help fighting the urge to upset something, be it a vase on a table or the slightly smug smile permanently attached to his face. We were seated in two outlandishly plush 18th c. upholstered chairs in the main hall directly opposite a massive fireplace already fired up by late morning.

"Well, Inspector, I do hope you've been able to make some headway in this matter. Such crimes are uncommon in this district and Lord knows we've had enough trauma over these past four years," Milner calmly said to me.

"I appreciate your concern, Mr. Milner."

"Please, call me Geoffrey. I've followed your career since you arrived, Inspector, and I'm quite pleased to finally make you a proper acquaintance."

"Thank you, Geoffrey. I'm equally pleased."

"I'm also determined to offer any assistance I can, be it as a citizen or as Steward of the Manor of the Leet. As you can imagine, though, since we've not been convened since the murder, I am unable to speak for other members of the court."

"I appreciate your honesty and candor, sir. I don't think that particular fact should affect the information I'm seeking," I said, glad to have the introductory phase of our meeting behind us.

"Well then, how can I be of help?"

"Most of my questions involve the participation of Mr. Alfred Potter."

"Yes, I know the gentleman," he stated simply, after a rather deep inhalation.

"I assume you're familiar with the basic circumstances surrounding the murder. I understand it has been a frequent subject for speculation by townspeople over the past few weeks."

"Yes, well, while I don't generally frequent the locale taverns. I'm a family man, Inspector. I gather the event has been on the minds of most inhabitants of Warwickshire and who can blame them? This European war has made most of us feel less safe, and such a brutal and undeserved murder in our own backyard seems to have dissolved any of the security we may have felt recently, believing the worst of the war behind us."

"How would you portray the concerns of Mr. Potter? I understand he was at least partly responsible for several of the more recent meetings of the court."

I noted a slight ill of ease in Milner's body language, as if the details he was about to reveal might be a slight ache, a congenital or chronic reminder that there were some things in life he couldn't control.

"Alfred Potter is a difficult man. While I admire his devotion to the influence of the Leet, he is not always as trusting or agreeable as most of the other bailiffs who have been on the court longer."

"Can you give me an estimation of those reasons for which he convened a meeting?" I asked.

"Nothing terribly important, really. Initially he seemed upset about the Italian prisoner of war camp located several miles from his property. He'd been hinting at his dissatisfaction since its installation, continually referring to them as Nazis, but practically no one else had any concerns. No other incidents occurred regarding those prisoners, and I made it clear to him that the court believed our overseeing of the camp was the least we could do for the war effort."

"Did your statements quell his dissatisfaction?"

"No. Not really. He's a stubborn man, Inspector, and I don't think he ever came round to the court's understanding."

"I see."

"The court gave serious consideration to Potter's complaints and after several months and a second meeting of the court, we resolved the matter. So, as you see, nothing particularly earth-shattering to report."

"No, I suppose not," I replied.

"I imagine, if you don't mind my asking, your investigation has shed some light on the possible involvement of any prisoners?" Milner asked.

"Yes, we've spoken to them. I'm not really at liberty to reveal anything of the investigation, however."

"Understood, Superintendent."

"And that's all the matters that came to your attention during those meetings?" I asked again.

"Yes, that was pretty much it. I'm sorry to have disappointed you."

I would, perhaps, have stood at that moment to express my gratitude to the gentleman and said my goodbyes had I not noticed one thing. At my mention of other "matters," Milner's thumb, comfortably folded into his hands sitting atop his bulging midsection, began to twitch. I couldn't be certain about the cause of this seemingly involuntary movement, but it caught my attention, and I decided to dig a little deeper while I had his attention.

"Are you certain, if you don't mind my asking, there were no other complaints offered during either of these meetings?" After a rather long pause during which the man neither moved nor blinked, the Steward of the Manor continued.

"Well, now that I can focus and recall…there was some shared apprehension about the health of some of the crops. As you might expect these concerns are frequently the subject of the court. Some members agreed that the war and our lack of certain products previously imported from the continent were most likely the cause of some rather lackluster harvests. It was generally agreed that with the war unwinding, our next harvest would likely improve immeasurably." I hoped he had more to say, but a lengthy pause followed.

I couldn't help but imagine there was more to that conversation than Geoffrey seemed willing to divulge. So, I decided to jump into the fray with one final question.

"And one last thing, Geoffrey. Has the court ever given any consideration to, how shall I put it, supernatural activities, claims of contemporary witchcraft?" An even broader smirk replaced the slightly smug.

"I must admit to being slightly aghast that the Metropolitan Police would give credence to such reports every time the smallest law is broken. Certainly, this investigation has more to show for itself than what you might have learned from the corner medium?"

"Without divulging the progress of our work, sir, it might be of interest to us to know how often these reports emerge amongst the general population, given the history of such speculation in our parts."

"While I cannot deny that I have heard such notions during my tenure as Steward, I can safely say that the court has never taken seriously any claims of interventions by the devil. And I trust, so that I may insure our constituents their police are not hunting ghosts, that you and your friends from Scotland Yard can make the same claims. Please tell me that is the case, Inspector."

I had to admire Milner's ability to turn the question around, nearly accusing our forces of the same proclivities I was suggesting his court had shown. I wanted to tell him that he should have been a lawyer but feared he might take such a suggestion the wrong way.

"I can assure you the leads we are pursuing show all indication of being part and parcel of the real world. So, you can assure the members of your community and the Leet that we are not chasing shadows."

I was reluctant to take this conversation any further and also confident he was not divulging every nuance of the court's last meeting. Though he no doubt knew intimately the myths and lore of his corner of the country, I found it curious he didn't want to address any of their details.

"I have no doubt," Milner continued, "the illustrious office of the Yard will be able to conclude this case in good time. And please send my regards to the Detective Superintendent - or is it Chief Detective Superintendent? Undoubtedly, we can all rest easier knowing the matter is in the hands of such a competent director."

Ouch! What a master of ridicule was our Steward of the Manor. He seemed to have reduced me to a mere peeler or bobbie, taking great delight, I imagined, in my exit through his grand entranceway.

Anticipating the mob that was probably awaiting me at the station, I decided to take lunch at my favorite café in town. This would give me time to decide my next move, confident Mr. Fabian had his hands full meeting all the residents of Quinton depending on his expertise for their protection. I suspected the experience would reveal a more humble leader.

Chapter Twenty-Six

Lower Quinton
Early Tuesday Morning
February 27, 1945

Clair was up on the ridge just above the crime scene freezing his toes and fingers, searching far and wide for onlookers, determined to keep their early morning event as clandestine as possible. Lower, just beside the road where Walton was killed, Sam, Eddie, and Edith stand huddled together for warmth, their eyes fixed on the ground beneath them. Though it had rained several times since the murder, all of them clearly saw the blood-soaked spot where Charles was slain.

"This is hard," Edie whimpered.

"Try to be strong, Edie. Let's give Sam the chance to bring him to us."

"Instead, let's think of all of us coming to him. Right, Edie?" Sam insisted.

"Yes, of course," answered Eddie.

"You need to join us, Clair. It won't work if all the energy isn't focused on this circle," Sam called to her new associate, who walked down to join the others. She then had everyone join hands. In her other hand she held a silver fork that Edie had given her, swearing her uncle had used it every morning to eat his eggs. She gripped the fork, rubbed it with her hands, then asked the group to close their eyes and imagine Charles standing between them.

"It's important that everyone concentrate, rid your minds of all thoughts that might take you away from this moment and the thought of Charles. Think of the photo Edie showed us. Think of Charles' kind eyes and the chronic pain he suffered due to the constant use of his back and hands. Remember his uniqueness, his generosity, and the love he showed for all living things."

A great quiet descended on the circle, so powerful that even the cries of the morning birds evaporated. Sam was certain their concentrated energy would transform their shared space, providing an avenue by which Charles' spirit could communicate to her, as she was the open source among them. All it would take would be the willingness of all to trust such contact was possible.

Time passed. Sam became increasingly tense. Sweat began to form on her forehead and between her breasts. Tears fell as she began to tremble, a movement each of them felt, connected as they were by human flesh and bones. What seemed an hour but was in fact no more than a quarter of that time, left them all nearly breathless, before Sam collapsed, emitting a sound resembling the final moments of a dying animal.

"Stand aside," ordered Clair, as he stooped down to feel her forehead, which was at a boiling point. Eddie and Edie panicked, thinking they'd caused the death of the young woman they'd only known a few days who had come to help them. She'd not even charged anything, having convinced them Charles was important to her, that she was beholden to him for her own devotion to the darker arts. How would they explain to Scotland Yard the death of someone else on the very spot where the crime had been committed?

Thankfully, it soon became apparent that Sam survived whatever force had engulfed her. She opened her eyes and took several deep breaths before Clair helped her stand. Stunned as she was, she seemed nearly reborn, more convinced than ever that they were on the cusp of a reunion with Charles.

"I felt him," she said. "He was here."

Edie began to cry, a consequence of the incident taking place on the very ground she'd visited only days before where she'd found the mutilated remains of her beloved uncle. Eddie took her into his expansive arms, unsure what to think of what had just happened. Every part of him had been reluctant to believe that human beings could communicate with the dead. But hadn't Charles shown him that he could speak to frogs, that the birds trusted him enough to let him feed them? Sam had become the only light in Edie's life. Shouldn't Eddie trust her enough to see if she can actually perform such magic?

It only took a few moments for Sam to recover, convinced she'd come close to making contact. Everyone else seemed to have witnessed a transformation that could only have been the result of otherworldly interference. She was excited and more committed than ever to finish what she'd begun.

"We were almost there, folks. I thought at first there were no vibrations, even though there are so many signs that he hasn't yet left us for the other side. But then, something happened, as if a new spirit had joined the circle." She motioned for everyone to break the circle while she walked several paces up the road, as the sun's light brightened, warming the early morning air. She seemed to be searching for something or someone, perhaps.

"What is it, Sam?" Clair asked.

"Someone is here with us."

"Yes, I think he's near, too," Clair agreed.

"No, no. Someone else." Sam's response mystified the others, as it appeared if they looked around there was no one else in view. Sam remained certain there was other energy at work. She left the three of them and moved swiftly down the road, stopping about twenty meters beyond them. She'd seen something close to a tree on the other side of the road. There, partly obscured, stood Roberto.

"Come, friend, join us," Sam said to him, as if she already knew he was there for Charles. Roberto calmly walked to Sam and took her hands, shaking them warmly, after which the two of them began walking together back to the group. Eddie and Edie greeted him as if he was a long-lost cousin.

"Roberto, it's you! Buongiorno!" called Eddie.

"I can't believe it," Edie followed.

***

That same morning I came to the station, just as I'd done the day before when I'd found what seemed half of the residents of Quinton awaiting entry. This morning the waiting area was empty, as if it were a morgue, in comparison. I immediately wondered if Fabian had completed his interviews. Was he, perhaps, already on his way back to London having found the killer?

Everyone in the office was exceedingly quiet. I usually expected to find friends among the staff greeting me with a morning smile. Not that morning. No one seemed the least interested in making eye contact, so I headed straight to my office without checking in with Scotland Yard. Before I'd been there five minutes Fabian was at my door.

"Good morning, Spooner." He seemed in a particularly sour mood and for the first time, vulnerable. I acutally found myself feeling empathy for the man, especially as I'd anticipated he might have been overwhelmed by the mission he'd chosen for himself.

"I seem to have found myself persona non grata this morning," Fabian said under his breath.

"I think you'll find most of them quite willing to forgive. What exactly do you think you've done?"

"I'm afraid I may have lost my temper. Yesterday was a certifiable disaster. I was confident at the beginning that the townspeople could be properly questioned in the time alotted, but right from the first group no one seemed willing to divulge anything about their whereabouts on the day of the killing. Without exception, they regarded me as an outlier. So, we got way behind in the groups and half of them remained here most of the day without being heard. I tried to impress them with the need to assist Scotland Yard, that the sooner we solved the case, the sooner life would return to normal. But absolutely no one seemed ready to cooperate.

"How strange," I said to him, privately enjoying his inability to cope.

“It appeared they were all reading from the same playbook, as if none of them could imagine anyone commiting such a crime. Even when I asked for their personal response to the murder or whether they knew Walton, they chose to say nothing.”

“Insufferable,” I said to him. Part of me had to agree. Why was everyone being so completely unhelpful?

“So I had no choice. I had to make it clear how unhappy I was and I had no choice but to... Well, I’m afraid I upset some of the staff.”

“I’ll have a talk with everyone, see if…”

“I think I’ve found the culprit, however,” said Fabian, as if he’d settled the whole matter, contrary to indications from everyone in the office. I was intrigued.

"It seems there was an organizer amidst the interviewees, a man, if you can believe it, one of the individuals who found Walton's body!"

"You don't mean Harry Beasley, do you?"

"Yes! What do you know about him? I think he’s likely much more involved than we originally thought. I checked our notes and it seems you spoke to him several days ago."

"I don't think Harry had much to do with anything, really." I had to fight the urge to break out laughing, imagining a face-off between Harry and Fabian.

"This man is a communist, Spooner! And everyone there seemed to know him! He was coordinating the crowd to be sure they all answered in the same way. I saw him with my own eyes, making sure our task was impossible."

"I'll drop by his place and talk to him again. I know Harry. I'm quite certain..."

"No need. He's here."

"Oh, well, then why don't you send him in," I suggested.

"No, Inspector, you don't understand. He's in the holding cell. Has been since late yesterday afternoon."

This information left me no urge to laugh, as I had a pretty good idea then why everyone in the office seemed as if they'd been to a funeral. Here was one of their town's oldest residents and, as grouchy as he often was, the idea that he would be arrested on suspicion of murdering his best friend had certainly not set well with anyone.

"Chief Inspector... Robert, I'm not certain that was the wisest of choices, given the reluctance of Quinton from the start."

"I felt I had to establish my authority. This man had been hampering an investigation of the Crown! When he began spouting the glory of the "People's Revolution" and demanding a "People's Tribunal," well, I'd just about had it. Especially when everyone else was treating me as if I was Hitler or Mussolini."

"I'm sure you're exaggerating, sir," I interjected.

"Do I appear to be a man who exaggerates, Spooner?! Fabian said firmly.

"No, not at all, sir, of course not."

At which point he and I reached some kind of an understanding, one that seemed to last throughout his tenure in Stratford. It may even have been the point when he decided the case might become his Achilles Heel. I don't think he ever pursued matters afterwards with the same verve or confidence he had before that day at the station. From that point forward he perferred going to each citizens' home for interviews and began working with the door to his office closed, as if he could no longer expect our staff to be trustworthy.

In the meantime, after clearing it with our great leader, I immediately went to retrieve Harry from the jail cell, curious as to the ways he might characterize the past twenty-four hours. He was huddled in the corner sitting on the bench, but contrary to my expectations – and confirming that he was a true enigma – he showed little spite or desire for retribution.

"Harry, please forgive me, man. There's been a real misunderstanding. The Chief Inspector was simply overwhelmed by everyone's attitude and..."

"Not to worry, Inspector. Your little escapade gave me the opportunity to begin forming the cells that will make our work easier once the armistice has been signed."

"Yes, I can imagine," I replied. And I could, actually.

"I'm beginning to think that Charles may have sacrificed himself for the greater cause," Harry suggested, as I ushered him out of the empty cell.

"Well, I'm not quite so sure about that."

"You needn't worry about my calling out the solicitors, Alec. I'm sure you're acquainted with the wisdom of first killing the lawyers," said Harry with relish.

"Yes, another gem we owe to the Bard, I believe."

"Exactly," stated Harry, as if to put a period on the whole affair.

"Let me suggest one thing, though, Harry. I would leave Inspector Fabian to his own maneuvers. I promise he won't be calling on your expertise again, should that be his suggestion."

"I shall make every effort to keep safe the secrets of the proletariat and expect Comrade Fabian will have made his exit before our revolution is set in motion."

"I, for one, will be sleeping more easily with that knowledge, Harry."

And from the stoop of our station I watched Harry walk away with new confidence, as if there was little anyone could do to stop the Bolsheviks from claiming victory aboard His Magesty's great ship of state.

Chapter Twenty-Seven

Lower Quinton
Thursday Morning
March 1, 1945

Had one stepped off a plane on this late winter day and landed in Geoffrey Milner's favorite spot for his grazing herd of Holsteins, they might have sworn it was late June. Even the cows seemed to be smiling, as if they'd just been released from a year-long quarantine. They were showing their appreciation by mooing long and deeply, their heads bowed to the warm sun and clear skies on a day even a fool would celebrate.

Though many men were envious of Milner's prosperity and revered station in the community, no one would ever claim he was a fool, even if a few made nasty comments about the breadth of his midriff. Regardless of his size or the remarks he knew were frequently uttered behind his back, Geoffrey was feeling especially satisfied that morning, as he lay on a blanket and, like his fellow cows, looked into the sky, soaking up its spring-like warmth.

He had much to feel good about. The numbers for his first fiscal quarter were looking particularly strong. Soon, once the war ended, his European markets would reopen, insuring an even brighter economic future. And, until further notice, his wife Margaret would be visiting family in Scotland. On top of that, it appeared to him that Scotland Yard, whose presence the Steward of the Manor believed would jeopardize

Warwickshire's tourist trade, would soon be moving on, unable to make any progress in their search for Walton's killer.

With little to regret, and seemingly no obstacle to his wellbeing, he gave some thought to the meeting he had arranged with Potter, whom he expected to see in his field later that morning. Geoffrey had been considering Alfred's complaints before the Leet and to the arrangements they'd made afterwards. When Potter reached out to him about some of his animals' recent illness, Milner suggested he sell him some of his herd at a substantial discount on a plan allowing him to pay over time. No matter how the investigation proceeded or to what degree they kept Potter within their crosshairs, Geoffrey was pleased that he might have an extra bit of insurance should either of the illustrious investigators come knocking on his door again. Not that he feared anything regarding his own guilt. He'd done nothing. He simply wanted to make sure he retained some control over Potter.

The better part of the previous afternoon had been spent determining which of the Holsteins he might include in the sale. Even with the great number of cattle in his herd – short of naming each animal – he knew most of them well enough to make sure the ones he'd marked would be in the field that morning. His work well done, he could comfortably pass the time waiting for Potter, indulge in one of his long afternoon naps he more frequently enjoyed as he neared his sixtieth year.

Even considering the disruption caused by the town's unusual murder case and its proximity to the magistrate's private affairs, Geoffrey felt particularly pleased. So, when he dreamed one particular dream – as he had on several nights before and after Valentine's Day's bloody murder – its details might evade his conscious mind, but the awful fears that lurked deep within his subconscious were increasingly near to breaking through.

***

Lupercalia, February 15, the pastoral festival and Roman feast, was about to begin. Inspired by the Roman god Februus (from whom we get the name of the month), the celebration became the basis for Valentine's Day, but its more pertinent application was related to the urge for purification.

Geoffrey stood at the center of the *Lupercal*, the cave named for the she-wolf, Lupa, overseen by the *Lupercalia* or priests devoted to the purging of the land through the sacrifice of a dog and a male goat. He looked around him, noting the numerous dogs by his side, their teeth bared. But where was the goat?

He was surrounded by the *Luperci* ("brothers of the wolf"), nearly twenty young men whose eyes remained glued to him. And nearby he saw the sanctuary of Rumina, the goddess of breastfeeding, as this sacrifice, like so many Greek and Roman rituals, was essentially about the importance of fertility. What, then, could his presence have to do with the festivities of the day?

And why was he unable to move? He looked down and noticed the rope tightly wrapping his ankles, and other rope holding his legs together. But where were his arms and why did he see only hooves where he once had feet? And when he tried to speak, he found no words would come to him, only bleats, sounds that would never be mistaken for authority or aggression, the tenor and language he usually employed to get what he wanted. Try as he did to make the chorus of priests understand he was not a four-legged animal, but a respected landowner, no man there recognized him as anything other than a stupid, dirty goat! How could this be? After all, he was a Christian father and husband; in fact, he was Steward of the Manor of the Court Leet!

Geoffrey was reminded of how he disliked beasts of the field, such as the huge, ignorant cows he tended, worth nothing except their bloated utters that provided him a livelihood. How often he'd wanted to kick them when they failed to respond to his orders, or serve them up for dinners, if only their meat was worth as much as the that of steers commonly slaughtered for the steaks and ribs found in Stratford's finest inns and restaurants. But goats! What earthly purpose was served by the existence of these rude, smelly, creatures? What right did they have to share nature's bounty? And how was it possible that he would be mistaken for one of these useless ogres?

He understood the importance of the ritual always performed on February 14, the means by which the populace insured that coming generations of men would have the same strength and power they needed to prosper. Such sacrifice seemed reasonable. Not just reasonable, in fact, but necessary, according to the earliest decrees of Jove, who recognized the ultimate supremacy of the human animal. Was not the face of man merely the representation of Jove himself? Was it not our duty to preserve this line of authority and wasn't Geoffrey's face the personification of Jove's? Why then was he being served up as if he was at the bottom of this holy line of succession?

Prior to the blood sacrifice, as the drums beat above hordes of morning celebrants, meat cakes prepared by vestal virgins are served by Jupiter's chief priest. Why was he not being offered a meat cake? All that anyone heard when he objected were louder bleats. They all seemed to be enjoying themselves, so delighted to be the designated Roman citizens responsible for the sacrifice that would lead to a feast. Was he to be eaten alive, he wondered?

No. He remembered the way this particular ritual proceeded. Following the blood sacrifice, two *Luperci* would approach the alter. Their foreheads would be anointed with the blood of the sacrificial knife. Then, the knife was wiped clean with wool soaked in milk. At which point – and it was this part that had caught his attention when he first learned about the sacrifice – the *Luperci* were expected to laugh joyously. How odd, he had thought.

So, when he was hoisted high and then thrown to the ground on his side, he trembled with the knowledge that after they slaughtered the hound to his right, his throat would be the next target. The black dog, covered in the red that oozed from its slit throat, with tongue looping to the side below astonished eyes in a lifeless stare, was dead.

Geoffrey knew his time on earth had dwindled to a few short moments, as the dog's body was pulled from the altar and shuffled off to the side. In desperation he tried to pull his legs free of the rope binding his legs, but any exertion was futile. The more he screamed in misery, the louder the bleats. When he looked into the face of the *Luperci* who held the knife above him, all he recognized was the sublime pleasure of being the chosen one to complete the sacrifice.

Unable to defend himself against the approaching darkness, he heard the exuberant laughter of twenty boys celebrating his imminent death. He closed his eyes and prayed in the name of Jove, of Jesus, of whomever might be listening at that moment.

When he opened them, he was staring into the fretful eyes of Alfred Potter standing over him. Milner's face and shaking body were drenched in sweat and his hand was twitching. He must have had a ghastly look on his face, because Potter thought the man was having a heart attack.

"Geoffrey, good lord, what's wrong wid yous?"

He lay there like a wet rag, still uncertain as to which world he was inhabiting, and fearful that Potter might be another priest come to deliver his severed head to the feast table. Only after several long moments did he recognize the farm manager, and even then, he remained unsure if he still had hooves. Thankfully, when he looked down, he saw shoes.

"You musta had an awful nightmare. I never seen yous like that," said Potter.

Milner had little to say. He was still in a state of shock, feeling as though he'd been executed and delivered to Elysian Fields. And what was Alfred Potter doing there? Someone's vengeful version of the Hereafter, if he was to be eternally sequestered with this man.

He finally had enough breath to request Potter's help. "Give me your hand, Alfred." Raising this corpulent specimen always took longer than anticipated and was generally accompanied by a symphony of squeals and groans. Once he was vertical, he wished he was still alone and horizontal, soaking up the sun. Though he was in no mood to return to his dreams, not the ones he'd been having lately.

"I've got the animals I promised, up the hill a bit, if you want a look?" Milner offered him.

"I trust yas," Potter responded.

"Do ya?"

"Well, sure, what do yous think?"

"I think it's bloody hard to trust most anyone these days, that's what I think," Geoffrey lamented, his eyes lingering on the man who had so abruptly interrupted his private world.

"If yous mean, well, what we discussed... about, well, you knows..."

"Yes, I know, Potter. Me, I know. And let's keep it that way, y'hear?" added Milner, irritated, as if he was naked.

"No need to worry. Thomas is a good man," answered Potter.

"Thomas?" Geoffrey's mind suddenly went blank. "Who?"

"You know," insisted Potter.

It took a while for Milner to recall Thomas' role. He had been nearly hysterical, but now subdued, he was inclined to go on about Thomas, as he liked the man. But he didn't have the energy, and really just hoped they could move to a new conversation.

"So, we're all set with this sale, right?"

"Thas, right. I's much obliged to ya, Geoffrey. This will make everythin' go down easier, if you knows what I mean."

"I'm sure I mostly have no idea what you mean, but I'll take your word."

"Thas, right. You see, yous can trust me," Alfred assured him.

"Yes, of course I can," Geoffrey said with a hint at finality. They were both as close as either of them would ever be to trusting one another.

Chapter Twenty-Eight

Lower Quinton
Thursday Evening
March 1, 1945

While it wasn't yet the Ides of March, celebrated one month after Valentine's Day, Sam was always sensitive to the Roman calendar, her studies having focused on early Christianity. She also knew that Julius Caesar had been laid to rest on the Ides of March (as I'd learned from a Shakespeare Memorial Company production), so perhaps, it was a reasonable goal to find some clarity by that date. Besides, if she didn't find a way to help Edie and Eddie, they would both be jobless. This was not a solution anybody could live with.

It was a whole new experience for Edie to have guests in her home. Other than hosting Harry Beasley on occasion, Eddie had been her and Charles' sole guest in their kitchen. So, it was astonishing that since Tuesday morning, they'd all been inseparable: Clair, Sam, Edie, Eddie and... Roberto! Two days of sharing their deepest feelings over a kitchen table. Everyone was also aware that Charles would have been the happiest at such a communion of new friends and delighted that Roberto's language barrier hardly mattered at all. They had all been taking their time enjoying a lunch of soup and sandwiches, in addition to some "deviled" eggs Sam had prepared at Edie's stove. She had fun introducing that dish to the others.

"Well, now that we've all been cursed by Sam's special eggs..." Eddie joked.

"No, no," countered Sam, "charmed, not deviled."

"Whatever power they may have, they are simply delicious," said Edie. Both Eddie and Clair nodded their heads in agreement, as did Roberto.

Just two weeks after the murder Sam had accomplished a large part of her main objective. She had gathered together the characters she needed to make contact with Charles. While it was important to be the one to solve this case – and for everyone to know it – she was also sincerely concerned about Charles' posthumous reputation and Edie's state of mind. She'd taken a real liking to both Eddie and Edie, as well as Clair, whose reputation also depended on Sam's ability to find the killer. With the new month upon them, she was beginning to feel an urgency.

"Oh, Sam, what would I have done had you not come along!" Edie proclaimed.

"We're not there yet, Edie. But all this coming together of Charles' closest will go a long way to helping us find him, because I know he's waiting for us." Roberto nodded emphatically.

"The question is, even if – with the help of Charles – we discover the murderer, how do we convince the world of the truth when our evidence or suspect's identification comes from the dead victim?" Sam's recognition of their huge task put a real damper on what had come to feel like a festive occasion. It seemed there was little anyone could say or do to defy that pesky Angel of Silence.

Sam was afraid she'd lost everyone's attention after failing their first attempt to contact Charles and each day lived meant there would be more distance between them. If only she were able to stop time in its tracks until she could figure out her next move.

***

Strangely, the atmosphere at the offices of the Warwickshire C.I.D. was not significantly different than that of Edie's kitchen. Having found his relations with both the staff in his office and the homeowners of Quinton strained nearly to the breaking point, Fabian decided to follow-up on two leads he'd found during his few interrogations.

All twenty-nine samples of clothing and items they'd submitted for testing in Birmingham came out negative. The tests they ran on the blood found on the shirt of the Italian POW – Roberto Rizzo – had also come up negative. It seems the blood on Roberto's shirt was that of a rabbit, not the victim. And suspicions regarding the other indigent "Italian Nazis" planted by Potter and encouraged by Milner were almost instantly scuttled after Fabian's visit to their camp. In addition to finding numerous alibis for each of the POWs, the chief was sincerely impressed by their integrity. He believed most of them would have gladly joined the Allied Forces. And all attempts to find Charles' lost watch had turned up several sacks of scrap metal, including many valuable items, none of which told the time.

What was the chief inspector to do if none of the residents in that corner of Warwickshire would give him any information? Some seemed reluctant to even share their names. He felt for the first time in his career as if he had no authority, no ability to collect the facts necessary for him to find the killer – or even come up with a credible suspect!

My work had also come to a stand-still. I knew that Fabian, convinced this case would be wrapped up by Easter, was frustrated by its lack of leads. He was understandably concerned that Warwickshire was capitalizing all his time, leaving other London matters unattended. We were both at a kind of crossroads.

Did I also see my opportunity to take over the case in Fabian's absence, thereby allowing me to explore the leads found in the myths that made Warwickshire famous? And did I believe that such a change in direction of the case to be necessary? Yes. I suppose I did.

"Is that all we've got?" asked the chief inspector, seated at the head of the table, intently puffing on his pipe during our last team meeting of the week. Silence.

"I wonder if we might want to consider the case of Ann Turner," I said.

Again, a great silence descended. Everyone in that room knew the tale, but no one was willing to admit it. My findings in the books from Chaucer Head were well known to the staff – thanks to office rumors – and they all understood the ramifications of taking them seriously, the rabbit holes we'd all have to enter in order to let the truth find its voice. But they also wanted to solve this case.

Fabian refused to look me in the eye. We both knew if he softened and agreed to look further into any connection between Ann Turner's and Charles Walton's murder, he would be accepting an entirely new worldview. How would he counter the realists at Scotland Yard who had championed their chief inspector for his cunning ability to consistently "smell out the rat?" Fabian of the Yard would be little more than a servant to the gods, dependent on otherworldly forces to determine the fate of the guilty.

"Listen, Alec..."

"Sir?" I thought for a moment I might miss him as much as I'd be glad to see him gone.

"Am I to understand that I should be open to the idea that Charles Walton was in some form or another a witch with supernatural powers?" Every eye turned to me.

"Only to the extent that others may have been convinced he was," I said. More silence.

"Mr. Spoon..."

"Er..."

"Spooner. If I accept the premise that this elderly, ailing, lover of animals was in fact an agent of the devil, rising to the level of a threat to the livelihood of an entire community... should I then celebrate the acts of those who decided the devil should be eliminated? You tell me."

"Yes, I suppose you might, if you lived in the 16th century."

"I wonder, sometimes, if I feel I might be, living as I am, in Stratford." One could sense the slings and arrows of outrage being quietly emitted by some of the local staff sitting around the table.

"I still think our Potter suspect is clearly the individual we're looking for," Fabian concluded.

"That makes the both of us," Sergeant Webb concurred. I had little trouble knowing which direction to take the conversation.

"Then let's bring him in. Certainly, we can find something to charge him with, which would give us the ability to thoroughly search his home and also observe the effects of any added pressure."

"On what charge, Spoon, do you believe we could logically depend?" Fabian asked, trying desperately to control both his embarrassment and anger.

"And he's no doubt well-acquainted with a good barrister," added Webb.

"Truth be told, he has no evident motive. We cannot arrest the man for not liking our victim, a fact to which he freely admits. I expect we'd have difficulties convincing a jury that he would have the physical strength to commit this murder in the way that it was executed. Our theory of why his prints were found on the murder weapon are easily countered by his claims that he tried removing the sickle blade while waiting for the authorities to arrive on the night of the murder. There is no case here!"

"There is the wife. We've yet to take her testimony," Webb interjected.

"And can we expect she will be any more forthcoming than anyone else in this damned town!" It wasn't the first time I felt the need to be a moderating force, still feeling the slightest empathy for a man who, despite his sometimes-prickly personality, was devoted to finding the truth.

"Why don't Sergeant Webb and I have a visit to Potter's farm for a little talk with this illusive wife we've all heard about," I suggested. "Your absence might be recommended, considering Potter's animosity."

"He's simply going to direct her testimony if he knows you're coming," Fabian cautioned.

"Perhaps, we can simply drop in when we know he will be elsewhere."

"I would be amenable to that. Sergeant?" Fabian asked.

"I am at your disposal, Chief."

Chapter Twenty-Nine

White Swan Hotel, Stratford
Friday Evening
March 2, 1945

Given the general sense on every side of the investigation that little had been learned since it began, when Friday night arrived nearly everyone decided to spend their evening drowning their sorrows in drink. Clair understood that his editor was losing patience, convinced his piece was never going to materialize. What would he do when he had to leave Sam, to whom he'd become seriously enamored? On the other hand, Fabian was beginning to accept for the first time he may have to walk away from a major case, unsolved. Not that he hadn't previously failed to solve a case, but never one so much in the public eye.

Though neither party knew of the other's plans for the evening, they all found themselves at the White Swan, aware that once their self-abuse had come to a close, they could simply retire to their rooms upstairs.

Clair and Sam had invited Roberto, Eddie, and Edie to dinner. Likewise, I accepted an invitation to dine with Fabian and Webb, suspecting such an opportunity would soon not exist. I did appreciate their company. Once they returned to London, life in Warwickshire would lack some of its luster. And I, alone, would be responsible for bringing this case to some kind of closure.

First to dine were Sam, Clair, Roberto, Eddie, and Edie. They all sat around a long table beside the largest fireplace on the floor. It was Friday night, and everyone was feeling the pulse of the moment.

"What are we drinking tonight, ladies and gents," offered Sam after taking a seat at the head of the table.

"I fear I may drink too much. What shall I do?"

"No worry, love," answered Eddie. It's time we all came together to remember... and drink."

"I hope my editor doesn't check the receipts too carefully," added Clair.

"Not to worry, it's on me," said Sam.

Once everyone had made their drink choices – mostly stout for the first round – they sat staring at one another, not quite sure if the evening was meant to be a celebration of new friendship or a wake. Roberto loved being included in their family.

The room was buzzing with all kinds of end-of-week gatherings. Even without Shakespeare in performance – and a war raging across the channel – Stratford could still attract a sizeable crowd of both tourists and locals on a Friday night. Eventually all eyes landed on Sam.

"You're all, really, all of you are my dears. And I say this without having yet consumed large amounts of alcohol, as I intend to do before the evening is through," preached Sam, with an enormous smile to hide the sentiment.

"Even Charles," said Edie, "a teetotaler all his life until just recently, would appreciate a night like this."

"Oh, I should explore that angle for my story," said Clair. "Something every red-blooded Brit will understand, don't you think, Sam?"

"You should have heard him when the three of us went out to celebrate my birthday not long ago," Eddie reported. "He opened up about his past, his youth, revealing things even Edie knew nothing about."

"We were both astonished. I'd never imagined, having lived with Charles and Aunt Isa those years after my mum died, how he'd gone to pubs and, well, become popular with the ladies."

"Edie and I laughed so hard trying to imagine how the girls would have loved his humor, even his "evil eye."

"I can attest to that "evil eye," Sam confirmed. "Doesn't surprise me a bit that he was so popular with the women. I was attracted, too!"

"Really?" asked Clair, feigning jealousy.

"Yes! He was a charmer."

"That was the night," said Edie," he told us about Ann Turner. I'd never heard anything like that story."

"Really?" Sam said. "I thought everyone was familiar with that tale, but I guess Edie," looking straight into her eyes with jest, "wasn't a regular at any of the pubs in town, living with her uncle, as she was."

"Goodness, no, Isabel would have been appalled!" Edie giggled.

"You told us, Edie, how the Ann Turner he found that night never reappeared after she revealed they were cousins?" Sam confirmed.

"Yes, that's right."

"He went on to tell us that he kept returning to the pub, hoping to find her again, but he never did," reported Eddie. "He would get quite drunk, I think, because he really loved this Ann, his Ann. He went on about her kisses."

"Good for Charles!" chirped Sam.

"But then it all came to a halt, right, Eddie?"

"Yes, the night he saw the black dog, and then... the headless woman."

Just then their waitress came to the table to take dinner orders. And behind her, from the lobby appeared first, Chief Inspector Robert Fabian. In single file behind him Sergeant Webb appeared, followed by yours truly. Fully fueled after visiting a few other pubs on our way, we bypassed the bar for a table only a few meters from Sam and Clair's table.

"Oh, my," remarked Sam, under her breath, "we seem to have the makings of quite a festive evening here. Best to be taking some notes, Clair. I may be too inebriated to remember all the details."

"What's that?"

"Lawmen at 2 o'clock."

"Oh, right you are," noted Clair, reaching for the small notepad in his breast pocket.

"Gentlemen, and I presume we are all gentlemen here this evening," chuckled Fabian, showing a kind of joviality I'd not encountered previously. I was also feeling the kind of release I hadn't known in a long while, since before the murder. Why the hell not let down some of our professional guardedness when we'd all soon be scattered to different parts of our island, as lost as we were when Scotland Yard arrived. How futile this all was, I thought. It was time to "throw caution to the wind," as my grandmother used to say.

"Robert," said Webb, apparently unaware of Eddie and Edie so close by, "you must share with Alec some of your most distinguished conquests."

"Oh, come, come," Fabian chortled, unable to mask his feigned modesty and more than ready to abide his sidekick. I gathered it was likely a regular routine, a sort of warmup act for the Fabulous Fabians' latest retelling of another killer found and punished.

"Well, countless robberies, a few blackmailers – some of whom were actors – and, well, that reminds me of another instance in which I found myself surrounded by those in the entertainment business.

"What'll it be, gentlemen?" barked their rather buxom waitress."

"Shall we stick to our customary spirits?" Without waiting for an answer, Fabian ordered for the three of us. "Jim Beams all around. Neat."

"I believe I know to which entertainer you may be referring," said Webb.

"Just another night in the West End, except for one young lad Jim Mahoney, 23, enjoying himself alone – as he never had before – at a club bar, a five-pound note burning a hole in his sad little pocket. Sad, because poor Jim suffered a speech impediment due to a cleft palate. No sooner than he'd sat at his table that he eyed the lovely Mary Heath – billed as "The Black Butterfly" – a gorgeous specimen with amber eyes and black hair, crooning out her heart before a five-piece band. Poor Jim took the unintended bait by flashing his note – all his week's wages – then ordering a bottle of gin. At which time Mary implored him to save his wages, but, then weakened, offering the lad the chance to see her home."

"Ah, the weakness of the fairer sex," cautioned the sergeant.

"Add to that the naked desire of a wounded boy who'd never known the likes of taxis, cocktails, and tempting women. When I arrived at Dover Street a few hours after midnight, the body of the slender girl – her white neck and delicate arms – lay beneath her scattered hair on the green carpet, covered with deep knife gashes. She'd been dead about four hours, according to the surgeon."

"Nearly as awful as the scene with our friend Charles Walton, I imagine," I noted.

"In the case of "The Black Butterfly" I couldn't help but feel I was mourning for both the victim and the murderer. I didn't know anything about him yet, of course, when I was pursuing all of her friends and coming up with no leads whatsoever. Sound familiar?"

"But that didn't stop the chief from carefully looking at every detail in that apartment," Fabian's second-in-command duly added.

"My eyes lingered over every item in her room, left just as it had been at the time of the murder. For whatever reason, the contents of a wicker waste basket caught my attention. In it I found a ball of tinfoil from a gin bottle. When I asked the girl's weary sister where "Butterfly" might have bought such a gin bottle, she suggested one of the several eateries near Dover Street. The only one with a license to stock liquor was the Cosa Roja. Apparently when she'd stopped in that night for a tomato juice at the bar, the owner mentioned that the man with her had a speech impediment. Upon hearing this revelation, the exhausted sister remembered that there'd been a man in the club speaking to her sister who had a speech impediment, most likely from a cleft palate. She hadn't liked him."

"You'll note," Webb interrupted, "the advantage of the witness bystander. No such animal exists on a remote Warwickshire road beside hedgerows, right, Chief?"

"I immediately escorted the sister to our Criminal Records Office, a registry containing files on nearly every felon in Europe. There it was. File 410 held 800 photos of criminals with cleft palates. It was a slender chance, I thought. With barely the energy to pick up the file, she dutifully turned its heavy pages until she came across the image of the man in the club. An hour later on Brixton Street, responding to my persistent knocking at his door, stood Jim Mahoney, his face covered in soap and his aromatic breakfast on the stove. Realizing the reason for our visit, he wiped the suds from his cheeks and said, 'The knife is upstairs.' Sometimes the numbers collate, a slight ray of light reveals a dark corner."

"The chief has a knack for those, these, ah, kinds of revev, revelations," the sergeant blurted out with a twisted grin, having been embraced by Jim Beam, not Jim Mahoney.

"Yes, Mr. Webb, as you are *want* to say." The sergeant took out his notepad, found the correct page, and announced:

"Poor Jim – who killed "The Black Butterfly" – was sentenced at the Old Bailey on March 6, 1939 and died at the Broadmoor Lunatic Asylum on July 2, 1940.

"Good, old-fashioned justice, I suppose," I observed.

"Another round. Let's not let the evening get ahead of us," warned Fabian, though I wasn't quite sure what he meant.

Apparently, Sam had been listening intently to Fabian's story, while pretending to hear Clair tell his own versions of reporting on several London homicides. Sam already knew those.

"Come close," she gestured to the others at the table. "I'm sure you understand who's sitting to our left."

"Oh, it's Inspector Spooner," said a surprised Edie. "And the other one from Scotland Yard."

"Yes, yes. I'm wondering if tonight is not the night to convince the authorities of the importance of contacting Charles. Eddie, what do you think?"

"I think there may not be enough alcohol in Britain to convince the chief inspector that any connection can be made between the murder of Charles and invisible forces in the night."

"So negative, Eddie," quipped Sam, "though you may be right. Which gives me the notion that our target needs to be Spooner alone. He is a good man with an imagination. If we can separate him from the pack, if you know what I mean?"

Our dinner with banter mostly directed by the chief inspector continued. Hearty laughter dominated both tables well into the night. The Fabulous Fabian delivered numerous other episodes of danger and redemptive justice, so aptly, I might add, that I became quite enthralled, nearly convinced the man was some kind of a judicial savior. Our two Scotland Yarders remained several sheets too many to the wind to take notice of those at the other table.

"I've not heard anything about your official conquests, Spoon," announced Fabian out of nowhere. "Surely your long career in this office has earned you some distinction, or you wouldn't still be here."

Taken quite off guard, with a head that was spinning from drink, I had no idea how to respond. Unlike the chief, I was not a raconteur. I'd never considered myself much more than a reliable constable. The story you're reading now has been my only attempt to write about any of my cases. Fabian would go on to write a bestseller. I recognized from the start we were very different kinds of detectives. Maybe even different kinds of human beings.

"I'm afraid you're going to have to ask my constituents, Robert. I have a tendency to put these episodes into the past, once I've become fully inured to their usually gruesome circumstances."

"Albert, I think the man is unusually sensitive for someone of his profession. In addition to being disgustingly humble. Have you had another shot? Waitress! Spoon, you must learn to celebrate your good deeds, not hide behind all that false modesty. It doesn't suit you. Such effacing of self is not good for your profile! You must let people know how special you are, if for no other reason than it creates fear in others, which will always play to your advantage. Am I right, Albert?"

Sergeant Webb had nodded off a bit and gave no response to Fabian's queries. The chief didn't seem to notice.

"I like to create fear differently, Robert. By being punctual and doing my homework," I uttered slyly.

A huge laugh erupted from the large Englishman that caught the attention of the remaining parties in the room. It was a loud expression of something other than delight, barely masking emotions that veered between contempt and disappointment. I never forgot that explosive response, recognizing for the first time a hollowness to this gentleman, signifying someone I believed could never recognize innate goodness. I began to believe he was, if not soulless, incapable of understanding Charles Walton and the real goodness to which he was devoted. At that moment I became determined I was the one to solve this case.

By midnight it was apparent to both Fabian and me that Albert would either have to move to his room upstairs or simply crawl into a corner by the fireplace. The chief understood that only one of these options was acceptable and began to lead the sergeant out of the room, as if he were an old, sleepy dog.

"Spoon, you're going to have to excuse us. It appears the sergeant has concluded his evening and that I have shown him once again who is the real drinker at Scotland Yard. Good night, for the both of us."

"Goodnight, Inspector." The two of them inched their way into the lobby.

As the hour was far later than I was used to, even on a Friday night, I stood and began to put on my overcoat. Before

I was done all five of those who'd been sitting at the table nearby moved to my table, where they sat, without saying a word.

"Heavens, good evening. I saw you all enjoying yourselves earlier in the evening. Forgive my not including you at this table."

"Not to worry," pounced Sam. I was somewhat taken aback, unaware of the person who'd just offered me her hand.

"May I introduce Sam Zawalich, who's been especially helpful over the past several days," said Eddie.

"Miss Zawalich, Superintendent Alec Spooner, Warwickshire C.I.D." I took her hand in mine and sat at the table again. She held it for a much longer than I was accustomed.

"This is my associate, Clair Dunham," said Sam.

"Good to meet you, Mr. Dunham."

"Likewise," replied Clair.

"And good evening to you and Edie and Roberto," I said to them. "I'm glad to see that you've been able to enjoy yourselves, even under the awful circumstances facing all of you."

"It looks as though we've all allowed ourselves a little joy when we needed it," Eddie replied.

"Well-spoken," I answered.

"I would ask you immediately how the investigation is going, if I was an annoying presumptive person, but of course I'm not," Sam said.

I smiled, admiring the woman's flirtatious irony, though I wasn't yet ready to provide information to someone without knowing their interest in the case.

"I'm not sure I can enlighten you much more than Eddie and Edie have surely done. I'm pleased to hear you've been able to provide them some, well, how exactly have you been able to be of help?" Edie and Eddie looked to Sam, not sure how Sam was going to handle things.

"Sam is an old friend of Charles who came to us because she felt so awful about losing him," said Edie.

"I'm an interested party, Inspector."

"I can see that."

"Inspector, what do you know about the supernatural powers that some of us believe Charles possessed? His ability to reach populations in the animal kingdom or even, perhaps, those who have found themselves in the hereafter?"

I don't suppose anyone had ever asked me that question so clearly or directly. And, of course, I didn't know quite know how to respond, having hedged the possibility that such phenomena exist. With the investigation at such a standstill, though, I felt there was no other option. I would enter this particular rabbit hole without knowing if it would turn me into a pariah or a hero.

"I have come to believe," I continued, "that Charles Walton was no usual human being, that what he believed many others came to believe: that there are forces at work way beyond our conventional understanding. You're a medium, aren't you?"

"I am. It has been my life's work to connect with unseen forces, the kind that Charles understood, even contributed to. Are you comfortable with that, Inspector?"

"I'm not sure I'd say I'm comfortable, but I do recognize that few other options remain. I'm willing to listen," I said.

"I trust you and Eddie and Edie," Sam supposed, "have discussed the night Charles, the young plowboy, having been jilted by the beautiful woman who first caught his attention in the pub, began to see the images of the black dog."

"Yes, I have read the account in Mr. Bloom's *Folklore, Old Customs and Superstitions*, if that's what you mean.

"And they have told you about Charles' own version of encountering the dog and the headless woman, after which Charles was informed of his sister's death."

"They have."

"As a medium, Inspector, I believe that such a moment is the rendering of a time that is not simply a part of the past, but remains a series of events that live outside of time and may be called up by someone with the will, the belief, and the openness to recognize such a liminal moment and, thereby, communicate directly with its participants."

"I'm not sure I follow," I said to Sam.

By now everyone at the table was in silent awe of Sam's careful construction of the moment that so dominated Charles' imagination that it changed the course of his life. Losing his Ann Turner, the granddaughter of the murdered "witch," and then seeing the black dog with the headless woman before learning of his sister's death, gave him the confidence to spend the remainder of his life communicating with nonhuman souls, those who observed life, but were unable to share their consciousness. And because this encounter became known to the community by means of chatter – the natural food of any small-town's culture – I began to understand why Charles had become such a mythic character, a mystery (or source of fear) for so many in Quinton.

"You see, Inspector Spooner, the ritual murder by pitchfork of the original Ann Turner in 1775, a woman claimed to have "bewitched the cattle and the land" of Quinton, only became problematic ten years later when a young Charles Walton – grandson to the original Ann Turner – saw the fantastic images as harbingers to his dear sister's death. So, of course, why wouldn't people think that Charles was as dark an angel as his grandmother?"

"You paint a picture, Ms. Zalawich, that begins to show things more clearly," I said to her.

"Thank you, Inspector. That's one of the nicest things anyone has ever said to me."

"Are you convinced Charles was able to speak to these animals, because it sounds as if you're as skeptical as I am that he was a witch?"

"I was witness," said Eddie.

"As was I," added Sam.

"I've never told this to anyone. Not even Edie."

"What?" asked Edie.

"Charles took me to his stream, just down the hill from The Firs. He told me we were going to confer with the frogs. Well, we did, and I was thrilled. They huddled close to him after he lured them onto the ground with a strange sound he made. And

I swear, they were listening and sharing their sounds with him. This was a conversation! He wanted me to say nothing to anyone. I think he was aware of being thought a witch. But we laughed and I promised him I wouldn't say anything."

"When I was a young girl," Sam began, "I latched on to Charles cause he loved horses, like I did. We would go to The Firs to feed the horses, sometimes clean or ride them. It was my first taste of freedom, riding through a field a top such a strong animal. Each of those horses knew Charles and connected to him in a unique way. They listened to each other. I mean, really listened! I'd never seen that before between a man and animal. I decided then I would find my way into that world and discover a universal language between species. That helped me connect to the other side."

"But even if we accept his supernatural powers, how will this help us find the person who committed this awful murder?" I asked.

Sam seemed a completely confident spiritualist who had devoted her life to investigating these kinds of phenomena, so my resistance to her was softening. She was also quite an alluring woman of an age who seemed to be approaching her best years.

"Inspector, if we were able to duplicate the circumstances surrounding his experience of seeing the dog, would we not perhaps find a way to speak directly to Charles? Recreate that instance in which the spirit world touched our material world. I think he might reach out to us if we invite him to a reenactment of that moment in time. At which time his killer might be revealed. Yes?"

I stopped, sitting back and smiling... no, laughing at myself, thinking such a theatre piece could conceivably solve a murder case! Had I totally lost touch with reality? Something out of *Hamlet*, by which the play's the thing? But then, where else did I have to go?

"Where then, if I may ask, does this investigation lead? Who do you think is responsible?" I asked.

"For some reason," Sam said, "I believe, certain people felt threatened by all that Charles represented, almost as if he held a secret power, the key to something nobody else had. He was different and apparently it was different people who wanted to destroy crops and make their animals sick."

"And besides, he was a witch."

"You're beginning to understand, Inspector."

Chapter Thirty

The Firs, Lower Quinton
Saturday Afternoon
March 3, 1945

Even though it was Saturday, and recent developments in the case meant we'd be going in new directions, I decided to catch up on some of the remaining interviews. I contacted Thomas Burns, who had been suggested by Potter as a bailiff in the Leet Court who could shed some light on their recent hearings. Having finally tracked him down, Burns told me that Potter was off to Birmingham on business and needed him to feed the herd and see to other duties that weekend. So, he suggested we meet at Potter's farm. I determined this opportunity to know Potter's world – including his spouse – was prescient, to say the least.

It had turned into a rainy night while we were partying at the White Swan, and by the next morning had gotten worse. But there was no way I could ignore these suspicions about Potter that I shared with Fabian. I felt great relief driving up to his house knowing he would not be there.

"In here!" Burns shouted to me when I got out of my car before I ran inside the barn trying to avoid the downpour. He was holding a pitchfork very much like the one used to murder Charles, though I assumed they all looked pretty much alike. This man holding that slash fork became an image I could not erase, and I made a note to take a closer look at the tool later.

In the meantime, Burns was filling the stalls with hay. Forever gracious and eager to please, he came over to me as soon as I entered.

"One hell of a day, isn't it? Sorry you had to drive in this."

"Just doing the job. Good morning to you," I said. "I assume this isn't the first time you've been called to this duty."

"No, no. I've been attached to The Firs for most of my life, long before Alfred took over. His father was responsible for my family getting my own farm, and I've had responsibilities here since I was a small boy."

"Well, thank you for meeting me."

"I hope I can be of help."

What a pleasure to be dealing with someone who seemed generous and cooperative. So unlike the farm's manager who had become the central focus of our investigation and was less than enthusiastic about helping us.

"Let me begin with an obvious question. Where were you on the afternoon and evening of Wednesday the 14th, Valentine's Day?"

"I was in and around my home for most of the day after I'd spent part of the morning with Joe Stanley at White Cross Farm."

"And you were there for what reason?" I asked.

"Joe had a sick heifer, so I was there to help out."

"And Alfred? Do you know where Alfred was?"

"Yes, he was with us, but we were finished there by noon, and I think Alfred came back here when I went home myself."

"I see. And you didn't go out again all evening?"

"No. I had chores on my own property and didn't hear anything about... the event until the next morning when I saw Potter."

"You work pretty closely with Mr. Potter, don't you?"

"Well, I been very close to his father who was a very decent man, may I add."

"You're not suggesting that his son is anything less than a decent man, are you?"

"No, sir. He can be a disagreeable man, for sure, but decent. He and his family have been very kind and I have often supported him when he needed it."

"Can you think of any time recently when he might have needed your help? Apart from farm work, I mean."

Burns hesitated and went back to his hay. I suspected he wanted to be very careful about the way he answered.

"Well, we both serve as bailiffs on the Court Leet. I got involved when Alfred joined just after the war started. We've often seen eye to eye on issues that have come up and I've been proud to be there when he needed me."

"Yes, I'm sure. What were some of those concerns that you both had?"

"I suppose you know about one of the things he was upset about. The POW camp they set up in Upper Quinton, the way the prisoners would come on his property and threaten his wife, even. So, when he asked me, I offered to testify on his behalf."

"I see. Did you find them bothersome or in any way a threat?"

"What's that?"

"Were you threatened by these POWs or Nazis, as Alfred called them?"

"Well, no, not exactly. I never saw one, actually. But I respected Alfred and stood up for his character."

"Of course, you did. Now, you say this was one of the things he was upset about. What was the other thing he brought up at the Leet?"

At this moment Burns became distracted, as if he'd just forgotten something. I suspected it was a diversion, so I dug in my heels when he dropped his fork and headed to the other end of the barn.

"Forgive me, Inspector, I need to change a bandage. I just remembered. It's a new fold with a damaged hoof. Such a sweet animal, come back here to see her."

I moved past the numerous stalls holding any number of animals until I reached the last one on the right. Burns was huddled beside a newborn filly, busy removing a bloody swath of cotton and refreshing the wound with a new bandage.

"You seem to have a knack for this work," I offered.

"Yes, I think it's why Alfred depends on me so much. He doesn't much like caring for animals."

"And yet he's a farmer. That seems a bit strange."

"He's more comfortable in his office," Burns said.

"I wonder, though, if you could remember what other issues Mr. Potter had presented to the court?"

"I hardly think it's worth mentioning, but Alfred seemed to get very bothered by the condition of our crops this past year. He wasn't alone. Lots of owners were very concerned about the harvest."

"And that was it? But how could the Court Leet do anything about the crops?"

"Well, that was pretty much what the court determined. There wasn't much they could do," concluded Burns.

"I'm still not clear about what was said. Wasn't Potter insistent the court should do something?"

"Inspector, you do know about the history of Warwickshire, don't you?"

"What sort of history do you refer to? I like to think I know my literature." I had to get him to broach the subject without my coaching.

"Its history of witchcraft, Inspector." Bingo!

"Of course, Mr. Burns. It is widely known. Do you mean to say that he blamed the lackluster harvest on witches?" I asked.

"He was concerned, as were many of the other farmers, that these very old threats to our crops had resurfaced. So the court asked him to prepare evidence."

Burns finished up with the filly, wiped the blood from his hands, and returned to the opposite end of the barn. I followed, still believing he was being unnecessarily vague, hoping I'd drop the subject.

"And did he prepare this evidence?" I asked.

"Yes, several months later he and I, along with several others from Upper Quinton, gave testimony of the damage to the court."

"Had you noted great changes to your crops, Mr. Burns?"

"Well, yes, of course."

"And you were convinced it was due to witchcraft?"

"My farm is very small, Inspector, and it was hard for me to assume that any harm had been done to my crops for that reason."

"It doesn't sound to me as if you were able to be much of a useful witness."

"I understood Alfred's worries, his history of running a large farm, and I supported his theories."

"You owed it to him?"

"Well, yes... I mean, no, I owed the court my honest observations."

"And these were your truthful observations?" I asked.

"Yes."

At which point, as he continued his chores, I walked around the barn, taking a closer look at the slash hook.

"Does the farm have more than one of these? And do they all look alike?" I asked. I checked to see if there were any identifying marks on the tool.

"Oh, yes, standard equipment at any of these farms, I assure you. Very useful."

"I can imagine. Excuse me, Mr. Burns, but do you have an available WC here in the barn?

"Closest one is off the mud room at the house." He moved to the doorway to check on the rain. "Looks to be dryer out there. Just go in that back door and it's the first door on your left."

"Thank you," I said, and scurried across the drive to the door leading to the mud room.

Of course, I had no interest in relieving myself. I wanted to find Potter's wife. There was very little light in the mud room, but I did see the door to the WC. Rather than go in I opened the door to the kitchen, expecting to find the wife, perhaps, but the room was empty. I listened carefully and heard nothing, so I ventured into a few other rooms, not quite sure what I was going to say should anyone find me there.

Then, it appeared I was in his office, looking at a table covered with maps and documents, along with mostly bills and receipts. I briefly shuffled through some of them, trying not to leave any trail of discovery. Among the receipts I noticed a list of several tools, including one of the slash hooks that I assumed were the ones in the barn. I wrote down the number of the receipt and the name of the shop where it was purchased. I lost track of time, and when I heard something behind me and turned, I was looking straight into the barrel of a shotgun.

She was so small I first thought it was a young child holding the gun, but she soon revealed herself to be a woman in her mid-50s, rather unattractive, excruciatingly thin, with what appeared to be half of her face heavily scarred. I had no choice but to try and turn this clandestine search into something more formal.

"Please excuse me, Mrs. Potter?" She remained silent, steadfastly aiming the weapon at my head.

"Forgive me, Mrs. Potter, but I'm here on formal business of the C.I.D. and can show you a warrant for a search of the property." I had no idea what I'd do if she actually asked to see a warrant. She said nothing, neither moving nor showing any emotion. I also wondered how long I could remain inside the house without raising Burns' suspicions.

"Mrs. Potter, don't you think it would be wise to put the gun down? After all, I'm not simply a police officer, I'm a friendly police officer."

She continued to silently defy my pleading, until she finally lowered the weapon. I looked intently at this frightened, shell-shocked creature, hoping I could keep the whole incident between the two of us.

"Mrs. Potter, I'm terribly sorry about coming into the house without your knowledge, but sometimes our job requires this kind of secretive work. But it's no small thing to be threatening a lawman with such a weapon and I wouldn't want to take this matter any further. So, why don't we pretend none of this happened. I'll simply leave you here and I won't say anything to anybody about the shotgun. And you mustn't say anything about my coming inside the house. Don't you think that's a good idea, Mrs. Potter?"

I doubt such a plea would have worked with most people, but I thought it might make sense to this waif. She gently nodded her head and stepped aside, gesturing for me to leave the way I'd come in. I couldn't bring myself to make an exit, though, until I'd asked one simple question.

"Mrs. Potter, can I ask you one thing? On Valentine's Day, a little more than two weeks ago, were you and your husband alone on the farm during the afternoon and evening? Can you remember?"

She looked at me without expression, showing just the slightest fear. There wasn't the time to wait for any response.

"Well, thank you, and remember, nothing's a problem as long as no one knows I was here. Right?" I immediately dashed into the mud room and out the back onto the dirt drive. The rain had let up and I saw Burns still shoveling his hay.

"I expect you'll be here for much of the day, Mr. Burns. It's a big farm," I said after coming back into the barn, trying to make small-talk."

"That it is, Inspector. Is there anything else I can help you with?" I was sure he'd be very glad to see me driving away.

"What do you know about witchcraft?" I asked.

"Mostly just what I hear down at the King George. Lots of whispering and pointing fingers over the years, mostly in jest. Folks've got to have something to blabber about."

"Did you think Charles was a witch?"

"Who? Walton? Never gave it much thought. Knew he was a healer, the way he knew just what to do with a sick animal. But a witch? I suppose there was something supernatural about him, but I found him to be very friendly and helpful."

"And others mostly felt the same way?"

"Like I said, everybody liked him well enough," Burns concluded.

"Even Alfred?"

"Yeah, I suppose. He hired him, didn't he?"

"Yes, he did," I replied. "Well, thank you for the time. I hope you get some time this weekend to enjoy yourself."

"We're farmers, Inspector. 24/7."

I noticed through my rearview mirror Burns return to his chores, even before I'd gotten a few feet down the drive. I imagined Potter depended on this man to do most of his work for him. How could Burns say 'no?'" By the time I'd driven to the end of his drive, I'd become convinced I knew very little about Potter, The Firs, or the woman who never left the kitchen. But, of course, having idiosyncrasies, disliking animals, and sharing your home with a silent, anxious, and incapacitated wife in no way makes you a murderer.

Chapter Thirty-One

Stratford-upon-Avon
Sunday Morning
March 4, 1945

When I returned home early Saturday evening, finally able to appreciate the solitude to which I'd come accustomed over the course of my career at C.I.D., I prayed no one was going to be needing me until Monday. I wanted to spend at least one day thinking of something other than the murder of Charles Walton. Every mundane matter I attended to seemed miraculous as it was accomplished alone, even as it provided what felt to be heavenly familiar. I had no work required, so I settled into my small library, turned on the BBC news, and sipped the seafood chowder I'd prepared earlier. Some men claim that having a wife to make these preparations is worth all the many tensions one must abide under a marriage contract. It was evenings like this one that sustained my belief in the benefits of living alone.

In fact, I reached such an absolute sense that all my concerns had melted away that I fell asleep in my office chair, leaving half of my chowder uneaten. It wasn't until very early Sunday morning that I was awakened by the ring of the phone. My first inclination was to let it ring, but then I remembered not only farmers are on call twenty-four hours a day.

"Yes, good morning, this is Alec Spooner." The voice I heard was instantly familiar, though it took a few moments to fully register. Had it been anyone else, I probably would have politely found a way to end the call.

"Oh, yes, of course, Ms. Zawalich. No, no, I've been up and around for more than an hour," I lied. "What can I do for you?" At which point this determined and astonishingly bright woman began what could be regarded a sermon. It was Sunday morning, after all. And, while I was very much like Harry Beasley and Charles Walton when it came to attending Sunday services at any of the many Christian houses of worship in Stratford, I found myself quite enchanted by her ongoing saga of befriending and coming to understand Walton at an age when she was especially vulnerable to the powers of an older male. So, after swearing to myself that I would not lend myself to the duties of an inspector on that particular Sunday, I agreed to meet the charming woman later that day.

After she admitted that her home, a smallish flat at the end of Church St., was not appropriate for entertaining, I suggested she come to my home later that day. At least I'd get a few hours alone, though I found myself thinking of little else after ending the call. Why, all of a sudden, had I become the center of her attention? How could she have known the investigation was at such a stand-still, and in what way would she benefit from this reenactment she had proposed? I also wondered, since she had wasted no time in contacting me, if she felt the same sort of fondness I seemed to be developing towards her?

I kept reminding myself as I showered and changed my clothes that there was no need to clean or arrange my living space. Ms. Zawalich was there for business, not pleasure. I made a pot of tea, then reviewed some of my notes from the past week. Fabian and Webb were still very much on my mind, especially as I was about to be consenting to an arrangement for a person who only appeared on the scene within the past twenty-four hours and seemingly had no connection to the homicide. Scotland Yard would be horrified if they knew I was taking these plans seriously.

3 pm arrived in what seemed to be minutes after my shower. It was good to be dressed in a football shirt and dungarees, items that had been difficult to procure during the war. When I opened the door I found Sam dressed as casually as I was, though it appeared she'd taken great care to be even more alluring than she had been at the White Swan. Or was that impression simply wishful thinking on my part?

"Ms. Zawalich," I greeted her.

"Sam, Sam, Sam."

"Sam, come in." She was in no need of directions and blithely landed on the settee. She was smiling, as confident as she had appeared the night before.

"Now, don't pretend otherwise, but I know you had absolutely no interest in seeing anyone today and deep down you seriously considered not answering my phone call."

"I expect it's futile to disagree with someone who reads minds, so I won't. Disagree, that is. Can I get you some tea?"

"That would be lovely, Alec."

I liked hearing her say my name and contemplated as I was pouring the tea into my best porcelain cups how good it was to entertain a woman in my home. I'm sure I would shock myself if I calculated the last time I played host to anyone. Today, though, I was feeling like a real human being again, not some extension to the town's jail.

"I trust you've been able to recover from Friday night's indulgences?" I asked.

"Oh, yes, fresh as a daisy," she chuckled. "It's funny, you know, Alec, how little I am affected by the over-consumption of alcohol. It really has little influence on me, especially when I am determined to accomplish something so important."

"Indeed, one of my first impressions of you was that you were determined, though I'm still not certain why or for what."

"Which is why I wasted no time in making sure I made myself clearer to you. Just you, as you are the central force behind the discovery of what happened to our dear Charles."

"Well, strictly speaking I am really second-in-command."

"Honestly, give me one good reason why I would want to impress or believe I could change the mind of Scotland Yard."

So, it seemed she was having similar feelings about the chances of Fabian cooperating with or believing in the work of Sam Zawalich.

"Honestly? I have the strangest sense that we've known each other before, either here in Stratford or..."

"Or, perhaps, from another one of our lives. We may have been very close in times past," she said demurely with a sly smile.

"Not what I was thinking, but I've promised to abandon my preconceptions."

"And remain open. An important concept, Alec. None of our hopes in this world will ever materialize if we don't stay open to possibilities."

"Tell me, Sam. Why risk the possibility of disappointing Edie again, when she's been in such a desperate condition since her uncle's death? What do you hope to accomplish? He's not your relative or even a close friend of late. Why this case?"

"It's a journey. Really begun when I met Charles. I'd been searching for ways to open the windows of perception between humans and those whose worlds are mostly closed to us. My study of early Christianity pointed me in certain directions that led to parapsychology, but I didn't know what I wanted or believed in until I met Charles. And like so many others I don't think I realized how precious he was until I lost him."

"But how would you be able to prove you've been communicating with the dead?"

"I haven't told you, but Clair is a news reporter writing a piece about the murder. If I can convince him and others around us who knew Charles that I had actually made contact with his spirit, I could reveal to the world a true story of two clairvoyants – one dead and one alive – actually conversing, and, perhaps even, helping solve a murder. I believe all this is possible and that you could be on the verge of something new, by helping us convince the world this is legitimate work."

It all seemed so simple when Sam said it. So rational, reasonable, even necessary. But then I'd try to formalize an opinion on the subject and feel like a complete fool.

"You know, I want to believe in this, because... I believe in you. But it's such a risky stab in the dark. I could lose my job."

She remained very calm and centered. She wasn't whining or trying to shame me, or even pushing very hard. This was one of the reasons I found her so appealing, so completely knowledgeable and mature.

"You ever been married, Alec?"

"Yes. A number of years ago. For only three years."

"Did you love her?"

I'd been young, only a year or so after joining the force. I loved her deeply, completely, and when I lost her I accepted – no, insisted – that there would be no one else. That's how much I loved her.

"Yes. Very much."

"Was there not a moment after you'd met and decided she was the one for you, a moment of doubt when your love seemed so enormous that everything turned into fear..."

"Yes. How did you know?"

"A fear that once your love was declared and you'd found yourself unmasked, something terrible would occur and that love would be gone. And you thought for more than a moment that it would simply be easier to abandon that love in order not to destroy your life?"

"Yes, I can't believe you know this, describe it so..."

"But then something embraced you, an invitation to take the necessary risk, because you knew deep down that life – living life to its fullest – means accepting danger. Because like life, love is dangerous."

"There was that moment. I can remember it as if it happened yesterday."

"And what did you do?" She moved closer to me, taking my hand and holding it strongly.

"I said to myself that this was hope. And with hope all things are possible."

"So you answer some of your own questions."

I felt something moving from her into me. Some force that I was able to hold tightly, that strengthened me. And afterwards I wasn't afraid. I clung to her hand, wondering if I let it go would hope disappear? To my surprise, having only known this person for less than forty-eight hours, I wanted to kiss her.

"There's something strong about you, Alec. And I don't mean simply because you represent the law or wield civic power. That, of course, you do, but I detect in you a sensitivity unusual for one so determined to uncover bad people. You have a gentler side that allows you to empathize when others simply clamp down."

"You mean I'd be more likely to forgive others for their criminal actions?"

"No, not forgive. You possess a sensitivity that allows you to calculate actions with intents not necessarily evil or criminal. Hence, you're able to see deeper into those actions."

Even as I continued to hold her hand as if it was some kind of lifeline, I wondered if she was simply feeding me compliments in order to win my loyalty. But I found I was unable to see her in that light. Rather, I was convinced she saw in me a gentle soul who was capable – like her – of reaching out to the better part of others. Almost as if we both possessed the power to see in most people a capacity for love, even if they no longer recognized it themselves.

"This is quite unexpected," she said.

"What is?"

"This bond I feel with you. I had no idea."

She held her other hand up to my face, gently touching its creases and corners, before she landed at my lips. I took her fingers into my mouth, getting my first taste of the woman I knew then had become the center of a new hope. Without any further thought I put my mouth on hers and embraced her as if nothing else in the world mattered.

***

My next conscious memory of that quiet Sunday evening found me sitting alone in my small kitchen alcove in my robe sipping tea. It must have been about 6:30, as streams of light were being eclipsed by deepening dark shadows. It was heavenly quiet. I listened carefully for any sound from my upstairs bedroom, soaking up the silence and treasured scents of my private space. The fact that for once in a very long while I was sharing that space with another human being provided a solace I remembered all my remaining days.

Then, without the slightest sound, she emerged from the living room dressed in only my football shirt, which covered her slight frame down to her thighs. She was smiling and looked as gloriously peaceful as I felt.

"Tea?" I asked.

She said nothing, seated herself opposite me, and kept smiling. We cherished the moment as if we both knew we were experiencing something close to the sublime. But we needed to deal with the consequences of the crime, especially since I'd agreed to be willing to use unconventional methods to do so. How I wished we'd met under different circumstances that weren't demanding our immediate attention. And I hated being the one to break the spell.

"You hungry?" I asked.

"I feel as though my hunger for almost all things has evaporated."

"You have a way with words, Ms. Zawalich."

"You seem to have unlocked my romantic inclinations, literary and otherwise."

"Lucky me."

We continued to be consumed by the sustained look of the other, unable to break away to face matters we both knew were waiting. Until the phone rang.

"No, not saved by the bell. Condemned by the bell. Hello, this is Alec Spooner."

At the other end I heard the voice of my boss, at least for the immediate future. He seemed pretty sure I'd like to know what he'd just discovered and gave me the basic details, a series of events I never imagined would be possible. It appears we'd lost one of the treasures of our community, in a manner that pointed to the serious nature of the Walton murder and its effect on others in Quinton. I listened and told Fabian I'd be in the office within the hour.

"It appears I'm not safe even on a Sunday night."

"What is it?"

"I don't know yet, but sometimes it seems as though the moment we discover a new friend, that friend is taken away."

"I know the feeling. I'm so sorry."

"Let me find out exactly what's happened before I tell you about it. In the meantime, we've got to make plans. Something's got to give in this case."

"You and I are ready to make that happen. Don't you think?"

Chapter Thirty-Two

C.I.D. Headquarters, Stratford
Sunday Evening
March 4, 1945

As I moved through the station's front lobby, I was reminded that Sunday was still with us, there being the minimum staff around the office. Even Fabian sat alone at our big table, his trusty sergeant nowhere to be seen.

"Sit down, Alec. It's all so grim."

I sat and for the first time felt as though the chief and I were having a serious, collaborative conversation, one that was not overshadowed by his need to prove seniority. We were just two coppers sharing our notes.

"I'd just gotten to know him. And like him tremendously," I said.

"I'm sure he never forgave me for putting him behind bars."

"I think he actually enjoyed his time with us. He seemed to be fully committed to the revolution at hand."

"Yes, and I guess I was the one he was revolting against," said Fabian.

"Harry embraced the revolution long before you came along, Robert. He lived for it. He regretted not being born in Moscow."

"At any rate, we're not looking at a murder here. No signs of violence, along with a note that once it's verified, should explain everything."

"And I guess it pretty much explains why he chose to end it where he did."

"It certainly tells us, "the chief continued, "how strongly he felt about Charles."

"Harry's beauty was the way he felt strongly about so many things. I'd like to see him."

"He's downstairs. I'll bring his note."

Robert led the way downstairs to the forensic lab. After switching on the light and adjusting to the drop in temperature, we moved towards the body beneath the sheet. The chief wasted no time in drawing back the sheet to reveal the corpse of Harold Arnold Beasley: born 1871, Lower Quinton, Warwickshire, England. He had a smile on his face.

All that I could think of were Sam's words about being open to possibilities. It seemed to me Harry was the King of Possibilities, a man who remained throughout his life open to change, as if change was what we lived for. Harry's passion for change, gardening, and his sense of humor inspired me to believe in his hope for the future. In fact, he and Charles, I think, shared a similar mission.

"He looks peaceful," said the chief. "Shall I read his note?"

"Yes, please."

Comrades,

Rather than wait for the people to recognize the superior powers of Charles Walton to bring together all species for the purposes of healing our broken world, I have chosen to take my place in his ranks on the other side. Having discovered little to recommend since Charles removed himself from our earthly battlefield, I have elected to march to the beat of a different drum: Charles' drum. I trust that once our Revolution here has been realized, all living beings will come to recognize the power and resolve of Charles' voice. I will have already joined his army.

Harry Beasley

"And you say they found him right at the spot where Charles was slaughtered?" I asked.

"Yes. He appears to have known exactly what medications would be necessary to bring his end. Some combination of opiates and over-the-counter sleeping pills, according to forensics."

"Funny. I remember his telling me about the fact that he and Charles were raised only a few houses away from each other, but hadn't been acquainted until they were of age to be drafted. They understood each other, he said. I should say there was much more between them than simply understanding."

"Well, of course, he was bonkers," Fabian said. "All that blather about the Communists ruling the world after the war. Pretty dangerous, if you ask me."

"I'm sure he would have been very pleased to know someone considered him dangerous, but I really think he was the least dangerous person I've ever known."

Strangely, the events of the day seemed to have thrown Fabian into a tailspin. He appeared distracted and unable to cope with Harry's suicide, whereas I was ready to celebrate a long life well-lived. I knew I would miss him terribly, though. His advice about what Sam and I were doing would have been invaluable.

I noted, before heading home where I knew Sam would be waiting, that Fabian seemed like another man than the one who arrived in Stratford shortly after Valentine's Day. The last thing he said to me indicated he was suffering a disturbance that would never allow him to sleep.

"Say, Alec, can I ask you?"

"What is it?"

"I realize it's late on a Sunday and the weather's rather nasty, but where do you think I might go at this hour to get a drink?"

"I often find myself down by the river at Cox's Yard or, because it's Sunday, the Dirty Duck, just a bit further south on Waterside. That might suit you better, I think."

Soon thereafter Fabian disappeared into the night without saying another word. Had I thought more of it, I might have been worried.

***

By 1 am the crowd he'd found earlier at The Dirty Duck had dwindled to about twenty or so hearty folks, mostly gentlemen. Fabian hadn't felt like mingling. Rather, he found himself huddled in a corner negotiating his third or fourth J&B. He'd pretty much lost count.

The Detective Superintendent felt he'd come to the end of the road in Stratford. While he'd never had Harry's inclinations to end it all along the side of a road, he found it difficult to even look at the others in the pub, several of whom he suspected had begun to recognize him, the only solo patron in the room. He felt an intense heat overcome his body as he noticed a party of three near his table who were certainly talking about him. A few of them were chuckling over their stouts, and while they weren't pointing at him, he knew who they were focused on.

Why had he been so bloody ineffectual here in England's heartland when he'd come to be so admired in London? Was he losing his knack in old age? All he'd asked for when he took over the investigation was to be trusted, so that he could do his work. But from the beginning, even those in the C.I.D. offices seemed reluctant to accept his authority. And now it seemed the entire town wanted no part of him, as if he'd become the King's fool, albeit one who showed none of the wisdom we associate with Shakespeare's fools. No, Fabian was just foolish, he thought.

After ordering another J&B he became sure that it was not just those at the nearby table who were mocking him. He was convinced everyone in the room found him to be the evening's laughingstock. These suspicions seemed to be intensifying his hot flashes, sensations he'd always assumed were exclusively experienced by women. Hence, his station in life, he thought, was more like a woman's than a man's. Weak and ineffectual. And how could such a man – he was sure the other patrons were thinking – pretend to be so powerful as to bring a killer to justice? Certainly not him, he thought.

He found himself short of breath and feeling as though everything from the neck upward was on fire. At that moment two gentleman stood at their table and began to move towards him. Sure that they intended to humiliate him even further, the chief stood abruptly, emptied his pockets of loose change to cover his drinks, and hustled out of the pub, sure that he'd saved himself from certain death.

Shaking outside of the Duck on Waterside, he suddenly headed South towards Quinton, though he understood the town was more than seven miles away. Barely able to put one foot in front of the other, he walked hurriedly, though there was very little light to guide his way and a slight mist made it impossible to see more than a few yards ahead. After checking to be sure he wasn't being followed, he thought, at last he was no longer a target for the town's disgrace.

And he walked and walked and walked, trying to make sense of all that occurred over the past few weeks: the town's lack of cooperation, a loathsome suspect who appeared to have all his angles covered, and now the suicide of a second fully decent citizen at the very spot of the murder. He'd not felt so alone since the death of his mother when he was sixteen.

Where was he headed? It was early morning now, not a soul anywhere on the road, but something drove him forward. He must be heading to the sight of the crime – and now suicide – but he was barely conscious of having any destination. All he knew was he had to walk, even while his joints ached and his feet began to slip within his shoes, soaked as they were from the mist, making walking that much more difficult. He'd found himself on Clifford St., still a few miles north of Quinton. While he'd come to know the road quite well since coming to Stratford, as it was the main thoroughfare between Quinton and town, that night it all looked strange, as if he'd found himself on a desert in dark Africa.

Soon, he noticed through the mist the moon appearing behind the clouds, giving him a clearer outline of the terrain, which had become hillier. Looking up, he realized he'd come to one of the few junctures with another road. At that moment in the distance he noted something moving quickly down Black Lane, running in his direction. He paused beneath the road sign and waited, part of him fearful of the object moving closer and the other half praying that he would be devoured by the creature.

Before he could fully determine the nature of the fast-moving object, a large black dog ran past him, passing within a few feet, not even slowing to recognize him. Fabian was thrilled, after first believing he was part of a dream, then recognizing that the running dog was the most real thing he'd ever encountered. He remained stunned, motionless, until he watched the dog turn onto Clifford Rd. and head towards Stratford. After only a few moments the dog had disappeared, just as the clouds began to clear in the east, allowing him to see much greater distances.

The experience of the dog had jostled Fabian, as if having seen the animal there was no more reason to be walking in the night. At which point he turned and began walking back up Clifford towards town in the same direction as the dog. His walking was no longer driven by the panic that had gotten him to Black Lane and, as he sobered a bit, he began to enjoy the rolling hills visible now in the moonlight.

He hadn't been walking more than ten minutes or so after seeing the dog when he noticed a figure walking in his direction. Who could it be at this hour of early morning? In just a few moments he stood face to face with a young boy, maybe a few years younger than Charles when he saw the phantom dog and headless woman. The boy looked frightened, so Fabian motioned to him.

"Listen, son, did you see a dog running up the road just a moment ago? Was that your dog?"

Without even coming to a full standstill, the youngster ran past Fabian, as if he was running for his life. And before the chief was able to get any further response, the frightened kid had faded into the distance. How odd, thought Fabian, having come to his senses enough to realize it was way past time for him to be back in his hotel room asleep.

In his dreams that night he fretted about the notion of reality, the ways of late he'd become convinced the earth was off its axis, that the laws of nature and society had been turned upside down. Perhaps, it was the war or maybe his increasing isolation from friends or lack of any romantic connection. He'd never been a man prone to depression, or even introspection, but he felt more and more as if he was in a box enclosed in cotton, unable to hear or feel the world around him. He was looking for a sign to know the way to move forward.

That sign was awaiting the chief inspector when he arrived late to his office the next morning. Just as he'd felt the morning he came to the station after putting Harry Beasley in jail, he sensed something ominous in the way the staff greeted him. When he asked if there was some reason he should be concerned, he was informed of a very bizarre gift found that morning just outside the gates to the Holy Trinity Churchyard. He and Sergeant Webb were advised to visit the site.

There they found hanging by its neck, "drawn and quartered," as they did during Shakespeare's age, a black dog, very much like the one Fabian observed earlier that morning. The chief didn't linger to inspect any of the details surrounding the killing. Nearly three hours later he and Webb were on the train headed back to London.

Chapter Thirty-Three

Stratford-upon-Avon
Monday Morning
March 5, 1945

Sam and I were standing just outside Trinity Church's famous churchyard around noon. After I'd arrived at headquarters in the late morning I was informed of Fabian and Webb's exodus. I wasn't surprised, but had never expected it would take this kind of 16th c. exhibition of the devil's work to finally drive him from town. I didn't blame him one bit. A part of me would have liked to make the same escape, though I supposed I would now be able to drive the investigation in an entirely new direction, taking for myself whatever reward or damnation might await its conclusion.

Sam seemed excited, empowered by the evidence suggesting the powers she was sure were at work had announced themselves, begging us to follow suit. I'd called her and told her to meet me at the church where unsurprisingly a crowd had formed. I'd realized when I got there that since Scotland Yard was no longer on the scene, it was my responsibility to decide what to do with dog's remains.

"Look at the faces," said Sam.

"Fear and wonder? What do you see?"

"Familiarity? As if they owned the event. Pride, maybe, that this wouldn't happen anywhere but here."

Such a response hadn't occurred to me, but I imagined she wasn't far off the mark. A number of people had brought their cameras and I noticed Clair jotting down some notes. Perhaps, he finally had the opening he needed for his article.

It was an upsetting sight, no matter how one might imagine the dog's slaughter occurred or what it meant. I ordered several officers to cut the poor creature down and bring the remains to the station. I figured it was worth giving forensics the opportunity to discover if there were any clues that might be pertinent to the investigation, though I doubted we were going to find anything useful. Sam seemed especially interested in the individuals in the crowd, as if she assumed the perpetrator always returns to the scene of his crime. She conferred with Clair, suggesting, I suspect, he write the names of those she knew in the crowd. Like me, Sam had spent her life in Stratford and probably knew more of its residents than I.

Sam, Clair, and I stayed around Trinity until the crowd dispersed, all but a few hard-core lovers of either horror or medieval history. None of the stragglers seemed familiar to either me or Sam, so we decided to have tea at the nearby Avonbank Gardens.

"I suppose we can take this as a sign to move forward, don't you think, Alec?" Sam asked.

"I trust we can make something happen within the week, since I'm going to need to head back to London soon," said Clair.

"I don't think we can wait much longer, either," I said. "To be honest, though, if nothing comes of this next... seance, shall we call it? What should we call it?

"Call it whatever we choose, it will take a few days to prepare. I'll need to do some research as to the best time of day, day of week, that sort of thing. Shall we tentatively plan for Sunday? One can usually depend on greater spiritual accessibility on the Lord's Day."

Clair put his notebook back into his pocket and got up from his chair.

"I'm heading back to the hotel to start putting together my article. As of this morning I think I've got plenty to get the damn thing started. Are you coming back with me, Sam?" Clair suggested.

She quickly looked my way to see if I'd taken any notice of Clair's tone.

"No, I'm going to confer some more with Alec about what needs to happen over the next few days. Right, Alec?"

"Right."

"Right. Then I'll see you back there for dinner." He briskly walked away.

That Monday turned out to be a stunning day, the rough weather having moved to the west with clear, dry air behind it. The bright sun reflected the deep blue of the River Avon as a steady breeze blew the trees branches. It felt as though it might be the peace after the storm, though I knew our real storm would not arrive until we reached out to the spirits that might be willing to listen.

"We'll return again to the spot where Charles was taken. The environment must be similar to the one Charles experienced the night he saw the woman, before his sister's death."

"That makes sense."

"We'll need a dog."

"A dog?" I asked.

"Yes. As close to the one pictured in Bloom's book as we can find."

"Let me think."

"We should be able to leash him to a tree for the effect we need, but I'm still working on that part."

"Ok," I answered.

"I'm going to portray Ann, the Ann that Charles met at the pub. The one whose grandmother – like Charles – suffered the same fate as Charles, the merciless sting of the sticking hayfork."

"I'm beginning to see where you're taking this. You even shared some of the attraction she felt towards Charles."

"I did. Ann is the key to all of it, the one thing Charles desired more than anything, and I think he'll be looking for her when he becomes aware of the moon and the dog."

"You're brilliant, Sam. I think this can really work."

"I seem to have been able to make you believe."

"You have. In more ways than one."

Neither of us said anything for a long time. We were both entranced by the beauty of the river and the ageless splendor of the ancient town in its background, begging to again play host to the works of its most famous forefather at the Memorial Theatre just down the shore, when the world came to its senses. Having landed on the river with a flourish, several ducks and a flock of geese caught our attention, bringing to each a smile we shared with each other.

Chapter Thirty-Four

Town Hall, Stratford
Friday Evening
March 9, 1945

Ever since Roberto's Christmas revelry with Edie and Eddie – and Harry's hilarious tirade about Santa's claws – Roberto had taken a keen interest in Bing Crosby. It appears he'd understood enough to gather that Bing's popularity, especially when he'd heard that the singer was in a hit movie that year, was worth investigating. Someone had said he played a priest, and despite Harry's claim that Bing was the devil, he'd loved *White Christmas* when he'd heard it on the wireless at Christmas. His family was full of priests, including his father and great-uncle. So, he wanted to make sure he understood this American variety that he'd come to understand through Harry was likely evil incarnate.

Besides, the only entertainment he'd found affordable while serving his time in Stratford was the movies – mostly American – presented by town authorities for a thruppence every Friday night at Town Hall on Sheep Street. American movies were everywhere during the second half of the war, believed to be the best antidote to Naziism and pessimism. With all the tragic events of the past month, Roberto believed he needed a spiritual lift. So, when he read that Bing's recent film hit *Going My Way* was on that week's bill, Roberto made plans to be there. He wasn't sure it would be appropriate to ask either Edie or Eddie to enjoy a comedy so soon after Charles' death, but when he mentioned his plans to Clair, who was spending more time alone than usual, the reporter suggested he'd like to go with him.

In order to better understand how America's greatest movie star of 1944 could also be the devil's advocate, Roberto decided to go to the library and, though he still had great difficulty understanding English, he imagined he could learn a few things about the man and the movie. In Italy, so inundated with priests, Roberto was already certain through experience that more than a few were taking orders from Satan, not Jesus Christ.

He found it curious that Crosby's priest was named Charles and that the supporting character Fortunio Bonanova – an opera singer – would be played by Tomaso Bozanni, the Italian actor, so he expected he'd feel right at home. He was more than ready to hear some music, both operatic and popular. Having spent nearly two years in a prison camp, it had been ages since he'd heard music in a dance hall. Feeling slightly guilty about the prospect of being entertained, he counted the hours until Friday and couldn't help mentioning to everyone he saw that Friday night was going to be special.

When the weekend arrived the night was quite cold and wet, making his walk from camp to town that much more difficult. Waiting out front, Clair signaled for Roberto to join him before they claimed good seats close to the screen. Even to someone living quite far away in Quinton, he recognized a number of familiar faces, including that of Thomas Burns, though he wasn't quite sure how or why he knew him. Perhaps, he thought, during those crazy few days when Scotland Yard was interviewing him at the station. Oddly enough, Burns seemed to recognize him, as well, and found himself sitting directly behind Roberto, who wished his English was better so he could ask Clair about him. Burns nodded his head in recognition just as the lights to the hall were dimming and the film was commencing.

The evening began with the usual newsreels, flashes from the front giving them glimpses of the Allied Forces inching towards Berlin. Roberto's jacket had gotten completely soaked during his walk from camp, so he stood and wrapped it around his chair, spreading the sleeves and pockets behind him so they'd dry.

"*Mi scusi, mi scusi,*" he said to Burns right behind him, not wanting to block his view or disrupt his enjoyment of the pictures from the war. He especially appreciated the photos of the Russian forces moving from the east in their race to be the first to behead the Nazi war machine. He remembered Harry's craving for Russian Socialism, thinking his return to the library might include learning more on that subject, too.

As for Bing, Roberto was having trouble picturing this gentle, sonorous crooner as anything but a kind lover of music – especially when he's joined by the wayward youngsters in the choir. He kept looking for some clue as to the true nature of the new pastor, but even when they get to Christmas Eve and Bing reunites the older pastor with his long, lost mother, Roberto could find no indication that the young priest was anything but a good angel who saves the day.

With or without the knowledge of Bing's possibly wicked identity, Roberto embraced the music, especially Crosby's rendition of *Ava Maria* and the selection from *Carmen.* Being Italian, of course, meant Roberto had been born with a love of opera, and this opportunity to hear even one operatic tune gave him the sense of being home again, bringing tears to his eyes and hope to his heart.

When the lights came up he felt like a new human being, reminded that the war was surely coming to a close thanks to both the Americans and the Russians. He could imagine being back in his small coastal village of Follonica embracing his mother and sister who were waiting anxiously for his return. He also knew he would miss his new friends in Stratford. As they were leaving Town Hall, he was trying to find the words to tell Clair how glad he was to discover that Bing Crosby was not really the devil, which tickled Clair no end. As they ambled down Sheep Street, Thomas Burns passed them, smiling in their direction. Clair knew him because I'd told him about his relationship to Potter.

When Clair suggested they get a drink at the pub on the corner, Roberto showed no objections and was grateful when the reporter volunteered to take him home afterwards. Their time at the pub and during the drive to camp would give Clair the opportunity to discuss the upcoming "event," for which both he and Roberto would surely play a role. Clair had decided to base his article on Sam's determined efforts to reach out to Charles, believing, as did Roberto, that Sam's powers would not only awaken the world to the legitimate uses of clairvoyance, it would also allow Roberto the pleasure of his adored Charles once again.

Chapter Thirty-Five

Stratford-upon-Avon
Saturday Afternoon
March 10, 1945

Having discovered that I'd missed playing host in my flat, I asked everyone to convene there on Saturday. Sam and I had spent the past forty-eight hours going over every detail we thought we could control of the "channeling." We certainly couldn't call it a reading, though I suppose that's what it was, but channeling seemed much more specific, better describing our intentions.

Rather than making our evening an austere meeting of some kind, we agreed to have some food and drink available for everyone. While I had little experience with mediums (none), practical sense told me that the better we all knew each other – and the more we talked about what Charles meant to us – the easier it would be to find a connection to our friend. Of course, I'd never met the man, but over the past several weeks I'd come to feel as if I knew him intimately.

I was happy to see that Edie's humours had improved. While she probably wasn't the jolly soul I'm sure she'd been while Charles was alive, she seemed to be inching toward an acceptance of his death. She would soon have a new husband, the war would be over, and all the angst she'd built up during the course of the investigation would be in her past. We were all looking forward to that moment and it wasn't going to happen until we knew exactly how and why her uncle was murdered.

Over the past few weeks we'd become quite a social circle, providing for each of us a needed connection to the wider world. Edie and Eddie were dominating the sofa while Roberto claimed the one comfortable armchair I had. Sam had no intention of settling in one place, convinced as she was of her role as supervisor, a position I was more than happy to accede to her. Clair sat atop a stool, his notepad in hand and I sat on the lower steps leading to the upstairs bedrooms.

"Have we finally decided on a date for the channeling?" asked Edie. "I got a call from the Arts Council earlier this week about coming back to work."

"That's what Alec and I have been discussing," answered Sam. "We agreed a Sunday would best fit the bill and it looks as though next Sunday's weather might cooperate. I've been channeling some of my sources at the National Weather Service."

"We want to duplicate as best we can the evening Charles saw the ghostly phantoms," I added. "Edie, have you told Sam all you learned from Charles about that night?"

"Yes, I think so. Right, Eddie? We've both gone over it with her several times."

"Listen, everyone needs to dig into the chips and sandwiches. There's also a chicken pot pie warming up. No deviled eggs, I'm afraid." Sam shot me a smile and even Roberto seemed to get it.

"One thing, Edie. I may need some more help with the specific looks of Ann Turner, the younger, Charles' paramour.

Were you able to get from Charles a sense of what she looked or sounded like?"

Poor Edie, who lacked self-confidence and tended to blame herself for most all mishaps, apologized to Sam for not being able to provide a truer picture of the girl. After all, their relationship and Charles' alcoholic binge that led to the sighting all occurred long before Edie was born. Neither she nor Eddie were properly equipped to convey her essence, though Sam was still trying to find a material possession of Charles' that could lead to a better understanding of his love for the girl many years ago.

"If only we could find that one object of Charles' that might be invested with his strongest feelings." Everyone looked to Sam as if she'd suggested they could all go to the moon.

"What are the rest of us going to do while you try to reach Charles," asked Clair.

"One of you will need to hold the dog."

"I'm still working on that one," I said.

"And we'll need someone else to portray the headless woman."

"Is good pie!" exclaimed Roberto, who'd put a bit on a plate and settled at the kitchen table to eat it.

"Excellent, Roberto!" I congratulated him on both his English and his pie eating.

"I think I know someone who might be able to help us with the headless woman," said Eddie. "She works at the Shakespeare Memorial in the props and costume department."

"Excellent, Eddie!" Sam declared.

"Goodness. All this excellence in one room!" I declared, and everyone laughed.

One thing we'd discovered during our previous get-togethers with the six of us was a better way to involve Roberto, whose English was still a major barrier to even a general understanding of what we were up to. Hence, it had been determined that a game of cards made it easier for us to include the Italian in our partying. By 5 pm, while Sam and I remained fixed on organizing our channeling, the other four rejoined their poker and blackjack, since Roberto had seemed happiest while playing those games. Sam and I thought this was a great way to proceed, as, frankly, she and I could get more done, just the two of us, and we both enjoyed hearing them all have great fun.

"Have we decided," I said to Sam, "what actions we can take if we feel like we're losing Charles once we've found him?"

"I thought about that. If we begin with just the moon at that particular spot, the same spot he knew, and he still isn't responding, I thought we could then introduce the dog. And then, if he still doesn't appear, we bring in the headless woman. Depending on what happens next, I can move the narrative along, so to speak, by going to the headless woman and asking her about the sister. Everything should work as if it was a scripted panto or something."

"Brilliant!" I congratulated Sam with a smile.

"Blackjack!" barked Eddie, pleased that he'd won three hands in a row. Roberto didn't mind losing. He was enjoying every minute.

"Let's try something new. Why don't we raise the stakes and add some betting," Eddie suggested.

"Oh, Eddie, I don't know..." Edie sheepishly objected. "Roberto hasn't got a lot of money. Neither do I."

"We could just bet pennies, with a thruppence maximum. Make it more exciting, no? What do you say, Roberto? Put bets on each hand?" Eddie explained by raising his hand. "Betting... gambling, si?" Roberto gazed at Eddie, still unsure of his intent. At which point Eddie pulled the insides of pockets out to indicate what they all needed.

"Ah, si, si, gioco d'azzardo! Ok, ok."

Eddie led the way by taking loose change out of his pocket.

"I haven't got anything, Eddie," said Edie.

"That's alright, love, I can lend you some."

Roberto then left the table to go to his overcoat, scoop out everything in his right pocket, return to the table, and drop it all in front of him. As he separated the various coins that landed on the table, Edie looked down and, unable to control a sudden impulse, stood so quickly that the table nearly collapsed.

"Whoa, Edie, control yourself, love!" Eddie blurted with a chuckle.

No sooner had she stood that everyone – seeing a face that turned instantly ashen – fell deathly silent. This was followed by Edie's huge intake of breath.

"Edie, what is it?" asked Eddie. She remained speechless before pointing at an old gold watch on the table. She took it gently into her hands and began crying helplessly.

"Oh, my dear," exclaimed Sam. "What happened?"

I immediately came over and put my arms around her. She was gripping that watch as if it was the crown jewels.

"That's your uncle's watch, isn't it?" She looked up at me, tears streaming down her face, and nodded. "Who had this, Edie?"

She simply looked down at Roberto and began crying even harder. By now we were all standing, except for Roberto, who was calmly seated looking quizzically at all of us, with no idea what he'd done wrong. How was this possible? It made no sense.

"Roberto," I asked, my stomach turning, "where did you get this watch?"

I recognized the light gold latch that perfectly matched the fob we had in our evidence bag. For as long as I'd known Roberto he'd been in a fog of misunderstanding, as I would have been had I been sitting around his kitchen table in Italy. So his response to the watch seemed similar to many other questions we had for him. But at that instant I had to admit we'd come across the strongest piece of evidence since the start of the investigation. I immediately began reconsidering the circumstances surrounding the first allegations about someone from the POW camp and the blood found on Roberto's shirt. Yes, squirrel's blood for sure, but could there have been other blood there, too? And those constant calls from Potter about the POW bothering Charles and his wife. I had to admit we had to take a whole new look at Roberto's standing in the case, which was terribly difficult, considering I'd become as fond of him as the other four had. I put my hand on his shoulder.

"Listen, Roberto... listening, but not hearing. Do you know who this watch belonged to?" I took the watch from Edie and showed it to Roberto. "Watch for time... gold watch... is this your watch, Roberto?" He looked up into my eyes, moistened now, and began to shake his head.

"Questo non è il mio orologio, Alec... Sam... I no understand. I no see watch, questo non è il mio orologio. Non, non."

Edie, I'm afraid, jumped to conclusions and left the table to get her jacket.

"Eddie, take me home... now!"

"Oh, dear," proclaimed Sam, distressed that all unity on her project had been lost. "Alec, what do we do?"

"Give me the watch, Inspector!"

"Edie, I understand, but I also think there might be an explanation."

"It is clear to me. Give me the watch."

"He might be right, love," said Eddie.

"Now!"

I felt as if I had few options. I knew Edie was in no mood to be pursuaded that she wasn't sharing a room with the man who killed her uncle and my only hope to change her mind would be to talk with her after she'd cooled down. I gave her the watch and she raced to the front door.

"Alec, I don't know what to do. Maybe she's right?" said Eddie.

"Go. Try to get her to calm down and I'll come see her later tonight."

"No, I don't want to see any of you ever again!"

We all heard the slam of the door, marking the end of a noble effort to find the true killer. Without Edie's cooperation there was no path forward. Sam knew it, as did Clair and I.

There sat Roberto, still at a complete loss as to why they'd all stopped playing cards and he'd been accused of something... he didn't know what.

I had no choice, and I think everyone knew it. How was I to ignore that Charles' missing watch, which might reveal some valuable fingerprints, had been found in the possession of one of our first suspects, a man we all knew was acquainted with the victim? Endeared as he may have become to all of us, I had no option but to hold him under arrest for the murder. I knew there'd be few objections. An immigrant and former Nazi, no less. I was certain the courts would like nothing more than to convict this gentle Italian awaiting his return to family after the war, just like thousands of others on all sides. I couldn't be the arbitrator, only the arresting officer. It's what I was paid for, even if I was convinced of the man's innocense.

"Roberto, my friend, I'm afraid you're going to have to come with me."

He looked at me as if I'd betrayed him, all the good times we'd shared, all the trust that I'd shown him as I sought new ways to solve the case. I knew at that moment all his dreams of returning to his village were evaporating and it broke my heart.

"Wait!" said Sam.

"No, no I can't wait, Sam. That's the sad truth, whether I like it or not."

"No, no, I understand that. But listen. The watch. That is the object, the one I've been looking for. You told me it was the one object that Edie insisted Charles loved the most. If I can get that watch, I think it will mean we can finally channel Charles. You must help me get that watch from Edie!"

Chapter Thirty-Six

Stratford-upon-Avon
Sunday Morning
March 11, 1945

What began as an almost joyful campaign on Saturday night to finally reveal Charles' murderer had on Sunday become a mournful collection of disparate friends looking to turn around a series of events that had landed Roberto behind bars. It had also been somewhat of an elated admission by Sam and me that we were sleeping together. This new information had, of course, not sat well with Clair, but it appears he came to some kind of acceptance without even speaking to either of us. He was more concerned about getting a news story that would jump-start his reporting career.

Sam and I sat at the kitchen table in robes wondering what our next move could possibly be. Roberto had said practically nothing to me as I drove him to the station. He appeared to be a sad, homeless puppy, unable to explain the appearance of the watch in his overcoat, swearing, as he must have been doing in Italian, that he never knew the watch existed. I'd tried to be encouraging, while simultaneously pushing him to get the truth.

"Roberto, did Charles give you the watch before he died?" I had no real way of knowing if he understood me, and it was too late at night to find a translator. I had no alternative but to leave him in the cell through the weekend. I instructed the overseeing officers to please treat him properly and make sure he got some decent food. They obliged and I headed home.

Sam, who had barely slept on either of the last previous nights, remained determined to come up with some plan so we could proceed with the channeling on the following Sunday. Our chances of reaching Charles were dwindling with each day. I think we both knew this would be our last chance to resolve the matter, but we spent most of that Sunday in bed or reading. With no clear strategy, there was little we could accomplish on a rainy Sunday in our ancient little town. Once Monday morning arrived, we had few excuses to avoid the decisions that needed to be made.

***

When I walked into Scotland Yard's former case room, almost nothing seemed to have changed, except for the presence of Fabian and Webb. I did miss them, damn it, especially on a morning when it appeared we might be forced to indict someone I believed was completely innocent. I could still detect the odor of Robert's pipe tobacco. Gertie came into the room with several notes on her clipboard.

"What have we got?"

"A call from Weston at the Oil Bureau, another from Edgar Goode, and a brief visit from Mr. Clyde Haven about some additional security for their upcoming conference on war veterans."

"Thank you, Gertie. Not so bad, all things considered."

"Right ye are, boss" she casually uttered on her way back to her desk.

"Oh, Gertie," I called, remembering. "Any trouble downstairs with our Italian war veteran in the bridal suite?"

"Is that what he is? No, nothing I've 'eard about, at least."

"Alright, thanks." How I wished these were our only concerns on the first day of the week, but they, of course, palled in importance when it came to the difficulties we faced in the Walton case. I would have sacrificed many things to have been able to head home at 5 pm with nothing on my plate but the usual thefts and criminal misdeeds we normally encountered in Warwickshire.

I had supposed that once Scotland Yard was out of the picture, it wouldn't be long before I got a visit from Warwickshire's Prosecuting Council, Edmond Longley, especially when he got wind of a suspect behind bars. It wasn't. Solicitor Longley would have favored the prospect of prosecuting a "celebrity" murder case with me in control and not our famous Fabian of the Yard. Longley wanted to be in the driver's seat and would probably regard me – if history was any lesson – as simply a liaison or high-level clerk.

"Good morning, Edmond," I greeted him, just as I was about to make a call to Eddie to inquire about Edie's condition.

"Well, well, well, Superintendent, strangers no more."

"It has been at least a fortnight."

"Longer than my second marriage," Longley chortled, as he winked at me and took the seat facing my desk. I couldn't abide winkers.

"What's this about the Italian POW? I thought you'd eliminated him as a suspect."

"We had. Until this past weekend when it was discovered he had the victim's watch, which had been the only item on the deceased to be missing."

"And how – if I might ask – were you able to find this item?"

I was in no mood to begin explaining to this man, who had no discernable imagination, our story of mediums, magical reverberations found in personal items, and our plan to stage a happening dedicated to conversations with the dead. So I lied.

"It was extracted by another prisoner who brought it to our attention."

"I see. Is this the reason Robert Fabian returned to London? Had he considered his job complete?" Good lord. Two lies on a morning before I'd even finished my first coffee.

"Yes, partly. He also had other commitments in town that required his attention."

"Well, I'm pleased. I feared this matter might take us through the summer, just as we'd all hoped the war would be over and our international visitors would once again be walking our streets and visiting our shops and stages. Good work, Superintendent. I'm sure our town fathers will be taking note of your accomplishment and responding in kind."

Such rewards were the farthest things from my mind and the ease with which everyone was assuming our investigation had come to a close really scared me. What are we all going to do when or if we discover the identity of the real killer?

"I just wanted to drop in to check on progress. I had no idea I'd be getting such good news. Of course, the prosecution and trial will most likely take us well into the fall, but at least this summer we won't be facing tourist hysteria."

I hoped Edmond had been given enough information to keep him at bay for another fortnight. His involvement would have put our plans in serious jeopardy, if they weren't already. Seemingly satisfied, the prosecutor collected his things and headed to his office, though I feared with Fabian no longer on the scene, he would be tempted to become more "hands on." Time would tell.

"Eddie, I'm glad I got you. What's the state of Edie at the moment?" Though he didn't say she had calmed down and would be fine with our plans for Sunday, I did sense several signs of hope. She hadn't fallen back into her nearly suicidal temperament and Eddie believed that once she could be convinced of Roberto's innocence, she would understand the greater importance of our channeling to prove that innocence. This was exactly what I'd hoped for, and I told him I'd drop by that evening with Sam. Perhaps, all was not lost.

My next chore was to check up on Roberto, not that I expected him to be on suicide watch or anything like that. I wasn't quite sure, though, how I was going to put his fears to rest, as I was afraid there might be little I could do. Thankfully, he looked as though he'd had a good night. He told me in his halting English that he'd had his dinner and gotten a good night's sleep. I asked as best as I could if there was anything he needed and he shook his head. I had to explain that I wasn't going to be able to let him out of jail, that, in fact, he may be indicted for Charles' murder and never see the outside of a prison cell. That explanation would be impossible without a translator, so I simply tried to put him at ease.

"I worry about you, my friend. I don't think you deserve what's happened to you, but I'm also at a loss because you seem unable to tell me how you got the watch." I doubted he understood anything I was saying, because his look indicated he may have accepted his guilt. I wanted to shake him, to beg him to try to remember how he got the watch.

"This watch... not il mio orologio. But nobody... nessuno mi ascolta. I love...vi amo tutti."

I understood enough Italian to know that he was telling me how much he loved me... or us. I tried to convey with my hands how much we all loved him, but wouldn't this fact make his incarceration that much harder to endure? I came away from our little meeting feeling even more powerless to stop what was feeling like a runaway train.

Chapter Thirty-Seven

Stratford-upon-Avon
Thursday Night
March 15, 1945

There we were, celebrating again, according to the orders of our resident medium Sam Zawalich. Why, you might ask? After all had seemed to be lost only days before? Apparently the first full moon, this Ides of March – the lunar origin of the Roman calendar – was not a date to be ignored by a scholar of early Christianity. Originally formalized by Claudius in 54 A.D., it was favored by Jupiter as another opportunity to slaughter sheep, one of the more important events that precluded the civil war leading to the rule of Augustus, so central to the formation of Christianity. It was simply a day of importance we needed to recognize, according to Sam, at least.

Sam's explanation of Roman history was meant to justify our gathering at The Dirty Duck, which had become my pub of choice since sending Fabian there on his last night in Stratford. More importantly, we were only three days away from our intended showdown with the spirit of Charles and I think Sam understood how she could use the Roman celebration to prepare us, considering Edie had not yet fully accepted what needed to be done. Perfect for our purposes, the Duck, as I'd discovered of late, was one of the few pubs in town that allowed some privacy at a large table away from the usual clientele.

"We're all here," I announced. "Well, not all."

"Thank you, everyone for coming," seconded Sam. "I know things have seemed as though they might all fall apart since our last meeting, but let me assure you we are still on schedule."

"What's all this about the Ides of March?" asked Clair, wanting to have a greater part in our organization since Sam and I connected.

"I thought you'd ask. You all know by now that I studied Christianity for a long time in Ireland. A lot of it stuck, and as it became clear that we could contact Charles, I noted how close we were to this important date in mid-March. With the accompanying full moon and our better ability to read the wishes of the gods, I felt it was important to take full advantage of this reckoning, in hopes that they would be more vulnerable and able to hear our pleas."

"But I still don't understand about Roberto. How could he have Charles' watch? How can we let him be a part of this?" Edie pleaded. I needed to support Sam.

"Edie," I said, "do you think Roberto killed Charles? Do you think it's possible, because I don't." Everyone else was nodding their heads.

"I know, I know. I couldn't believe it myself. But there was the watch. And how does one challenge what the eyes can see?"

"I asked the same thing, Edie," I pleaded, "but isn't that exactly what Sam is asking us to do? To put aside what only the eyes can see and to trust what we all feel? I, for one, believe Roberto, the sweet soul we've all come to know, is not capable of lying or committing the kind of crime we've witnessed. My eyes tell me that, too."

"I understand what Sam and Alec are saying, Edie. Sometimes we have to trust our intuition, even when the evidence seems to contradict us. 'Outer beauty is what the eyes can see, inner beauty can only be seen through the heart,'" Eddie concluded.

"I want to believe you and Sam, and Alec, and Roberto, but he doesn't, or can't tell us, how he got it."

"It's the language problem," I added.

"It's a problem of the spirit," said Sam. "After knowing Roberto, seeing the way he joined us, what he knows about Charles, his desire to be with Charles again, I don't think any of this will work, really, unless Roberto is a part of it."

"Edie, think about how much Charles loved Roberto," Eddie chimed in, "how they behaved on Christmas, as if they were two long-separated brothers, laughing and hugging. My eyes tell me that story, too."

Everyone at the table fell quiet, knowing that if we couldn't all agree now and forever that our mission was clear and necessary, all of us would regret it for all time going forward.

"All right," said Edie.

We all let out a communal intake of breath, as we settled into our stouts and Scottish ales. Nothing hard core in the alcohol department. We were going to need clear heads to fully comprehend the plans Sam had for each of us. She then began to lay out on our huge table – with the use of maps, lists, and bits of dialogue we were all going to have to learn before

Sunday – her plans for the channeling, as if we were headed for a battlefield.

Chapter Thirty-Eight

Upper Quinton
Sunday Night
March 18, 1945

There were all kinds of reasons I thought Sam's choice of Sunday night was perfect for our channeling, above and beyond the more esoteric reasons only Sam could understand. It was highly unlikely there'd be any activity other than ours on this little sliver of road in Upper Quinton on a late Sunday night. Enough time had passed since the murder that it was also doubtful anyone was still focused on the crime. The fact of it being a Sunday had also made it much easier for me to release Roberto from jail without being noticed. And should any other criminal activity occur during our gathering, there would only be one other officer on duty, and he'd be under my supervision.

From my perspective, sitting just off the road in a small ravine about sixty meters from the crime scene, Sam's research into the likely weather had proven invaluable. With a little more than an hour before we were supposed to begin, I could see darker clouds forming over the western horizon heading directly for the glorious full moon. While the time of year didn't exactly match that of the night Charles saw his visions, the weather looked as though it was going to provide a stage set that captured the essence and spirit of that night long ago.

Thank goodness Sam and I had gotten a lot of rest after Friday night. I discovered she was shifting into an action mode, which included an almost Zen-like concentration on her mission. The place I was located had become off-stage central, where we'd collected our "props," all the items and costumes we'd be needing to make the experience as real to ourselves as we could. Afterall, the point was not to entertain an audience or prove to them a scene was real; we needed to convince our unconscious minds that years had slipped away and the actions of that evening in 1885 were as real on this night as they were then.

The temperature had gone down quite a bit since we'd landed at our current positions and the mist that Edie and Eddie said Charles had mentioned several times was now beginning to pervade the atmosphere. Two areas would be the focus of our action. As before, we'd try to stay as close to the exact spot on which Charles was slain. This would be where Sam (as Ann) would make her plea to Charles, after coming down the road to join Roberto, who would commandeer that position from the beginning. Sam had determined that since Roberto had told us – as best he could – about his extended conversation with Charles during which neither of them said a word, he should be the one to attract the energy, to be the focus of the spirit's communications.

Our second – or upstage – area would be on a rise in the field with a tree about twenty meters north of Roberto. This was where we'd planned to tie the dog, from whom, we were promised, we were likely to hear – if the moon was full – a series of blood-curdling howls. The animal I'd found from a farmer I knew in Stratford would be one of our featured players. He was with me, leashed and muted.

The decision of how to portray the headless woman was easy, once we'd gotten Edie to understand the importance of proving Roberto's innocence. Eddie had sought help from his friend the production designer at Shakespeare Memorial, and I couldn't wait to see how effective her costume work was going to prove.

Determining how best to use Clair and Eddie was more difficult. Eddie was a big man and Sam wasn't quite sure where he would be most effective. Clair, with a diminutive body type – slight and small-boned – proved perfect for the job. So, it was decided he would represent Charles, the boy at age 14 who saw the headless woman. This would leave Eddie, like me, to be an observer or more precisely another stage manager to make sure all the production elements came together as planned.

We weren't exactly clear about the time the original incident took place, but Sam estimated – with the help of her study of the Roman calendar and the moon's placement that evening – Charles saw the visions soon after midnight, so we aimed for that beginning. That left us about an hour to make sure everything was in place.

I thought it quite miraculous that the ambiance seemed so perfect for our intentions. One could sense the ethereal overwhelming the mundane. I'm not a believer or religious type in any form, but I was beginning to feel a kind of openness to all around me, as if every atom in my body was absorbing something eternal. A communal consciousness, perhaps, allowing a different set of natural laws into our systems, the kind that Harry told me about in his garden. Were we not appealing to a sort of natural law that human civilization abandoned long ago?

I wanted to check on Sam, but her instructions had been to take this time to ourselves until we met during the channeling. This would give each of us the opportunity to concentrate on Charles' meaning, on his supremacy in this moment, so that if his spirit happened our way he would know everyone was there for him.

Thus instructed, I sat quietly with my black canine friend, who was to stay with me until just before the ritual began. About five meters from me sat Roberto, happy to be out of a jail cell and sitting quietly, using his time as Sam intended, to conjure his dead friend. Edie and Clair were close to the tree up on the ridge, but not yet visible in their set positions. I wasn't quite sure where Eddie was, though I assumed he was near to where Clair and Edie were meditating, awaiting the cue to take their places. Sam, I knew, was somewhere near, hovering, because I could feel her.

How extraordinary it was, I thought, to be on the cusp of another world, waiting to connect to another time by clinging to – and embracing – a particular incident and place. I remembered reading how our concept of time was beginning to change, that we needed to accept it as more fluid than we had previously. These studies I'd read in a popular psychology magazine seemed to confirm Sam's vision of time. She believed that once a moment – an event or action – occurs, it doesn't disappear forever. If we were to employ the full potential of our minds (a difficult task, considering we only use about 5% of its capacity), we could find ways back into those moments. All it took was a shared communal objective and the courage of a group to embrace possibility.

I checked my watch to see how close we were to starting. Charles' watch – as well as his hayfork and the spoon he ate with – were all in Sam's possession, as she continued to claim their vibrations would ultimately make the difference in our ability to contact Charles. By then I totally trusted Sam's instincts and entirely believed we were about to witness that eerie night back in 1885 when Charles first became aware of his clairvoyant powers, determining the way he was to live the remainder of his life.

I remained mesmerized, soaking up the quiet of the evening and staring at the magnificent glow of our lunar lamp. So much did this atmosphere capture my mind and body that I nearly fell into a deep sleep, only to be awakened by Eddie, who'd come to take the dog.

"Don't leave us, Alec," he said. "I think we're about to start."

I nodded my head and checked my watch. He was right. I gave him the leash to the dog. His instructions were to leave the muzzle on until just before the hound took his place and I hoped he would behave in the meantime. Eddie and the dog disappeared, and I waited for the next action, which was to be led by Roberto, whom I could see was fully concentrated and about to move to his beginning marks.

I still had no idea where Sam was located, until I noticed a figure moving along the side of road. At least thirty meters from the crime scene and barely visible, a woman with a shawl dressed in a 19th c. length dark skirt stood holding the slash hook. She was staring at Roberto who had seen her and solemnly moved to his position at the spot where Charles' blood had soaked into the ground. Roberto's figure, dressed in a long Catholic-looking robe, held his hands together before him, clenched as if in prayer. The sound he was making resembled a low "oooom," nothing like anything I'd ever heard in a Christian church. It was a deep and foreboding sound that raised the hair on my neck.

"Chaaaaarlie... Chaaaaarlie..." the hooded woman called, as she slowly walked towards Roberto, who had now gradually begun turning around counterclockwise. I wondered if that little element was important. Apparently, Sam told me, Ann had been the only woman in his life who called him Charlie, not Charles.

Everything seemed to be happening at half-speed, as if all our subjects were deep in water. Just as Ann was about half-way to Roberto's position, the clouds broke apart, allowing the light from the moon to brighten our playing area, as if someone had gotten the cue to turn up a lighting instrument.

Meanwhile, the chanting of Charlie's name continued, sounding more and more like the lyrics of some foreign lament, made even more eerie by the sight of Ann holding the slash hook, raised high as if it were the cross of Jesus in a Christian church.

Once Ann reached Roberto, she joined his circular movement, the two of them now holding high the slash hook.

"Chaaaarlie... Chaaaarlie," Ann continued.

The next movement that caught my eye was Clair's, dressed in a young boy's outfit, moving to a spot not far from the tree. Once he reached his place, he began his chant.

"Aaaaan...Aaaaan," he bellowed. Who knew Clair had such talents? "Aaaaan, I'm here for you. Aaaaan, I'm here for you. Aaaaan... Aaaaan"

I was mesmerized, as the three voices all blended together. They all seemed attuned to each other's rhythms and tones, as if it had been rehearsed, though I don't think they'd ever prepared that fully. And, as if he appeared out of nowhere, the black dog was standing quietly by the tree. Then, right on cue, we heard it's spine-tingling howl.

"Ooooooo... Ooooooo"

At which point Clair's young boy pointed his finger at the dog, repeating his mantra.

"Aaaaan...Aaaaan"

All the sounds seemed to encourage our black dog to continue his bellowing at exactly the right intervals. This mesmerizing potpourri of sounds continued unabated for at least ten minutes until the moment the moon shined most brightly, illuminating a spot about five meters from the boy and the dog. Into that spot stepped the headless woman, the most accurate – and upsetting – of the visions Sam had created. Anyone would have sworn there was no head on her body. I literally lost my breath.

Clair's boy was now instructed to point in the direction of Roberto and Ann, who then stepped away from their circle. Roberto stopped too, continuing to hold the slash hook above them and lowering the volume of his throaty sound, not unlike the one Charles employed with his frogs. I could see Ann holding Charles' spoon and watch, rubbing them, as she began speaking to the spirit.

"Charlie, I reach out to you now, with all my heart, heavy as it is to have lost your touch and smile. Come to me now, join with me now as my cousin, my lover, my everlasting connection to all that is joy, so that I may see again your dark eyes, and feel your lips on mine where the gods intended they should be."

She then looked to Roberto, hoping some response would be forthcoming through this vessel, his friend from far away. This was the moment we all hoped to hear him or even, perhaps, to see him, rejoining our spirits so that we could all be together again. All eyes were on our Italian. But so far none of us detected any change in Roberto's expression or sound. Sam waited, allowing the ambiance to sink in even further. Then she spoke again.

"My dearest Charlie, you must know I only stayed away after discovering we were family because of my fear, not because I stopped loving you. Your connection to our grandma only made me love you more, but that love was so strong I feared if I rejoined you another night I would lose you. I thought about you every night for thousands of nights afterwards and I come to you now to reclaim what is mine, what is ours, our love eternal."

At that moment, a voice that I imagined sounded much like that of Charles, emanated from Roberto, whose face suddenly morphed into that of a glowing saint, as if he was looking into the face of the sublime.

"Ann. Ann. Ann."

I thought to myself this must be him. The voice was nothing like Roberto's, no sounds of Italian, only the sound of what must be Charles. And he seemed to be addressing Ann, right in front of our eyes.

"Ann, all the years I've waited, and you've come."

"I am here, Charlie, yes, as the gods intended, by your side."

"You fill me with such joy."

"As you do for me, my dear Charlie. But you left us. How, Charlie, could this have happened? Tell us how, Charlie." A long pause followed, after which Charles spoke again.

"I trusted him. I'd known him nearly all my life, so when he took my hook, I thought it was just to put it aside."

"Oh, Charlie, my poor Charlie, who, who took your hook, Charlie?" Another pause.

"The man who worked for him, the man who did his deeds."

"Who was that Charlie? Whose deeds?"

The next moment, the one I replay in my mind nearly every day since, happened so quickly, in such a flash that when all had settled it was as if I'd been transported to a new planet. After Charles' last words I saw a flash and looked up towards a small mound to my right where I thought I'd seen the first light. Then a second flash; this time I also heard the blast that came with it. There on the mound stood Potter, and next to him, Thomas Burns. Potter was holding the shotgun, still smoking. I swallowed hard, then looked to Sam, who was crouching over Roberto on the ground, still holding the slash hook. God in heaven, I heard myself say, how could this have happened again? Except now it was the blood of our dear Roberto seeping into the ground of Quinton.

Chapter Thirty-Nine

Stratford-upon-Avon
Tuesday Morning
March 20, 1945

It's not as if I expected when I got to the station on Tuesday morning after our channeling that all would be forgotten – or forgiven. I'd been instructed to take Monday off, but the twenty-four hour reprieve had only allowed the horror to metastasize, claiming all my conscious thoughts.

A man had been killed. I was heartbroken, nearly apoplectic, when the reality of what had occurred sank in. There we were in the dead of night (an expression I now understood viscerally), pitch black once the clouds had overtaken the moon, and no one knew what to do. Roberto, like his blood-brother Charles, had probably died instantly. All of us were thankful for this one detail, as we were all equally hysterical once the murder became clear to us.

Sam was inconsolable. After checking Roberto's vital signs – and finding none – she collapsed, wailing over his body, pounding it, as if the strength of her blows could somehow revive our treasured friend. By then I knew Sam well enough to understand how devastating this incident would remain for the sensitive and caring woman I'd fallen in love with. I felt completely powerless to bring her any solace or effective means of forgiveness for her actions. I was cursing myself for allowing the whole exercise to happen, trying, I suppose, to make sure she knew I shared in the responsibility for Roberto's death. She would have none of it.

As for the others, Edie and Eddie were in shock, having relived a murder they'd spent the past month trying to forget. This time, however, they were eyewitnesses. Impossible to imagine, nearly unbearable to endure. Clair, too, was in a catatonic state, so much so that he'd forgotten his name and the reason he'd found himself so far from his London circle of friends. How would he be able to write anything about such a heinous turn of events? As for Potter and Burns? Gone. Disappeared, as if they'd never been there.

So, when I found Prosecuting Council Edmond Longley sitting at my desk upon my arrival I was hardly surprised. But having gotten practically no sleep since the murder, I feared I would be unable to reasonably navigate its repercussions. My intentions were so far removed from those of the visiting solicitor that I imagined I might commit murder myself, if he so much as rubbed me the wrong way.

"How are you feeling, Alec? I cancelled everything on my schedule when I heard about what happened Sunday night."

"I'm not feeling much of anything at the moment."

I sensed Longley was not going to move out of my chair and wondered if this was a sign of future intentions, so I settled in the chair opposite him. His calmness and lack of any recognizable distress made me squirm.

"I'm sure you must be entirely unsettled. Were you able to get any rest yesterday?"

"No."

I knew he wanted me to continue, but all the events of that evening had been running through my mind since they happened, and I was resisting having to review them again – for anybody.

"I hope you understand I've only spoken to a few of you involved, and I'm going to need your full story to proceed."

"Yes, I suppose you are." Even so, I couldn't seem to get out anything more. I sat there staring out into the room from an angle that made it all seem new to me. The prosecuting solicitor waited, losing patience with each second that passed.

"Alright. Alec, what in God's name were you doing that night? Six of you, were there not? Dressed in ridiculous costumes, apparently making odd sounds, what? Baying at the moon, were you not? What were you trying to do?"

It was as if the words being spoken were in a different language, none of it making any sense or touching me in any way. Who was this person? And how did he know what had happened that night? He wasn't there.

"And what were you thinking, releasing our prisoner – our one prime suspect – taking him to the crime scene dressed in some robe, where he could have escaped. And then you allow him to be shot and killed! It all seems beyond comprehension."

At least that statement made sense to me, but none of what he was saying moved me any closer to some kind of confession, or whatever he was seeking.

"And who were these people you had with you? Some newspaper reporter for *The Mirror*! Just perfect. Exactly what we want, this story all over the London press, connecting our Superintendent to the accidental death of an individual about to stand trial for a murder that's already everybody's favorite topic of conversation. It was our duty to protect this individual who was under our jurisdiction. And if that's not enough, you enlist a medium, some female psycho who was there for what? As if there wasn't already enough talk about this witchcraft murder, another mark against our precious town in this quiet corner of the Empire – at this point in time when we're all celebrating democracy – and sanity!"

He was, of course, making an argument that would make perfect sense to any jury or judge recruited to put all these events into proper prospective, but none of it made sense to me. I had simply been taking the next step in finding Charles' killer. The irony, of course, was that I'd found him.

"I take full responsibility, of course."

"You're damned right you do! You've put me and this office in a very difficult position, to say the least."

"Yes, I suppose I have."

"That's all you've got to say?"

"Potter and Burns. What about them?"

Longley began feeling ill at ease for the first time. I had the sense he'd already spoken with them, already solved the whole case together, perhaps.

"Yes, well, we've talked, of course. They came in first thing yesterday morning, very upset. They explained what happened, how they'd been hunting that evening, heard the... what shall I call it? Heard the commotion coming from the very same spot where Walton was killed. They said they mistook the sounds of the howling dog you had there, saw the movement below the ridge, and fired at what they thought was an armed trespasser, as was their perfect right, may I add, as protectors of their property. If you have anything to add to this version of the story, I'd love to hear it."

I couldn't believe what I was hearing. Already, it seemed, the authorities had come to an understanding with the suspects in this crime. Except I was hearing there was no crime – certainly no murder – only what had been decreed a wreckless manslaughter, something like a hunting accident. I was furious!

"Now you listen to me, Longley," I barked at him, "How can you walk away from this insisting there was no murder? A man who had become my dear friend over the past few weeks..."

"This lowly Nazi prisoner of war, this foreigner and murder suspect – the man who killed Walton – had become a "dear" friend of yours?"

"Roberto was not the murderer!"

"That's not the way it's looking to me."

"Roberto could never have committed such a crime, I swear to you. But I know who did. And your actions are going to set this man free."

"What are you saying, Inspector? Potter? But you had no evidence to charge this man, and you know it. After weeks of coming up with nothing, we finally had the suspect in our jail, we had irrefutable evidence, and you just blithely set him free. And what does he do? He returns to the scene of his crime where a man who understands the danger of the suspect simply takes measures to protect his home and family. It seems pretty clear to me where this is all leading."

I wanted nothing to do with this version of events intended to cover up both murders. Yes, my job meant everything to me, but if my continuing as Superintendent of Warwickshire D.I.C. was dependent on buying into this big lie, I'd sooner find employment with the road department. Once I understood what I was up against, however, I knew I had to try my best to clarify why we were in Upper Quinton the previous night.

"Edmond. Do you believe in God?"

"Yes, of course. I've been a proud member of the Church of England since birth, as well as an active Deacon of the Stratford Parish."

"But do you believe in a transactive maker of Man who oversees your actions, whose presence you can feel and who listens to your pleas?"

"I trust in a God who represents Good over Evil."

"But do you always know who represents Good and Evil, or does the devil often work in circuitous ways, deceiving good men into following evil men?"

"Well, yes, I suppose, but what has this got to do with Walton's death or the death of this POW?"

"Charles was an unusual man because he devoted his life to understanding the ways in which God speaks to us. And God can speak to us, correct?"

"Yes, if we are listening."

"Exactly! If we are listening. And Charles was one of a few men – as was Roberto – who listened. And what he heard he believed came through the animals on our earth, not from other humans."

"Rubbish!"

"Why rubbish? Who are we to deny this kind of transaction? You said yourself that God was transactive."

"Who's selling you this bill of goods? That libidinous medium I understand you're cohabitating with? Come on, Alec."

"No. Look, I'd never met Charles, but I came to understand he'd affected many peoples' lives, all of whom swore he had innate powers to converse with creatures who'd never been able to connect to other men or women. This power also enabled him to converse with the Italian who knew almost no English. Yet they had countless exchanges without the use of verbal language."

"You don't expect me to believe any of this?"

"But believing in such powers is nearly universal amongst those whose ancestors understood their Warwickshire inheritance included a belief in the supernatural. When none of our usual investigative tools seemed to be working, when even the "Fabulous Fabian" couldn't find our suspect, I chose to follow the leads I found in books about those supernatural powers. I was simply performing the duties of a serious detective, was I not?"

"But how can you put any stock in these fairy tales?"

"For the same reasons you can claim to know a transactive Deity."

"How do you expect this office to endorse the actions of an obviously fraudulent clairvoyant responsible for the death of a man we were on the verge of convicting for Walton's murder? Do you understand how big a story this has become? How many people were demanding the case be solved? It had become a scar on our Metropolitan Police. Now they shall all become the laughingstock of the Commonwealth, so inept that they needed to enlist the aid of a seer, a so-called medium able to communicate with the dead."

"Which she did. Through Roberto. Walton spoke through Roberto, I swear!"

"You can't be serious, Spooner. You're telling me that had this prisoner not been killed we would know the identity of Walton's real killer?" Longley asked incredulously.

"I'm telling you he'd already spoken by the time they shot him. He revealed the real killer." Longley became silent, walked a bit around my office, then sat again, trying to control his growing temper.

"Even if I believed you and it was confirmed by the motley group of spooks you assembled that night, who else would believe it? How would we prove this individual was responsible? You're not thinking clearly, Superintendent, and I will not allow you to forever besmirch the reputation of this sterling office of the law."

"This sterling office of the law has no interest in the truth. It's only concern is saving the reputation of those at the top, moving so-called justice along so it doesn't interfere with life as we know it."

I could sense the solicitor's desire to do me physical harm, to see me disappeared from his world and all that I'd come to know as my world, too.

"I suppose, then, that you want me expelled from this position," I ventured. "You're sitting in my chair."

"If only such things were so easy."

He paused again for the longest time. I could sense his mind searching for the best re-entry into our discussion. Because I also knew I had him in a bit of a bind.

"You know, Alec, I've become quite fond of you over the years. You've got a fine mind and frankly I'm wholeheartedly disappointed you've been so easily duped by this woman who has so carelessly turned this office upside down. Isn't this a case of a man following his hardened member, not his logical mind?"

I wanted to plumet his body until it disappeared.

"I did nothing but follow my gut instinct – as strong today as it was before our channeling – so that I could bring the real killer to trial, as I could do now, if you'd only allow me to do my job."

"You can't be suggesting I indict Alfred Potter! On what grounds?"

"On the grounds that we witnessed the identification of the killer by the victim, at which point the killer silenced the voice of the one person who knew the truth. Faced with these facts – and the added testimony of the person who actually committed the acts – the indicted suspect would confess to both murders. I know it."

For a few lingering moments I thought Longley had truly heard me and was open to other solutions. It was a momentary lapse in disappointment. No such window for restorative justice was going to be opened. The question now was simply finding a way for all these actions to be kept undercover. Longley already knew the direction his office would have to take. He'd never seriously believed that anything I had to say would change his mind.

"Frankly, if this had not become such a national – even international – incident, and I was free to find serious remedies, I might accept your resignation and simply close both these cases, explaining that the suspect killed in the second incident had been guilty of Walton's murder. As I believe he was."

"And I know he wasn't."

"There is no doubt that Sunday's incident was simply an accident, an unfortunate ending to the POW's sojourn on the British Isles."

"Sojourn! What do I tell Roberto's...?"

"Let me finish, Alec. I also know that should you be relieved of your office, you would be free to speak to the press, raise all sorts of questions about possible mishandling of the case, and bring misery to the lives of your co-workers. No doubt we would hear all about your friend's mystical powers, her supernatural ability to talk with the dead. Perhaps you'd be foolish enough to continue pointing the finger at Potter."

"That will certainly be the case should you declare Roberto guilty. I will not report to his family, who are waiting for his return after the armistice, that he was guilty of a crime he didn't commit."

There we were, both of us fully aware of the awkward position in which the prosecutor had found himself. I was perfectly ready to be thrown overboard, to be demoted to civilian, should that solution be determined the best. But I would not feed their big lie to the extent that Roberto's fate should include a conviction for murder.

"There will be a trial, won't there?" I asked. "Certainly you intend to prove that Potter was guilty of manslaughter, at least."

The prosecutor was silent. Was he embarrassed? He certainly should have been, though I doubted he was capable of holding such a high regard for the truth. At that moment I doubted there was anyone in the British justice system who had any regard for the truth.

"Alec, listen to me."

"It appears I have little choice in that matter."

"If I indict Potter, everything about this matter will become part of the trial testimony. Your job would most certainly become untenable. How could you expect people to have the same trust in you, knowing you're guided by some ridiculous belief in ghosts and goblins? Can you imagine what the press would make of that situation? I mean, what did you have in mind letting that reporter put together a story about reaching out to the dead to solve a crime?"

"I felt I had no other option. I didn't believe Roberto was guilty and I wasn't going to let the wrong person be convicted. That was my job."

"No, your job was to provide evidence, which you did, and let me take the suspect to trial."

He was right about that. Somehow the missing piece of evidence – Charles' watch – had fallen in our lap, a fact that still bothered me. Out of nowhere. But it was what we'd been looking for. And so it seemed we'd both found ourselves at this standoff.

"I intend to put the matter in the hands of the Alcester Court Leet, to do exactly what that association was created for,"

Longley said, taking a paper from his pocket and reading, "to take cognizance of grosser crimes of assault, arson, burglary, larceny, manslaughter, murder, treason, and every felony at common law."

Into the hands of the very people who committed both these crimes. The perfect kind of paradox that Harry talked about. I was witnessing it firsthand.

"As both you and I know very few members of the press – certainly the international press – take note of their docket, so we can rely on the whole matter being settled with as little notice as possible. You will keep your position, Potter will pay his price according to the verdict of the bailiffs, and..."

"And you will see that Roberto is not charged with Walton's murder, that the case remains cold."

He waited a long time to confirm this final addendum, realizing, I suppose, that such an agreement would take some persuasion. Ultimately, though, Longley understood he had little choice.

But I did have the choice. I could abandon my place of privilege, make my theory known to the town and the rest of the world, for that matter. The guilty parties would likely never be brought to trial, but suspicions of their guilt would follow them to the end of time, and I would be free of my own guilt in covering up a double murder and a suicide that left me even more bereft. If I had been half the man I thought I could be, or that Sam believed me to be, truth might have been the winner. It wasn't.

Chapter Forty

Stratford-upon-Avon
Saturday Morning
March 24, 1945

A week now since the channeling. It had been decided I should continue my suspension until the Court Leet meets, as Longley explained to the rest of the office, to "mediate the misunderstanding." With every new day I felt more and more like a phony. I decided to grow a beard, hoping, I suppose, to reach a point in time when I would no longer recognize the righteous lawman I used to see in the mirror.

And Sam, my Sam. I'd not seen her since the evening of the shooting, and I had no idea where she was. She'd left a number of her items in my bedroom. Every time I came across a new one I sat on my bed, numb, fighting off the tears that had overwhelmed me right after the incident. How, I asked, could I have allowed her to escape without my knowing her state of mind, without having the chance to share our grief.

So, as you can imagine, I spent much of my time gazing out into nothingness, imagining what demons might possibly be possessing the mind of Samantha Zawalich, unable to provide any remedy or human kindness. She had often spoken of her love for Ireland, the ease with which people there understood the unspoken, the spiritual life of their ancestors, the clarity by which both God and the Devil take sides. They possessed their ancestors in ways unknown to the more proper and restrained British. Perhaps, she returned to the comfort of those she knew in her youth. Should that be the case, I worried that I would never set my eyes on her again.

I was also inundated with phone calls, a ceaseless cavalcade of interested parties who insisted I reach out to friends, respond to reporters, go out for a spot of brew, you know. I finally decided I wanted none of it and simply let it ring.

But then I thought. She might be trying to reach me. Probably not, but what if? Why can't someone invent some kind of a voice recorder for telephones, I thought. Funny. Didn't happen until about ten years ago, but I certainly could have used one then. At the time though, it all depended on what mood I found myself when the damn thing rang.

"Hello? Edie. How are you? Yes, I know. I can't believe it all either. Are you both alright? I know, we should."

I knew she and Eddie would want to get together to talk about the terrible events of the past week, but I couldn't bring myself to admitting how things had been resolved. I felt as though I'd deceived them.

"No, she's not here."

What could I say about Sam? I knew how attached they'd become to her, that she'd become the most important member of our coterie.

"No, she's not here, Edie. No, I actually don't know where she is. Yes, I know it's crazy, but..."

Just get off with her, a voice kept saying. How will they ever remain your friends after what you've agreed to?

"Maybe, maybe I'll hear from her soon. I'll let you know, ok Edie? My best to Eddie."

And suddenly she was gone, and I decided not to pick up any more calls.

That morning, though, that Saturday after Roberto left us, I saw a note slipped under my door. Hope. It was handwritten.

"Meet me by The King's Stone at The Rollright Stones, Sunday Communion, 11 am. SZ"

***

Sunday was a warm day, as if late March had morphed into early June. I had thought of nothing else but our meeting since receiving the note, which I'd stared at for what seemed like hours, unable to believe that Sam had not disappeared into thin air, as I'd thought.

I remembered reading about the Rollright Stones, nearby the bottom of Meon Hill, where the Celtic King met his demise and where women came to enhance their fertility. I immediately referred to its mention in *Phantom Dogs*, the book I had taken back from Fabian, along with Bloom's volume, before he returned to London. I read that chapter over and over before setting out on that gorgeous Sunday morning.

What was Sam saying to me by suggesting we converge at this ancient corner of Warwickshire, this sacred space to many women who believed they could live as comfortably in the underworld as in the Celtic graveyard where I was standing? I was early for the meeting, as I'd been unable to find anything to do before coming, my whole body so overwhelmed with expectation.

I sat just below the King's Stone, imagining it was the original Celtic commander standing above me, surveying the land in which he'd rest for eternity. I felt like eternity myself, a part of this lucent landscape so pregnant with meaning, so alluring for its mystery and the rich stories it had birthed over the centuries. As I thought about Rollright and its appeal to Sam, I began to better understand why she had chosen this place. I also came to fear that this would most likely be my last encounter with Sam.

I found myself lying down in the long grass, letting the warm sun seep into my bones. I felt so content after a week of near-suicidal angst that I fell asleep, awaking only when I felt a warm breath on my cheek. She was lying next to me, her head nestled between my shoulder and arm, her hand under my shirt just above my groin, playing with hair around my naval. I took a deep breath, preparing to ask a million questions, but she put two fingers to my lips.

"Let's just lie like this. For eternity, maybe."

And so we did, and had it been for eternity I would have been the happiest man alive. I took deep breaths, inhaling her scent, feeling her beating heart at the spot I believed my heart to be. Indeed, I was the happiest man alive, for at least an hour, after which she began to whisper her deepest thoughts.

"I wonder, my love, had we met when we were young, would we be married with a horde of children at our feet."

Her suggestion gave me such joy, just in the imagining.

"I can only wonder too..."

Her fingers went to my lips again, suggesting I should listen first. I understood, but still had so much to say.

"Perhaps we'd be living on the Irish coast, harvesting peet, just to keep all those fingers and toes warm. But we didn't. We found ourselves now, even so different as we were. As we are."

"But we found we shared so much, and..."

"Perhaps not so much, but we did share a dream and a belief that beyond this temporal realm – and beyond the strictures of formal Christianity – there lives a spirit, a language we can all learn from, if only we take the time to listen. Charles taught me that."

"And then you taught me," I answered. "And you could teach me more. We could find a life together still."

"Oh, Alec, that might have been true. Maybe two weeks ago, but..."

"But Sam, listen. What happened last week. Few people will know about it."

"I will know."

"There will be no trial. And Roberto will never again be accused of Charles' murder. I will be able to continue in my position. Time will heal our catastrophe, I swear."

"I would never be able to walk the streets of Stratford without feeling I should have been punished for causing Roberto's death."

"I am as guilty as anyone, if not more so," I insisted. "It was my responsibility."

"And the murderers would be walking with me through the streets. Or sitting with me in a pub sharing a drink. I would be looking for them at every turn. And they would be looking for me."

"I can't imagine life without you, Sam."

"As you said, my love, time will heal our catastrophe."

My dread returned, the thought of moving beyond my time with Sam, of having to face Eddie and Edie without feeling I'm an enormous disappointment, as both investigator and human being. And with Sam out of the picture I would have no one to return home to, to remind me that I may not be completely lost, at least when I looked into her eyes.

"He told us the murderer. In his voice, through Roberto, just before the shots. You know that, don't you?" I assured her.

"I expected you knew what Charles' words meant, yes. But then everything exploded, all of it. My life became a lie, at least my life here."

I felt weak, as if I was a child holding my mother tightly, trying to stop time.

"Please tell me we can still find a life here, Sam."

"I will always be here with you... a part of me. And you will always be with me."

"These are such fancy words, but what do they mean?"

"I can't tell you what they mean, but I can show you. Here, on this spot where women have been coming for thousands of years, to awaken their inner sanctums, to fill themselves with God's wishes."

She swung her leg around, so she was kneeling above me, taking my face into her hands. She then loosened her top, button by button, and bent down so that I could take her breast into my mouth. My tongue tasted her sweetness, as she maneuvered herself into a position that allowed me to enter her. She moved gently at first, then with such a passion as I'd never witnessed in my lifetime. I felt the ground below me disappear and our bodies melded together, as if any attempt to separate us was impossible. I knew, too, that our final crossing had a purpose that would outlive our worldly desires.

And because this encounter occurred in this field, at the very place where generations of men and women have come to comingle with those of the underworld, its result would be rich with the best of us both.

Sam's Field

Chapter Forty-One

Alcester Court Leet
Monday Morning
May 7, 1945

The last place I'd hoped to be on that May morning, as the entire world waited for word from Berlin about Germany's capitulation, was the 15th c. courtroom of the Alcester Court Leet. There we were on the verge of a global celebration of peace after five years of a war that saw the slaughter of tens of millions in the name of "making the world safe for Democracy." Yet, there was I, at the center of another court hearing being conducted by, perhaps, the most outdated, if not undemocratic, institution in the Free World. If I wasn't in fear of being convicted of aiding and abetting what had finally been designated an involuntary manslaughter, I might have better appreciated the irony in the proceeding.

I'd spent the weekend alone at home, much the way I'd lived all of my days since our catastrophic channeling of Charles Walton. Because of the questions surrounding my involvement in the shooting, I was still on a temporary paid suspension, which meant I'd gotten to know my small apartment better than I'd ever imagined possible. I'd tried to cheer myself – and the cohorts I'd enlisted to follow me and Sam to the edge of consciousness – by remembering that in two weeks Eddie and Edie would be married along the shores of the Avon and peace would be breaking out around the world.

Certainly, my own sad circumstances seemed mundane compared to more compelling events that were defining this mid-century moment, all of which would hopefully help us forget the personal and civil losses of our recent past. Was there as much hope for me as there was for Edie?

I had been led to believe that the Leet's inquiry was just that, not a trial or indictment, and would last most of one day. The morning session had been fairly straight forward. The bailiffs sat in a separate section of the hall and those of us designated witnesses to the "accident" sat in an opposite section. Steward of the Manor, Geoffrey Milner, sat between us on a small, elevated stage, the closest thing the hearing had to a judge or mediator. It all seemed perfectly judicial, the kind of session that often took up the time of the Court. There being so many other more important events occurring that week – including the restoration of democracy in Europe – the press had shown little interest in the Court's schedule. In fact, little of what was decided that day would ever find its way into print or onto any wireless.

A week or so before the inquiry I finally met with Eddie and Edie. Clair had returned to London shortly after the shooting, happy to have finally remembered his name, but disappointed that none of his Stratford experience was likely to find itself in an article with his byline. And, of course, as far as the four of us knew, Sam had disappeared off the face of the earth.

Though I had dreaded the moment I would have to recount Sunday's disastrous outcome with Eddie and Edie, I knew they had to understand the way in which the Metropolitan Police would be handling the case. I had to explain that our testimony needed to be trimmed, that our wish to connect to Charles via the medium was a fact we couldn't share with the Court Leet.

"You mean to say it will be as if we had no intention of finding Charles, as if Sam never came to help us?" she asked when we met over lunch at the Dirty Duck.

"Yes, I'm afraid that's the situation," I replied, humiliated that our search for Charles' real murderer would never be acknowledged. It was an act on my part of complete capitulation, even as I helped Edie recognize that no one was ever going to be held responsible for her uncle's terrible death.

"At least we can give Roberto's family a memory that doesn't include his role as a murderer. We owe them that," I said, hoping to console her.

"So, after everything we've done, no one will ever be convicted for killing Charles? asked Eddie.

"I'm afraid not."

"But we all know the killers, right? When you told us what Charles' words meant that night, you said you knew who they were."

"But we'd never be able to prove it, Eddie. Not after Roberto's killing."

Edie became silent, then looked at both of us, pleading with her eyes for her ordeal to simply come to a close.

"We'll say whatever you need us to say. Right, Eddie?"

"Of course, love."

As he had in the morning, Milner would be conducting the afternoon session of the court. Having heard from Potter and Burns, as well as Edie, Eddie, and myself, in the morning, the

Steward of the Manor decided he and the leading bailiffs would take their lunch hour to finalize the court's summation of the accident. Then, after asking a few final questions of those involved, he would announce the summation in the afternoon. Milner and the other bailiffs would make no mention of the existence of either Clair or Sam.

The portly steward looked as though he'd enjoyed his lunch, jesting with a few of the bailiffs as he took his seat at the center of the room.

"This meeting of the Alcester Court Leet is now in session. Let me first congratulate the members of the Municipal Police for their cooperation in this inquiry. The unfortunate loss of life during this incident, so soon after the unthinkable murder of Charles Walton, has tested the resolve of that institution, adding, of course, to the grief of the Walton family. We are reminded during the current restitution of civil law here and on the Continent that this great war has affected all of us, regardless of age, citizenship, or wealth. Let us all be thankful that we have found a way to resolve this matter without further injury to the members of this community who have waited so long for an end to the sickening hostilities of a world war."

I couldn't help wondering in what ways Milner had been inconvenienced by the war, other than to interfere with his free marketing of milk. It was my understanding that Milner's two grown sons, both of whom worked for their father, had somehow escaped the draft, having proven they were indispensable to the war effort by providing milk to the Allied Forces. But then, according to Harry, Charles had been less than enthusiastic about fighting in the First War, where Potter had first proven his abilities to kill. Once a killer...

"Before the court makes its final determination, let me ask the witnesses a few questions. Miss Walton."

"Yes, your honor," Edie replied.

"Please, you need not address me in such glorious terms. I am merely the Steward."

"Yes, your honor, sir."

"Miss Walton, can you swear to me and to the residing bailiffs that your appearance at the crime scene on that Sunday evening in question was merely to aid Superintendent Spooner in his attempt to evaluate the suspect's actions on the night of your uncle's murder?"

"Yes, that's correct."

"To your knowledge there was no other reason for your attending?"

"Not to my knowledge, sir."

"Thank you, Miss Walton. Superintendent Spooner."

"Yes, sir." Thankfully we were done taking any kind of stand and I remained seated during this part.

"There is little doubt you've served this community faithfully during your tenure with the C.I.D. We can only be grateful we've had the expertise and assistance of both you and Inspector Fabian during this ordeal, but I am dismayed by your decision to conduct this investigation late at night, risking the escape of a prisoner, putting Miss Walton in harm's way, and facilitating this accident. Your decision-making seems to be less than stellar, and this court has seriously considered rather grave repercussions."

During which I wondered if Mr. Milner's authority hadn't overstepped its boundaries. Had he fully explained to me the debated concerns of the Court Leet when Potter introduced his suspicions of witchcraft, I might have trusted there was legitimacy to his authority. But I couldn't help feeling he had much more invested in Potter's wellbeing than he was letting on.

"Bailiff Alfred Potter."

"Sir," Potter replied.

"As an active bailiff of this court I hope you've come to understand the seriousness of your lapses in attention while using firearms, as well as your lack of respect for our local laws that clearly forbid hunting after dark. Your well known reputation as a metaled veteran of the First War aside, I am disappointed that your actions have facilitated the death of another individual not yet convicted of any crime or misdemeanor, even. Do you acknowledge these blatant failures to abide by the critical laws of this court and town?

"I do," the farmer uttered, barely audible

I could not help envisioning a school master shunning a first-form student for smoking behind the building. I kept waiting for the Steward to wink at his bailiff. And I can't abide winkers.

"With these concerns in mind, the court has determined that Mr. Potter shall be relieved of his duties as bailiff to this court for at least two years, until he is able to rebuild the trust this community might have in his continuing to serve. As for you, Superintendent, you are hereby sentenced to six months suspension from your duties, with two months served. At such a time as you will be reinstated, followed by a period in which you will serve six months on probation."

I couldn't deny that I, too, was being slapped on the wrists, confirming my certainty that this entire exercise was for show. How embarrassed I would have been had Sam witnessed this masquerade of justice.

"As for the legal outcome of the Walton murder case, in conjunction with the office of Prosecuting Council Longley, it has been determined that neither his office nor the Court Leet is able to formally convict Roberto Ricci for the homicide of one Charles Walton."

I looked to see if there'd be any response by Potter to this bit of information? Was it a look of fear? Or just a confirmation that he and Burns would have to remain vigilant?

"It is regrettable that such an important case as this must remain unsolved, but there is simply too little evidence to assign guilt. I therefore order that the body of Roberto Ricci be returned to his family in Italy, along with our condolences."

I wondered how such a word, "condolences," would be translated to Roberto's native tongue. I was sure that if ever such a word existed, it would never begin to adequately express my regret or love for their son.

"And by the authority vested in me as Steward of the Manor I must report that this case remains open until such a time as another suspect becomes known to this court. And with that I hereby declare this session of the Court Leet adjourned."

Chapter Forty-Two

Nuneaton
Tuesday Evening
October, 1970

Since moving to Nuneaton after my transfer in 1959, I've had little reason to return to Stratford with any regularity, except to spend several lazy afternoons reading at the Chaucer Head, which relocated from Birmingham. Prior to moving, over the course of my fifteen remaining years in Stratford, I attended on several occasions Eddie in the tavern scenes of *Henry IV* and *The Merry Wives of Windsor*. I had to agree with Edie that good Eddie – and he was such a good man – had no need for lines to impress. I regretted never seeing him on the same stage with Olivier, whom I so admired at the Royal Shakespeare Company the year I moved to Nuneaton. Though I'd never been able to forget the grisly image of Roberto killed in the dead of night at Meon Hill, Olivier's death in *Coriolanus* came very close to substituting that hideous memory.

My work as Superintendent in Stratford continued, as did the crime, though I never encountered another case like Charles Walton's. I was able to continue to contribute, I believe, to the safety and well-being of Stratford's citizens. If anyone other than the small circle of individuals caught in the web of that murder ever came to know the way in which it was resolved, I never knew about it. I did, however, feel a certain fissure had been created between myself and Longley who, thankfully, never again winked at me. One must appreciate small rewards. We rarely socialized afterwards, and I sometimes felt he was using his knowledge of the case as a sort of quiet threat should my work as investigator not please him.

As for Robert Fabian, we never had the occasion to cross each other's paths again, except at a distance. It was, of course, impossible to be unaware of the man's celebrity when he published his memoir *Fabian of the Yard* in 1954. I'm sure, like every other member of Scotland Yard or local Metropolitan Police force, I was one of the first to read his "best-seller." In addition to recognizing several of his tales of conquering criminals from our evening at The White Swan, I was curious about the way he'd portrayed the Walton case, as it clearly wasn't his finest hour. I have to admit to being disappointed that his version of the case took no more than five pages: Chapter 16 *Under the Shadow of Meon Hill*. And I was, of course, terribly jealous that he'd actually published his book, whereas my memories of the investigation remain a part of this unrecognized tome. I suppose I should congratulate him for including this less than congratulatory episode of his career, but the knowledge I accumulated over the course of our investigation suggests something far richer than the story he references. But then, I'm no book critic and he is "the Fabulous Fabian."

I never did marry. In fact, I rarely found myself in the solitary company of single women. I suppose I did get lonely on occasion, but I never envisioned any relationship would ever come close to replacing what I'd found with Sam.

Just as I'd imagined, Sam Zawalich returned to Ireland, where she continued her work as a medium, but also distinguished herself by working with wayward mothers in a school just outside Dublin. Though we never saw each other again, I discovered about a year later that I had a daughter, Christine Anne, who since the age of thirteen comes to visit several times a year. She remains my sun and I, her moon. Looking remarkably like her mother, she exhibits the same self-confidence, sterling intellect, and saucy sense of humor. She shares with me her exuberant belief that life is worth living to the fullest, even when disappointment seems to overwhelm all else. When she's in Stratford, we often walk together down by the river where her mom and I found so much peace. We have also visited the spot near Meon Hill where she was conceived, a journey that always reminds me that time can confirm our faith that we have not lived in vein.

As for my reason for putting this story in print – other than to challenge Robert Fabian in a quest to give this case the notoriety it deserves – I hope to leave a living document that brings attention to the need for listening. To what, you may ask? To the voices of the dispossessed, I suppose. To the wronged visions of those convicted of witchery – men and women – who are no more than seekers of spiritual truths we refuse to acknowledge. To the hardworking individuals intent on seeking justice, even when those that hold power and influence do everything they can to silence their voices. And to the souls of our animal cousins, who no doubt understand better than us the value of loving openly.

So, when Valentine's Day rolls around each year, I find myself on the same crusade, walking the quiet streets of Quinton and visiting the same shops in search of the man who walks free today, despite my knowledge of his guilt. And, while this annual quest to confront Walton's killer – also the man responsible for snuffing out the lives of Harry and Roberto – generally alienates me from those who know why I'm there, I continue to hope this saga has one last chapter. Perhaps, those of you who have witnessed the crimes in this journal will find a way to reveal these truths in my absence.

Alec Spooner
(b.1904, d.1970)